FORTY DAYS

✣

FORTY DAYS

❖❖

Bob Simon

G. P. PUTNAM'S SONS
NEW YORK

G. P. Putnam's Sons
Publishers Since 1838
200 Madison Avenue
New York, NY 10016

The author acknowledges permission to reprint lines from
The Poems of Dylan Thomas, © 1953 by Dylan Thomas,
courtesy of New Directions Publishing Co.

Library of Congress Cataloging-in-Publication Data
Simon, Bob, date.
Forty days / Bob Simon.
p.   cm.
ISBN 0-399-13760-2 (alk. paper)
1. Persian Gulf War, 1991—Personal narratives.   2. Simon,
Bob, date-   —Captivity, 1991.   3. Simon, Bob, date
—Journeys—Iraq.   4. Television journalists—United States—
Biography.   5. Persian Gulf War, 1991—Journalists.   I. Title.
DS79.74.S56   1992   92-3872 CIP
956.704'3—dc20

Book design and composition by The Sarabande Press

ACKNOWLEDGMENTS

❖❖

W HAT follows is the story of what happened to four newsmen during forty days of imprisonment in Iraq. It is a highly personal narrative, drawing on no sources other than what I saw and heard, thought and felt at the time.

When we were freed, it came as no surprise to learn that friends and colleagues had been working hard to secure our release. What startled us all was the intensity and breadth of the campaign.

I have tried to tell that story, briefly, in an epilogue. To explain it all would be another book, and an uplifting one. All I can do here is thank a very few of those who helped and apologize to the hundreds of others who are not mentioned but will not be forgotten. I believe to this day that, had it not been for their efforts, we would never have gotten out of Iraq alive.

By the time the Gulf War began, Soviet President Mikhail Gorbachev was virtually the only world leader with any diplomatic leverage in Baghdad. He used his influence persistently and effectively. His spokesman, Vitaly Ignatenko; his Middle East envoy, Yevgeny Primakov; and his ambassador to Iraq, Viktor Pasovoluk, were tireless in their efforts to keep the issue on the agenda.

Dr. Henry Kissinger was instrumental in keeping the Russian ball rolling. He told me later that our case had been very real to him as his greatest fear over the years was of being taken hostage himself.

Their Majesties King Hussein and Queen Noor of Jordan informed the Iraqi leadership of their personal interest in our safety. I also thank them for the gracious hospitality they offered my wife, Françoise, during her difficult days in Amman.

General H. Norman Schwarzkopf found the time during some rather busy days to brief our CBS colleagues in Saudi Arabia on fragments of information he was receiving from Iraqi POWs. Secretary of State James Baker was in constant communication with CBS executives in New York.

When I joined CBS twenty-five years ago, it was as much an extended family as a news organization. Those ties have been shaken in recent years by relentless economic pressures. But that family core resurfaced within hours of our disappearance. Word came from the top — from CEO Laurence Tisch, Broadcast Group President Howard Stringer, and Senior Vice President Jay Kriegel — that no stone was to be left unturned, no expense spared.

Eric Ober, the newly installed president of the News Division, did not know any of us personally, but behaved like a Dutch uncle immediately, directing the division's campaign and, after it had been crowned with success, offering us anything and everything we needed to get back on our feet.

Dan Rather made every call he could make and told our story every night as if, magically, keeping us on the air would keep us alive.

Executive Vice President Joe Peyronnin and foreign editor Al Ortiz told all bureaus that our well-being was to take precedence over news coverage.

Vice President Don DeCesare spent most of the forty days prowling the region and kept knocking on those human-proof Saudi and Iraqi doors until, eventually, they opened.

Former Foreign Editor Sam Roberts headed the task force in New York and probably got a lot less sleep during the ordeal than we did. I also thank him for his trust in turning over his logs to me.

My good friends Jack Smith and Doug Sefton had the unenviable task of caring for two anguished women: my wife, Françoise, and Geraldine Sharpe-Newton, Peter Bluff's fiancée. No two men could have shown more devotion and sensitivity.

Tom Goodman, publicity director, and Donna Dees, his deputy, managed the flow of information during our captivity so effectively that neither the truth nor our survival prospects were compromised.

Former CBS News people rejoined the fold to help shoulder the load. When Saudi authorities withheld permission for DeCesare to visit the border region, Keith Kay, working in Dhahran for ABC, jumped in his car and drove there, bringing back the first sighting of our abandoned vehicle. Alain Debos, in Dhahran for "La Cinq," spearheaded a petition campaign and plumbed his extensive Middle Eastern intelligence sources for word on what was going on. Sanford Socolow, former executive producer of the "CBS Evening News," offered to go to Baghdad to lead the search.

The entire news community took time out from one of the biggest stories of the decade to lend a hand. There is no way I can mention all our colleagues who helped, but CNN must be singled out for special thanks. Peter Arnett was the first and the only reporter who received and reported reliable information that we were alive. CNN, the only network seen in the region, gave our story far more air time than it deserved, just to let the Iraqis know that it was an issue which wouldn't go away.

Ron Koven of The World Press Freedom Committee turned up the pressure from Paris while Pierre Salinger of ABC pushed the many buttons he had at his disposal.

In London, Sir David Nicholas and Trevor McDonald of ITN and Jonathon Dimbleby of the BBC mobilized the resources of the United Kingdom.

Richard Holbrooke, managing director of Lehman Brothers, took the time to give Françoise what turned out to be extremely valuable advice on how to proceed.

Toby Bernstein, Harriet Weiss, and Anne Reingold dedicated themselves to giving Françoise and Tanya as much support as my wife and daughter were willing to accept.

Much later, Michael Carlisle, vice president of The William Morris Agency, went from stranger to friend in record time, leading me through the strange world of publishing with kindness and courtesy.

Two women are largely responsible for whatever merit lies in this book. My favorite Vietnam Vet, Gloria Emerson, urged me to write it when the time was right and offered countless helpful suggestions. Andrea Chambers, executive editor of Putnam's, just wouldn't take no for an answer. She assured me that reliving the pain would produce something worthwhile. I hope she was right.

For Françoise and Tanya

CELLS

❦

I CAN'T see my hands, and the pain in my stomach is getting worse. There is no window in my cell, but an air vent near the ceiling lets in enough light for me to know when it is daytime. Dawn is far away. I drank the last of my water before going to sleep and now I need more. Something is chewing away at my insides, crawling down from my abdomen to my groin. Dysentery. Can I survive another bout? I reach my hands under the blanket but this is not my body. The legs are sticks. The chest belongs to a skeleton. I need to use the toilet but I don't remember where the toilet is. The floor seems soft tonight. Did I put another blanket underneath me? I don't have another blanket. I turn on my side. There is something in the corner. It looks like a lamp. Did they put a lamp in my cell? Of course they didn't put a lamp in my cell. I close my eyes, try to sleep, but my stomach is about to explode. I push a button and the lamp in the corner lights up. This is not my cell. It is larger. The walls are white. I am in a bed. I think my wife is in the room next door. I need to feel her against me, see her smile. I push another button.

A woman comes in. She is wearing a white gown. She is smiling. I ask her where am I. She says in London, in a hospital. I tell her I hurt. She takes my hand, leads me to the toilet. I ask her what time is it. One in the morning. I lie in my bed, light a cigarette, and watch television until I feel dawn coming on.

It had been my first nightmare in forty days. It had been my first night of freedom.

BORDERS

❖

Rivers make the best borders. Even though the Jordan is little more than a lively brook at the level of the Allenby bridge, even though the two banks—lush vegetation trailing up to mad lunarscapes—are mirror images of each other, crossing over from Israeli territory to Jordan, as I did on August sixth to begin covering the Gulf crisis, always carries a sense of transition, of the forbidden, of moving between enemy camps.

There is none of that at Al-Ruqi, the inland border post between Saudi Arabia and Kuwait. Here the white desolation seems uninterrupted even by the horizon: the immigration and customs houses are Lego pieces carelessly strewn about in a sandbox by imperial children. There is no logic to the border. If you moved it a mile or ten miles in any direction, it's hard to see how anyone would notice or why anyone would care. On the twenty-first of January, four days after the bombing began, there were no soldiers anywhere near Al-Ruqi, no sights or sounds to suggest that anyone was preparing for war. There was just the wind, the hot dry wind which dazzled the fine grains of sand and threw them in the air, sewing curtains of dust between us and the white winter sun.

We were on the roof of the customs house, interviewing an old Saudi, an immigrations official. He was the only man left in the complex, the only man we had seen since we drove past allied lines twenty miles to the south. We met him at an abandoned gas station near the border. He seemed neither pleased nor surprised to see us, even though, he told us, we were his first visitors in four days. The other officials, he said, had left as soon as the air war began. Were they ordered out or did they just leave? we asked. He smiled and offered us tea. We told him we were reporters. That didn't seem to faze him even though, according to allied press restrictions, we had no right to be anywhere near the border or, for that matter, anywhere outside our hotel without a military escort. We asked him for an interview and he seemed happy to oblige. We asked him to take us to the border so we could film him there and he offered us more tea. But after some coaxing, he led us, in his Land Cruiser, to the customs house and to this excellent camera position on the roof overlooking the no-man's land and, in the distance, Kuwait. In the interview he told me how hundreds of Iraqis had defected over the last few days and were being held in a football stadium nearby, how the first Iraqi lines were six miles to the north, how the Iraqis had abandoned their border post on the other side of the no-man's land.

I did what is called a "stand-up" in the trade. Standing on the roof, squinting as I looked into the camera, I predicted that the silent and sea-less beach behind me was destined to become a battlefield before long. It was midday. Shining a reflector in my face so my eyes would not look like black sockets was Peter Bluff, a forty-six-year-old Englishman and the CBS News bureau chief in London. Once the favorite field producer of every foreign correspondent and cameraman, he decided last year that, with middle age descending, he would have to accept the offer of a "grown-up" job even though he knew he would hate it, which he did. The take-every-available-body syndrome of the Gulf crisis forced the CBS bureaucrats to answer Peter's pleas and let him out in the fresh air with his mates. He had just arrived in Saudi Arabia after working several weeks in Baghdad. Peter and I were close friends. We had worked together in Beirut, India, Israel, and the West Bank.

Behind the camera was Roberto Alvarez, thirty-seven, a free-lancer out of Miami. Roberto had just celebrated the thirtieth anniversary of his family's arrival in America from Havana — on a plane, he always pointed out, not on a raft. He had covered just about every war and insurrection in Latin America since 1979, and had never been to the Middle East. A week earlier he and I worked together for the first time. His perfectionism was evident: his courage was well known.

Soundman Juan Caldera, twenty-nine, the son of a wealthy Nicaraguan rancher, had soft, sad eyes which revealed his warmth and vulnerability but not his street smarts. He had started in the trade in '83 as a fixer-driver for NBC in Managua, and had just arrived in Saudi Arabia. None of his Latin American experience would be terribly relevant here—aside from the fact that of the four of us he was the only one who had ever been imprisoned, briefly, in Nicaragua and while covering Panama.

I had been with CBS News twenty-four years, most of them overseas. I had been posted to London, Vietnam, and Israel. I had reported from sixty-seven countries including every major nation in the Middle East except Iraq. That was about to change.

Our Saudi friend disappeared after the interview. Peter and I were chatting; Roberto was taking some long shots when suddenly I realized he wasn't there anymore. Then I heard his engine start. Peter and I looked at each other, then down to the road, to see his Land Cruiser speeding off, away from the border. I took a step toward the stairwell, as if to follow, and then stopped. Roberto hadn't seen anything. He was immersed in his viewfinder. Juan was staring off into the distance.

We decided to get a few shots in the no-man's land, maybe shoot another stand-upper, to flesh out the story. We parked the van behind a building at the border crossing, walked past the closed white gates which, on better days, lifted and fell to let cars pass, and strolled across the border. We figured we'd be away from the van five to ten minutes. Roberto left the key in the ignition. Juan left six thousand dollars in his bag; a cash advance he had just taken which he didn't want to leave in the hotel. We took no extra camera batteries or cassettes. Without the hint of a curve, the road stretched out in front of us like a thin black ribbon, cutting through the desolate sands.

Aside from a faint, intermittent rustle from the wind, there was no sound in this vast empty lot. But I had grown accustomed to the desert. I found the silence neither strange nor menacing. Later, when I thought about these moments and compared them to other moments in other wars, I could only conclude that I had been exceptionally lucky over the years — that this stroll was no riskier than a hundred other walks I had taken at other times, in other places. Had we made it back to our bureau in Saudi Arabia that night, I would have told my friends about the massive buildup we had seen on our way to the border, about Hafr el-Baten, the deserted desert town where we had spent the night. Our short stroll across the line would have been hardly worth mentioning. It was no big deal and it didn't seem like a big risk. The Iraqis had deserted their border post two miles north of us. Iraqi lines were six miles away. The Saudis had told us that.

There were blanched sheep bones on the soft shoulders of the road — very moody material for a talented cameraman like Roberto. Peter warned him not to step off the asphalt: the sands could be mined. I looked hard at the road for any signs that mines might have been planted under the surface. There were none. In the distance, several miles away it seemed, a small vehicle, resembling a boat more than a car, sailed slowly to the east along a road north of us. Roberto shot that too. After a few moments it tacked and headed back along the same road. Roberto turned around and took some pictures of the Saudi border post, probably never shot from this perspective before, not in this war, anyway.

There were large green signs on both sides of the road fifty yards ahead of us. We figured they might mark the actual frontier, delineating which part of the no-man's land belonged to Saudi Arabia, which to Kuwait. We walked ahead, slowly. We thought we might be fifty yards away from a Kuwaiti dateline, but we were wrong. The signs were just arrows pointing to parking lots.

We turned around, started heading back to the Saudi border, less than 300 yards away. Roberto held the camera eighteen inches off the ground as we walked: a tracking shot of legs, a road, and a desert.

Peter said: "That vehicle is heading towards us."

I turned around. It was still quite far away. No one could tell what kind of vehicle it was, but it certainly was off the road, crossing the sands, and it certainly was heading toward us. We quickened our pace, but no one broke into a sprint.

In the days to come, we spent many hours thinking about that moment. Why didn't we run? Were we exercising some form of denial, hoping that if we ignored it, it would go away? Thirty seconds later I turned around again and saw that it was an army jeep. It was making tracks, kicking up sand. By then it was too close, too late to run, and we're lucky we didn't. They would have shot us at close range.

The jeep pulled up a few yards from the road. The driver got out and slowly came toward us saying, "Peace." He was not carrying a rifle. His pistol was in its holster. Two other men were getting out of the back of the jeep. Defectors? More defectors? Peter extended his hand to the driver. Roberto was filming the scene. It was television.

The two other Iraqis were out of the jeep, on either side of it now. They had AK-47s, but were not pointing them at us. In fact they joined the "peace" chorus, adding the refrain, "No more war, no more war." Peter was calmly talking to the driver, clearly the man in charge. "We would like to interview you. We work for CBS." He said it slowly: "C–B–S, American television," Peter's way of talking to foreigners. It all seemed so familiar and benign. Peter and the driver were shaking hands.

It was Peter who first realized what was happening when he tried to withdraw his hand and could not. I understood when another hand copped me on the back of the head and shoved me into the jeep. Roberto told me he knew when he looked at me and saw that I had turned as white as the sand.

Then we were speeding across this huge, gritty rug. When we reached the "abandoned" border post on the Kuwaiti side, Iraqi soldiers peered at us from their reinforced foxholes, machine guns and mortars pointing south, toward Saudi Arabia. We crossed log bridges over the deep ditches we had heard so much about, the ditches Saddam promised to fill with burning oil if the allies came. I was seeing things I was not meant to see.

I knew it was really happening. There was no sense of disbelief. But there was something strangely cinematic about it. Troops came out of the bunkers which dotted the desert, waving their rifles dramatically in the air. Where were the camera positions? Where was the director?

I started singing what would become our aria in weeks to come. "*Zahafi*, press," I said. "We are *zahafi*. Not soldiers, *zahafi*."

"Yes, yes," the driver said.

"Where are we going?"

"To see some people."

"Will you take us back to the border?"

"Yes, later I'll take you back to the border." I tried to believe this, but the light in his eyes was pointing toward a different scheme. He was one happy Iraqi, the happiest Iraqi in Kuwait. His smile curled past his mustache. He had just trapped four westerners without firing a shot. He was taking his booty home for dinner.

Right then I felt more embarrassment than fear. I was ashamed that I had let this happen. I turned toward Bluff. He looked at me, knitting his brows as if to say, "What have we done this time?"

"Yvonne will never forgive you for this," I said. Yvonne was the power behind the throne in the London bureau, Bluff's Moneypenny, who happened to adore him.

"I know," he said.

The jeep lurched to a stop. We were yanked out, thrown to the ground. We were surrounded by soldiers, their rifles pointed down at us. I felt cold metal on my cheek. An officer was poking me with the barrel of his gun. He had light hair and a dark scowl. He shouted, "Give, Give!" He pointed the rifle at my pockets, shouted again. I took out my notebook and pen, my cigarettes and my lighter, a memento I valued. He dropped his weapon and went for my throat with both hands. He ripped the chain off from around my neck. It carried my press credentials. "Please," I said, "I need those."

A brick fell on the back of my head. That's what it felt like, anyway. I went down on all fours, looked around, and saw the soldier who had just knocked me with his rifle butt step back and take aim. "Don't move!" someone shouted. I lowered my forehead to the sand and waited to hear the shots.

BUNKERS

✧✦✧

I T is axiomatic in prisoner-of-war lore that the most dangerous moments are the ones immediately following your capture, before you get injected into the system. I heard no shots and when I raised my head, I saw that preparations were being made for the next leg of our journey. What I didn't realize then, what I realized only much later, was that my life had already been saved—for the first, not for the last time that day—by a bureaucratic error which had been made some three weeks earlier, something so trivial that it bordered on the miraculous. In fact, had I been a believer, I might have concluded that a bit of military incompetence had been written by a divine hand.

I covered the buildup in Saudi Arabia from the beginning, in mid-August 1990, until early December, when I took a two-week vacation at my home base in Israel. I returned on the second of January to the International Hotel in Dhahran, an unassuming airport hotel in quieter times, which was now joining Saigon's Caravelle and Beirut's Commodore in the mythology of wartime media haunts. All it lacked was a bar. CBS shared a banquet room with CNN. ABC took over a wing of bedrooms; the wire services, newspapers, and weeklies commandeered suites ordinarily reserved for American arms salesmen and European contractors. The burgeoning American military information establishment was also making its home here. The corridors were swarming with captains and majors in khaki camouflage and smartly polished desert boots which looked as if they'd never touched the sands and probably hadn't. I'd always gotten a kick out of army deskmen who waltz around in full combat gear, as if they were about to hit the beaches of Normandy.

When I walked in that second day of the new year, the Joint Information Bureau was in high gear, distributing army uniforms and gas masks to journalists who had signed up for their "combat pools," handing out credentials. I already had my Saudi press card. I stood on line in the corridor to get my International Red Cross ID card from a major sitting at a plywood desk. A Red Cross card is standard issue for anyone working in a combat zone. Aside from your picture, name, nationality, and rank (or position), it lists your blood type in case of injury and your religion in case you have to be buried quickly. When the major handed me mine, I saw that next to "religion" it said "Protestant." "Hey, that's not right," I said.

He was painfully polite. "I'm sorry, Mr. Simon. You weren't here when we drew these up, so we looked at your Saudi visa application sheet and you didn't specify your religion there so we put down 'Protestant' because most people are."

"Well, that's not right," I said. "I'm Jewish."

"No problem, sir. We can change it. We'll give you a new card tomorrow morning."

"Thanks a lot," I said and started walking away.

"Mr. Simon, one minute please." I turned around. He was a stocky man, the major, with a pasty complexion which had never encountered the desert sun. He had thick round glasses and he was looking at me with a strange intensity that betrayed a deep concern. "Mr. Simon," he said, "are you sure?"

"OK, forget it," I said. It just didn't seem that important.

The military manuals all say it: the most dangerous time is the period right after capture. As we cowered in the sand, I could hear warplanes overhead. There were the dull thuds of bombs exploding not too far away. The men pointing rifles at us were angry, confused, and frightened. If my Red Cross card had been accurate, they would have shot that Jew in army pants right away.

In weeks to come, the deepest panic was brought on not by thoughts of death but by fear of separation. I was feeling that now. For the first time since our capture I could not swallow and I wanted to scream. Juan and Roberto had just been shoved into a jeep. It drove off. Peter and I were pushed into another jeep and we followed, at breakneck speed, along a parallel track. But we could not see them. Peter leaned out. "Where are they? Fuck it, where are they?"

Then we saw the first jeep, swerving wildly through the

sands. We caught up. The drivers shouted at each other. We changed directions, then again. Our captors were lost. The driver slammed on the brakes. The other jeep pulled up next to us. The four of us were shoved out again. They had forgotten something. I felt a cloth being tied tightly behind my head. My hands were being tied behind my back. I was being blindfolded and bound.

Back in the car, I realized that I could see straight down. When I thought I could get away with it, I tilted my head back, shot a glance through the bottom of the blindfold out the window. It was like Saudi Arabia. There was nothing, no one.

Then we came to an area where I saw some mounds. I heard the sounds of soldiers. The jeep stopped. Someone took my arm, quick-stepped me through the sand. Then I was being led down steep stairs. I was shoved onto something soft. My hands were untied, my blindfold lifted. I was on a bed. Juan, Roberto, and Peter were led into the room, a small, tidy room with three neatly made beds. We were in a bunker, well-constructed and very clean. Three young officers came in. It was their room. They spoke English. They were calm and they seemed, inexplicably, to have been expecting us.

"How are you? Are you thirsty?"

We drank water. We were offered cigarettes. We smoked.

The men were smartly dressed, clean-shaven and spiffy, with sharp creases in their pants. They were nothing like the ragtag band of hungry peasants the Saudis and the Americans had told us were dug in here. One of the officers had studied in England. Another had been to New York. He wanted to know how the Mets were doing.

It was warm in the bunker, the bed was soft, and I felt safe. An enlisted man came to the door carrying a tray with four glasses of steaming sweet tea. "Room service," I said to myself. I heard planes now and then, the thump of bombs impacting and loud bursts of antiaircraft fire, but the officers didn't take notice, so why should I? I put a pillow against the wall, leaned back, closed my eyes, and thought I might doze off. I remembered other times I'd been taken into custody for being places I wasn't supposed to be. The British arrested me once in Belfast for taking pictures of Long Kesh, the IRA prison camp. The Israelis arrested me several times for being in "military zones" on the West Bank. It had always ended like this, with tea, cigarettes, and a chat. Then we would be released.

We told the officers our story, how we were just nosing around on our own, trying to size up the situation. They seemed slightly amused and entirely sympathetic. "That's what journalists do," the Mets fan said. They wanted to know why I was wearing army pants. I told them it was to get past allied checkpoints. It worked — too well, I said. Then why weren't my friends wearing army gear as well? they asked. I told them discipline wasn't very tight in our unit. They laughed.

Peter told them about his good friends in Baghdad, Latif Jassim, the Minister of Information, Naji al-Hadithi, his sidekick. Peter asked them to get word to Baghdad, let his friends know we are here. Then everything will be clarified, sorted out right away. They nodded. I hoped it would happen quickly. After all, I had a story to do that night. We were lucky Peter was so well connected. I asked whether they could get us back to the border before nightfall.

"No, that's not possible."

"Then what's going to happen?" I asked.

"We think they will want to see you in Baghdad."

Juan and Roberto were looking at me. I asked Peter how his friend the minister will react when we are brought to him. "Oh, he will pretend to be angry," Peter said. "He will say 'Peter, Peter, you naughty boy. What have you done this time? I can't leave you alone for a minute.' Then he will ask if we want to work in Baghdad."

Peter and I looked at each other. Maybe we had lucked out once again. We knew there were no CBS people in Baghdad. CNN had the story to itself. Peter said, "We still have our office in the Al-Rasheed Hotel, room 502. Our equipment is there. Our phone is there." Roberto wanted to know if there was an extra camera, extra batteries, and a charger. Peter said he thought so. We talked about how quickly we could get operational. I asked the officers if they thought we might get to Baghdad by tomorrow morning. They nodded.

I said, "They'll take us to the ministry, then we'll go to the hotel and go up to the office and we'll phone New York and we'll say, 'Listen, we heard you had some openings in the Baghdad bureau. We took a shortcut.' Can you imagine?"

What I can just begin to imagine now is what those

smartly dressed, well-educated officers of the Iraqi army must have thought of those bounding idiots in their bunk beds, those pathological dreamers who thought they were still news reporters. They must have had some idea of what was in store for us. They must have known.

But they were courteous, hospitable, and exceedingly polite. We were their guests, and it was turning into a social evening, collegial, hanging out with exchange students in the dorm. The enlisted man came back with plates of beans and rice. He was deferential, the practiced Arab waiter, bowing his head as he distributed forks and paper napkins. Peter tried to decline. "Eat," I told him. "From now on we eat whenever we're offered food."

Dinner talk came around to Peter's country house in Oxfordshire and to the centerpiece of his life, his tree. Peter could talk for hours about his tree. He turned to it, far more than he did to people, whenever life got a bit tense. It was a Cedar of Lebanon and, in fact, I'd first heard about it when Peter and I were in Lebanon together several years ago. It's at least two hundred years old and a hundred feet high, Peter was telling our hosts. "It's a really big one," he said, "really fat and chunky. It has great, thick branches that sweep down to the ground, like a giant creature standing in the corner of the garden." As soon as he got home, the first thing he would do would be to hug it. Then, he told the officers, he would go buy a dog. That didn't go down well. Iraqis don't like dogs, never touch them or let them into their homes. Peter also noticed that they didn't like hearing about his lady friend, Geraldine. That day, and for the rest of our stay as guests in Iraq, Geraldine became Peter's wife. Back in England, Geraldine was also pretending she and Peter were married, in her fierce campaign to get him freed.

Françoise, my wife, was in New York. We lived in Israel, where I'd been based for four years, but she left a few days before the Scuds started falling on Tel Aviv. She wasn't scared, really. Françoise was comfortable in combat zones; we'd lived in Saigon for a year in the early '70s. But Tanya, our nineteen-year-old daughter, a student at Columbia, was nervous about both her parents' being within firing range, told her mother, ominously, that she didn't want the Gulf War to leave her an orphan. Luckily I had a short period of grace before they'd realize something was wrong. I told Tanya before I left Dhahran that I might be out of touch a couple of days.

We smoked after dinner. That is, we all smoked except Peter. He is usually militant about people smoking in his vicinity, but was not protesting now. I stopped eight years ago but just started again. We were escorted to the toilet one by one. It was in another bunker, so it was a welcome occasion for a stroll. Night had fallen. A guard flickered a red flashlight to lead the way. Around me, the black and barren sands ran without the hint of a hill all the way to a rim of light marking the horizon. I remembered hearing how some holy men in Saudi Arabia still believed that the earth is flat, and I could understand why. The bombing had resumed. I could hear explosions and gunfire from what seemed to be a few kilometers away. Silhouettes of soldiers crept slowly through the darkness. This was only the fourth night of bombing, but there was no panic in the air. The sounds of war had already faded into background music.

Back in the bunker, I told the officers I felt safe with them but was worried about the bombing. They did not seem to share my concern. Every time we expressed anxiety, they countered, "Don't worry, no problem." Their arrogance was like a hard glaze which they kept polishing; a shield against the next moment. They were confident in their bunker, disdainful of American bombs. "The Americans bomb us for days," they said, "and what did they hit? Nothing, not a thing."

All of us were worried about getting stuck in this friendly bunker, for we were all convinced the Americans were going to invade Kuwait, and soon. But even with all the beans, cigarettes, and civility, it was beginning to seep in that we no longer had anything to say about where we would go or when we would go there.

The waiter came back to the room, but he wasn't carrying a tray this time. He beckoned me to follow him. Peter winked. "Correspondents first," he said. I was led down a long, well-lit underground corridor to a smaller room. A heavyset major was sitting at a desk. Two men were standing on either side of him. The major was writing. The social part of the evening was over. This was a formal interrogation. The idea excited me somehow. I'd always done well at tests. I liked answering questions. It was what I did best.

"What is your name?"

"Robert Simon."

"Where do you live?"

"New York City."

"What is your address?"

"Five twenty-four West 57th Street." That's the address of CBS News, the only permanent address I've had for twenty-four years.

"Is that where you live?"

"No, it's where I work."

"Where do you live?"

The honest answer would have been, "In a suburb of Tel Aviv." Before 1987 we lived in Bethesda, Maryland. We still own a house there, but the question had rattled me. I was more nervous than I realized. I couldn't remember the address, so I made one up. "Seventy-eleven Bethesda Avenue," I said. And I stuck to it through all the interrogations which were to come.

My credentials were on the desk. So were my pen and my notebook, reminders of an identity which was slipping away. The major wanted to know what I had seen on the Saudi side of the border. I decided to tell him what I would have reported on CBS had I made it back that night, and to rely heavily on understatement. I talked about military traffic heading north and described it as fairly heavy. In fact, the four of us had been stunned by what we saw. What was amazing now was the idea that we were on that road only yesterday. It seemed such a very long time ago.

We weren't expecting to find anything monumental when we left our hotel in Dhahran, 250 miles south of the border, early Sunday morning. We weren't combing the desert for scoops, revelations, or prizes. We just wanted to break away from the pack because it was becoming clear that the Pentagon was not planning to lead the pack anywhere anything was happening. Two days earlier—on Friday, the day after the air war began—Bluff and I had gone up to Khafji, the coastal border town where we found a burning Saudi oil refinery which had been hit by Iraqi artillery, a U.S. Marine unit under fire, and Saudi army positions abandoned by their defenders: three items which had not been covered by the military pools and which would have gone unreported that day had we not taken the drive.

On Sunday we expected to see military convoys heading north. What we found instead loomed as one never-ending convoy: hundreds of trucks, tank carriers, artillery pieces, starting, like the desert, beyond the horizon and driving right off the planet. Or so it seemed. It had the four of us shaking our heads in disbelief. Where did all those tanks and trucks come from? How could anyone doubt that Bush planned to wage a ground war? We stopped many times to film. The soldiers were, as always, delighted to see a television crew and in a high state of excitation. After months of waiting they were on their way, or thought they were. Hosts of helicopters, Cobras mainly, flew just above the turrets of the tanks. The pilots waved at us, gyrated the choppers when they saw our camera.

It was because of the traffic that we didn't make it back to our hotel in Dhahran Sunday night. By the time we got to Hafr el-Baten, the northernmost Saudi town, it was dark and we decided to sleep over. Monday morning we continued toward the border. There was not much traffic on the road. The traffic was in the desert, alongside the road. A Syrian convoy, trucks and artillery pieces, was heading north. We stopped and filmed. Having been based in Israel four years, it excited me, being so close to so much Syrian firepower.

"How did you know they were Syrian?" the major asked.

"Two officers came up to us when we were filming from the road. They told us to leave. They were Syrian."

"Did they tell you they were Syrian?"

"No. I know their uniforms. I've been to Lebanon."

"What did you do then?"

"We got back in the car and drove north."

"What did you see?"

"Nothing," I lied. "Nothing between them and the border." I waited to see if they knew better. We had passed an armored battalion from the American First Cav a few miles north of the Syrians.

The movie sense came back. The men facing me were playing their parts as officers and interrogators. Their costumes were good, the accents just right. I was playing mine. We were all aware that these were just the opening scenes, and we were anxious not to fluff our lines.

Peter later told me he was very pleased with himself when he remembered that the Syrian vehicles had small wheels in front and big wheels in back. The interrogators, he said, were also impressed.

It was so cordial, I decided to bring up an annoying detail, a detail which troubled me then far more than I will ever fully understand. "I had a lighter," I said. "It was given to me by the French Foreign Legion. It was taken from me this afternoon. I see you have my pen and my notebook. Do you have my lighter?"

This created a flurry of fast talk in Arabic. They asked me to describe the officer who frisked us, the kind of uniform he was wearing, his rank. One of the soldiers left the room. This felt very reassuring. These were officers and gentlemen, I decided. What's more, they were Arabs, and I was in their tent, their prisoner, perhaps, but their guest as well. There were codes to be observed. Petty thievery would not be tolerated.

While they waited for the soldier to return, there was a pause, and then a subject change, a few words delivered matter-of-factly, which put it all in some context. "You realize you were captured in a war zone," the major said. "We are obliged to consider you prisoners of war."

"But we are journalists. I told you that. You have our credentials."

"We must consider you prisoners of war."

How frightening that phrase sounded in that bunker. How I was to long for it when I learned, weeks down the road, that compared to other possibilities it was a status devoutly to be wished.

The interrogation appeared to be over, but we chatted awhile. We were having a break, talking about our kids between takes. I told them how naked I felt without my pen and my notebook, lying so close, just a few inches away, on the table between us. Can I have them back?

"Maybe later," the major said.

I was taken back to our room. There was a guard standing at the door but no soldiers inside. My friends were alone. I spoke quickly and softly. I told them what I had said and what I had omitted: many Syrians, no Americans. I had just finished telling them we were POWs now when the guard came to get Roberto. He was taken away.

I told Juan and Peter what, at that moment, I really believed. The POW label, I said, is good news and bad news. Bad news because it means we're not going to get sprung right away. Good news because it means we're safe. We're in the system. It sounded logical. Perhaps there was a certain logic to it. It also showed how little I knew about the system.

Suddenly it got very noisy. There was heavy cannon fire, much shouting inside the bunker.

"We got one." One of the officers charged into our room, very excited. "We shot one down," he said.

We sat on our beds, avoiding each others' eyes. I could hear movement in the corridor, men running, rushing upstairs.

"Do you want to see?" I looked up. The officer was talking to me. "Do you want to come see?"

"Yes, of course."

Two of them took me by the arms, led me up a back flight of stairs. The sky was painted red and orange and white. The image was inescapable. I remembered the first time my father took me to the George Washington Bridge on the Fourth of July.

Tracers and phosphorous bombs were the floodlights

illuminating a landscape of bunkers, revetments, artillery pieces. War can be astonishing in its terrible beauty.

They may or may not have shot down a plane, but there were dozens more in the air. I couldn't see them but I could hear them circling overhead, the whine turning into a hoarse roar as they plummeted down on bombing runs. I felt privileged right then, the same extraordinary sense of privilege I'd felt so many times over the years when I found myself in the center of the action, witnessing history, licensed to experience the raw event. I remembered driving overnight from Yugoslavia to Bucharest almost exactly one year ago, saying to a colleague in the car, "There's nowhere in the world I'd rather be right now than Romania." Bucharest was the place then. This was the place now. Whatever happens next, I thought, I will have seen the bombing of Kuwait; the view from the ground. I didn't feel like a prisoner on that mound, looking at the sky. I felt as if I'd been called upon to impersonate a prisoner just to get here, to this forbidden territory beyond the line.

When I was taken back to the bunker, Roberto had returned. Now Peter was missing. The officers were asking Roberto about our car, exactly where had we left it? They said they wanted to mount a commando operation, rescue the vehicle. I pounced on this idea. How good it would be to have our Land Cruiser back! I remembered the things I had left inside, chose not to think about the cassette I'd left in the tape deck: a recording of the Verdi Requiem. Roberto was drawing a diagram, putting an X by the building where we'd parked. I looked at the officer.

Our eyes met and I realized that there was no commando operation in the works. I felt disappointed. This man, whom I'd come to trust, was conning us. I didn't understand exactly why. They certainly had their own diagrams of the border complex. But I knew we'd have to start being more careful. We'd have to fight this instinct to trust people who treated us kindly.

Peter came back. Juan smiled and waved as he was led away. Peter seemed to have come out of his interrogation with a heightened sense of urgency. He told the officers how they must get word to his mates in the ministry, Jassim and Hadithi. They must do it now. I thought about how I was investing so much hope in the intervention of two men I had never met. Peter's pleas were interrupted by a firm voice: "You are in the hands of the Iraqi military now," the officer said. "The Ministry of Information has nothing to do with you."

Exhaustion claimed every bone and muscle. I didn't want to think anymore or talk anymore. I just wanted to lean back and go to sleep, so I did. I was vaguely aware of Juan's return, then that we were alone in the room, then that several men had come in. "Come," a voice said. "Come, it's time to move." It was the major.

"Why? We like it here," I said.

"This place is not suitable. We will take you someplace suitable."

Even now I find it painful to confess that I was on the verge of saying, "Don't worry, one of us will sleep on the floor." I thought he was suggesting the place was not suitable because there were four of us and only three beds.

Who I was and what I'd been until a few hours ago was shriveling, fading into the vastness of the night.

Peter said, "Will you come with us?"

The major smiled. "What do you mean?"

"I know if you're with us, we're safe. Bad things won't happen. Please come."

"I can't."

It was so warm in the room that I'd taken off my jacket, or, rather, Peter's jacket. He had lent it to me—an olive-green windbreaker with a hood—some eight hours earlier. I hadn't wanted to wear the army camouflage jacket for that stand-up on the roof at the border.

"Here. Take your jacket back," I said.

"You wear it. I'm from the north," Peter said. "I can take the cold. You'll need it."

I didn't realize it then. How could I have realized it? But that was the second time that day that my life had been saved. During the next forty days and nights, I took that jacket off only once or twice and only briefly. I would not have had a chance without it.

We were blindfolded, our hands tied behind our backs. A soldier gave me his hand to lead me upstairs. It was small and smooth. I grasped on to it tightly and thought, Please, never let me go.

He led me slowly and carefully to a vehicle, lifted my leg to guide me in. From the other side a familiar voice said, "Mr. Simon, I'm sorry. We did not find your lighter."

40

A MORE
SUITABLE PLACE

❧❧

Now I cannot remember the particular question or answer that prompted the first cane to come crashing down on my leg. Maybe it wasn't a particular question or answer. Maybe it was just time for it. Or maybe it was random, haphazard. I screamed and lurched forward in my chair. It was a wooden chair with a high back. I imagined an electric chair. My hands were tied behind it. I was blindfolded. A cane came down on my other leg. I did not scream that time and another cane came down. I felt welts rising on my thighs. Then the canes were beating me on the head. There were two men doing the beating, one on either side of me. There was another man in the room shouting the questions.

I'd been beaten up before. I'd been the victim of a mob before. But I'd never been systematically brutalized or tortured. The most frightening thing now was my sense that there were no limits. There was no code, no higher authority, nothing they could not do. I sensed that they would not kill me, at least not now, but anything else was possible.

The prelude to the beating, the warmup, had been a trip on a highway, moving fast, not long after we'd left the bunker. It was dark and our eyes were covered, but at one point, peering out from under the bottom of my blindfold, I could see large road signs overhead, the kind you would expect on the approaches to a city. This must be Kuwait, I thought. Baghdad would be ten hours away. The four of us were squeezed into the back of a jeep, our legs pressed against each others', uncomfortable, but very comforting at the same time. It was cold. Even with Peter's jacket, I was shivering. Our escorts were a new crop of guards and drivers, not officers and gentlemen anymore. This was an entirely different breed. They poked us with sticks and collapsed into high-pitched, hyena-like laughs when we grunted or squirmed. When one of us tried to whisper something, one of them would shout, "Don't speak anything!" That was, apparently, a popular line in Iraq. We were to hear it often in weeks to come.

I have always managed to sleep in cars and planes, and I think I dozed a bit then. But when I came around and sensed from the number of turns we were making that we were in a city, I knew it couldn't be Baghdad. We hadn't been driving long enough. This must be Basra, a place I'd never been and never planned to go to, a city I knew only by reputation as the filth-infested focal point of the Iran-Iraq war.

The car lurched to a stop and we were dragged out.

There were men waiting for us. I was shoved inside a door, pushed against a wall, thrown to the floor. I had the impression I was in a long, wide corridor. I heard my friends being pushed down against the same wall. We had apparently arrived at "the more suitable place."

I was the first to be interrogated. I was taken into a room off the corridor. The door was slammed shut. My hands were untied and retied behind the back of a chair. There seemed to be a lamp in the room, but that was all I could make out. A deep voice said, "I will ask you questions. You will choose. You will answer the questions or I will make you answer them. Do you understand?"

I said I understood and would answer his questions. I was frightened, but a corner of my mind was doing a critique. We need a new scriptwriter, I thought. These lines are too hackneyed. If we have to go through all this, does it have to be so unremittingly grade B?

The line of questioning was familiar. What had we seen? What were we doing? Why were we there? When the beating began, after the initial shock I felt that I was wandering in and out of consciousness, but in a tactical sort of way. My mind would retreat during a flurry of blows and then come back when it was over, when it had to cope with another question. It was as if I were punching into a program I had never used before because I'd never needed it, and I didn't know it existed. I felt I would make it through the beating, not because my assailants would exercise any restraint but because my mind would know how to absorb the blows. It would tune out when the pain got too intense.

But the universe had turned savage. Mad dogs howled in the distance. I had never heard animal sounds like that before. I pictured them being tortured too. We were in an isolated house, I imagined, surrounded by moonlit moorland. The packs of wild dogs were roaming the barren hills, their cries responding to my own.

I didn't try to control my screams. I sensed that any display of control, even were I capable of it, would be seen as defiance, would egg them on. I couldn't see them, of course. But I imagined them young and inexperienced; hoodlums on a binge, not professional interrogators. The tactics I had stumbled on unconsciously seemed more subtle than theirs. They never asked the questions which would have tempted me to say the things I had decided not to say. I just hoped that my screams weren't terrifying my friends.

Then they turned the tables on me. They opened the door to the corridor and I knew why. They opened the door so I could hear Juan, Peter, and Roberto scream. The three of them were being beaten at the same time. I could hear the sticks come down on their heads and their cries of pain: no words, just shrieks. That sound was much harder to deal with than anything that was being done to me. I had never seen Peter out of control in any way before. The image of him sitting on the floor and screaming was more than I could take. I shouted, "No, No. Stop!" and for the first time got a cane in the face. Then the door closed and it was over.

A memory came to me, startling in its incongruity. I remembered my first contract negotiations with CBS in the late 1960s. I remembered how, taking a bus before the session, I read an article on corporate negotiating techniques. Later, in the CBS business office, I was stunned when I saw how many clichés from the article were there. The executive's chair was higher than mine. The door was left open so that our "confidential" conversation could be heard by anyone passing by. The interrogators had their own manual. But it was just as transparent. I had read that article, seen that movie too.

The toughest thing in that interrogation, and in many to come, was convincing the Iraqis that there was no more to our "mission" than I said there was. In their eyes it just seemed too trivial: A little scouting? A few pictures? Some sheep bones? And for that, you took this risk, of winding up here, in the hands of your enemy? For that, you let us beat you and threaten you and perhaps kill you? I could understand their skepticism. The lack of proportion was evident. I tried to explain to this interviewer the nature of network competition, how I'd just been trying to keep one step ahead.

"Did you dream last night?" he asked me.

"What do you mean?"

"Did you dream you were Rambo?"

For the first time that night, I laughed. Here we were, an Iraqi intelligence goon and a New York Jew and we had the same cultural references. We had seen the same films. I realized how important humor would be. "There is no fate that cannot be surmounted by scorn," Camus said. I remembered that line from his essay "The Myth of Sisyphus," which I read thirty years ago. Long-lost memories were being mobilized and heading toward the front. Everything I'd ever known would help me through this.

But the most astounding revelation, as I was being led out to the corridor, was the realization that it simply hadn't been that bad. I'd been beaten. One beating was over. My legs were swollen. My head hurt. But I was OK. It was uplifting, somehow. If they beat me again, as they may, as they probably will, I thought, I will survive that too. Faces can be rebuilt, I told myself, teeth can be implanted. If they leave my eyes and my balls alone, I'll be all right. It's not such a big deal after all.

Then I was back up against the wall in the corridor listening as, one by one, my friends were taken into that little room in Basra for their interviews. I couldn't hear the questions or the answers, or the sound of the sticks; just their screams. Juan's were somehow the toughest to take. It may have been just because his voice is normally higher-pitched than the others. But his screams had a childlike quality about them. I was listening to the sounds of a little boy being tormented. With Roberto and Peter, I had the impression that what was being done to them was no worse than what had been done to me. It was their voices I heard, it was identifiably them. But Juan sounded like he was being carried over the edge, falling into a black and bottomless pit.

I tried to focus on the baying of the dogs, but that didn't work. I couldn't lose consciousness now. I couldn't command my mind to float off the way it just had on its own when I was in that chair. I had to be there in that corridor. I had to be there and listen.

I found myself repeating a phrase, a strange and technical phrase I hadn't thought of in years. "Transferred pain, transferred pain," was in my head. I remembered: when I ruptured a disc a few years ago, the doctors explained that while the injury was to my back, I would be feeling the pain in my leg. It was transferred pain, and no one ever told me that in years ahead, the agony of other men being beaten would move down a grimy, airless corridor to assault me. Now I was feeling the hurt which evoked the screams, cringing with each imagined blow, opening my mouth to add my silent scream to theirs.

I felt I was invading their privacy. People should be allowed to scream unheard by anyone. There shouldn't be any witnesses. It's a very intimate thing, the way you scream. Even worse was my deepening sense of guilt. It was because of me that this was happening to them. It was a crazy Bob Simon escapade. Even if Peter had known better, he had never been able to say "No." Juan and Roberto had just faithfully tagged along.

I started saying to myself, "I'm OK, they'll be OK; I'm OK, they'll be OK." It must have been audible. I didn't hear a guard walk by. I just felt a sharp blow to my head. I might have gone out again then because I remember a strong arm pushing me up to a sitting position.

It was strange, not being able to touch my wounds. I didn't think my skull was cracked. I wasn't sure if my head was wet with sweat or with blood and, several times, I tried to raise my hands to find out, only to discover anew that they were tied behind my back.

When it was over and we were all back up against the

47

wall, it was silent except for Roberto's quick and shallow breathing a few feet from me and the demonic howling of the dogs. Then the Iraqis, a group of them, started marching up and down the corridor, slamming their boots on the floor. It was the first time I thought of the Nazis. But what buffoons they are, I thought. Even as fascists they don't make the grade.

They stopped in front of me. "Roberto," the interrogator asked. "Is he Cuban or American?"

I didn't know what this was about, but thought I'd better stay close to the facts. "Roberto was born in Cuba," I said. "His father is a friend of Castro."

They marched off, turned around, and stopped again a few feet from me. "Roberto," I heard them ask, "are you Cuban or American?"

"I was born in Cuba," he said. "I am an American citizen."

"You told us you are Cuban," the interrogator screamed. "You are American."

Those were, I think, the last words spoken that night in that building in Basra. For the next few minutes the silence was broken only by Roberto's screams as the canes came thrashing down on his head.

For some reason I thought the cell was in the shape of an igloo. It was small. It was pitch-black inside. I had been shoved in after a fifteen-minute drive. A metal door had been slammed shut behind me.

I had no idea what time it was. My hands were still tied behind my back but I could feel that my watch was gone. I didn't know when it had been taken, but I knew it was gone. I hoped there would be many more hours of night. I knew we would be taken back to that house in the morning. Interrogations are never over. That had been just the opening session.

I rocked on my heels to keep warm. I didn't want to walk. I didn't want to sit. I just wanted to stand here and feel that, for a little while anyway, nothing else would happen. Then the door opened and closed again. A man had come inside. He walked right up to me. I could feel his breath on my face. Somehow I did not think he was going to hit me. "Can I have some water?" I said. "I haven't had a drink all night."

"You shouldn't drink the water here," he said. He had a soft voice. He sounded young. "We can drink it, but it will make you sick. You will go to Baghdad in the morning. Then you can drink, eat, everything."

"When are we going to Baghdad?"

"Nine o'clock."

"What time is it now?"

"It is four o'clock."

When he left, I managed to untie my hands, felt my head. It was covered in bumps which were capped with crusted blood, but they weren't bleeding anymore. I took my blindfold off, nervously, and kept it around my neck, thinking, if I hear the door open I will have time to put it on again. But there was nothing to see. I walked around the room slowly, trailing my hand on the cement wall. I stumbled over a pail. Liquid spilled from it. I lowered my head to the floor and smelled. It was urine.

I could feel some air, some wonderfully fresh air, coming in from an opening in the wall opposite the door. I stood there and took deep breaths. I didn't want to sleep. I was full of nervous energy. It was too cold anyway. I sat down, sat cross-legged, my back against the wall. An idea came to me which was little short of astonishing. I had been a prisoner less than fourteen hours.

I started rocking back and forth against the wall. I started whispering what I sensed would become my mantra in Iraq. "POWs survive, POWs survive," I whispered. "Most POWs survive, most POWs survive," repeating the phrase over and over again until there was nothing in my head, nothing in the world, but the sound, the sound fighting off the horror of the night. "I will survive, I will survive," I said, the sound struggling to become a belief, the sound reminding me of the time I was a boy, sitting in the back of a bus with my mother, shouting some phrase from a nursery rhyme until the sound became nonsense, and people looked at my mother and told her to make that child stop.

Dawn revealed a small square room with a solid steel door and a barred window which looked out over a sewage-filled ditch. Small birds frolicked in the slime. An army truck was parked nearby. Hours passed. I didn't know how many, but I knew it was well after 9 A.M., the promised hour of our departure. "Never believe anything they tell you," I told myself, "never believe anything they tell you." I quick-stepped the four steps across the cell to test my legs. They hurt but I didn't think anything was broken. I felt the way I did in high school the morning after a football game.

The door opened. A soldier beckoned me to come out. It was a sunny day, but he was wearing a woolen balaclava over his head. He carried an AK. My cell was one of about a dozen, all part of a concrete row. He led me along a lane to a separate, small building. The door was open. He pushed me inside. It was the toilet. But there was no way of getting to the stalls. I was standing by the door on the one dry spot in the room. The rest was a shallow lake of liquid and excrement. I'd spent a lot of time in the third world. I knew the sights and smells. But this stench made me choke. I thought I was going to be sick. I didn't move. I stood there, unzipped my fly, took a leak, and walked out. On the way back to my cell I saw something which must have made me smile or stop in my tracks, because the guard slapped me and screamed at me to hurry. Peter, in his black V-neck sweater, was being led, blindfolded, from the cell next to mine to the shithouse. We were still together.

Later, I heard someone go into Peter's cell, close the door, and talk to him. Even putting my ear to the wall, I couldn't hear the conversation, but it sounded warm and friendly. I had the impression Peter was being given food. I felt jealous. It wasn't because of the food. I wasn't hungry. I was jealous that Peter had someone to talk to. Then I heard screams from farther down the block. It was Juan.

Much later, days later in fact, when we could talk freely or thought we could, Juan told me he started screaming because he thought the Iraqis were beating me. Peter told me he had not been given food. Because of his blindfold, he could not see his visitor. And the conversation, he said, was not warm or friendly. The Iraqi wanted to know if Peter had ever heard of a man named Bazoft.

Bazoft was the British journalist executed by the Iraqis a year earlier. He had been accused of espionage.

THE ROAD

✥

THE weeks following our release, when there was little in my world beyond memories of Iraq, I felt I was beginning to understand the process of mythmaking. I could see how, when the need is great enough, a series of random events becomes infused with meaning; how, in retrospect, days which were ruled by coincidence and chaos become coherent stages in a voyage of discovery.

I will always remember that drive from Basra to Baghdad as the day I learned there is nothing that can compete with unremitting pain, not fear or hope or even thirst; not even immediate threats to one's life, like bombs impacting a few hundred meters away. I remember even hoping for a direct hit just to ease the pain in my hands.

It may not have been much after nine when we were led out of our cells. I knew we were all there. When a blindfold is not put on by a professional, you can see straight down. I could now recognize my friends by their shoes. All six of them were there, shuffling around on the sand, near mine. We were also developing a surreptitious language. We all grunted as we stood there. We could recognize each other's grunts.

For the first time they secured our hands behind our backs with real handcuffs. We were gagged, too; a strip of cloth was tied around my head, through my open mouth, tied tightly so it cut into the sides of my lips.

We were put into a station wagon. Guards sat up front. I was wedged between a back door and Roberto. I knew it was a station wagon because, from the sound of his breathing, I could tell that Peter was lying on a surface behind me. There were guards there as well.

Later, we estimated that the drive lasted ten hours. It was light most of the time; it was all on a highway. Along some stretches, we drove very slowly, swerving around bomb craters. Often I could hear voices from outside directing us off the road where it had become impassable.

Objectively it may well have been among the most dangerous hours of our captivity. In fact, many of my friends back in Saudi Arabia, journalists and soldiers, were convinced we were dead, because they knew we would end up on the road to Baghdad, and they knew what was being done to that road by allied warplanes.

But none of that mattered at the time. The only thing that mattered was my hands. The cuffs were tight to begin with. Every time the car hit a bump and I was jerked back against the seat, they tightened a notch more. I could feel the swelling. I could also feel some blood. When the car stopped, as it did several times, and I could smell gas, it was even worse. Movement at least carried with it the notion that the journey would eventually end.

When I was hospitalized with my back problem in 1986, I could ease into positions which would be tolerable for a while. But here, nothing was tolerable; no motion was possible. When I tried to lean forward, a guard from up front shoved me back against the seat.

I'd had nothing to drink in almost a day, but my gag was wet with saliva. That loosened it a bit, enough to permit me to mumble. I leaned forward, toward the guard, said, "Hands, hands."

He said something in Arabic and a guard behind me loosened my cuffs. I wriggled my hands, managed to touch my fingers. They felt like balloons. The relief disappeared after a little time and a few more bumps. The metal was cutting into my flesh again. I repeated my plea.

The guard leaned back, smashed me in the face, and tightened my gag. I did not complain anymore about my hands. I was learning passivity.

Peter must have managed to loosen his gag as well, because I heard him ask, "Can I turn? Please, can I change sides?" I heard him say that two or three times, but I never heard the sound of any motion.

We never had the impression we had arrived anywhere. Suddenly we were just dumped. It was dark. It was cold. A raw wind cut into my bruised cheeks. We definitely were not in a city street. There were a lot of people around, a lot of scurrying about, considerable excitement, but, it seemed, no plan. None of that made any difference, though. The essential thing was that our handcuffs were removed. My hands were retied in front of me with some kind of cloth. Peter later told me he thought they were preparing to shoot us then. The idea didn't occur to me. I was too busy flexing my fingers.

I was standing, and I could tell that my friends were not far, because Iraqis were shouting at them and the shouts were close by. "*Ameriki, Ameriki,*" they shouted. Swinging my body back and forth, I managed to knock up against Roberto. I knew it was Roberto because his arms felt hard and muscular. Juan had thin arms; Peter's were softer.

From nowhere, it seemed, I received a rabbit punch in the stomach. I doubled over. Whoever hit me pulled me up by my hair and started slapping me across the face with his free hand. Then I felt a leg come behind my calves. I was pushed backward and fell to the ground. My head was lying on what felt like a rise in the pavement. I propped myself up and sat on the curb. Peter was next to me. He muttered through his gag, "I think we're in an aluminum plant."

"Why?" I asked.

"I heard the guards in the car talk about ALCAN." ALCAN was Iraq's large aluminum-smelting corporation. It made sense. This was how Saddam had been using his foreign "guests," scattering them around the country, keeping them in strategic locations to discourage allied bombing.

I don't remember getting up from that cold curb. I don't remember being taken anywhere. The next thing I remember is sitting on the floor in the corner of a cell, knowing this was not an aluminum plant, knowing my friends were in the same cell, and feeling surprisingly good. We had survived another transition and we had already found out that transitions were the most precarious times of all. We'd been slapped around a bit, but in a roughhouse sort of way. There had been nothing really menacing. We were together and we were OK.

I lifted my bound hands to my face and slowly lowered my blindfold just below my eyes. It was the first time my eyes had been uncovered since I'd left that cell in Basra. We were in a rectangular cell now, each of us in a corner. This one also had a steel door, but there was a barred window near the top, giving me a glimpse of the nighttime. There must have been a fire nearby because orange light flickered on the ceiling. There was another barred window in the wall opposite the door. A candle was planted on the floor in the middle of the room. I looked at my hands. They made me think of floats in a parade. There were bloody gashes around my wrists. I looked at Peter. He was sitting in the corner diagonally across from me. His dapper red kerchief was tied tightly across his eyes, his arms were around his knees, his head was tilted toward the floor. I whispered, "My God. I didn't know."

That was, for me, the instant of recognition, or, if you insist, the moment of truth. Peter looked like a hostage. That picture of Peter in the corner brought back those haunting snapshots of Terry Anderson. I couldn't imagine what I looked like, but I realized I had never seen Peter despairing before, not in Beirut, not in Nablus, never. I knew now that this was not television. We would not be rushing back to some Sheraton with our story. We were hostages. We were American and British—not to mention Jewish—hostages in Iraq.

I have put some thought into that moment recently and my reaction now is a slightly sardonic, "Well, Bob, good morning. What had you thought for thirty-six hours, after two interrogations, one brutal beating, and a ten-hour trip on a road under fire from the air—that this was another game?" And my answer even today is a defenseless, patently inexplicable, "Yes, it appears so." It appears that reality takes a while to register, that I had clung to thoughts of that two-bit lighter and that two-minute story I hoped to file from Baghdad as mechanisms to block an awareness of what was really going on.

I whispered loudly, "Peter!"

A face appeared at the barred window to our cell. "Don't speak anything."

Soldiers came in and out of the cell, telling us we could take our blindfolds off before others wandered in and ordered us to put them back on. It was chaotic but not threatening. Everyone seemed to want part of the action. In Peter's favorite metaphor for Iraqi behavior, everyone was kicking the ball at once.

Again, I was the first to be led away. I knew I was being taken for an interrogation, but as soon as I was led into the room, I was not afraid. You quickly learn to see through blindfolds, technically and psychologically. You can sense the level of light, the proportions of a space, but more important, you can sense the mood of a situation, whether it is hostile or threatening. Here, I knew I was back in the hands of army people, not thugs of the Muhabarat, the intelligence service that worked us over in Basra. Even the requisite threat was veiled with some elegance.

"Please cooperate with us so we will have reason to treat you well." Thank God, the scriptwriting was getting better.

"I will answer your questions," I said. "But my hands are swollen and infected. Please untie them. There is no reason for this."

"There is reason for it," came the reply. But there was some hesitation in the voice.

There were many men in the room, I sensed, many men but no bravado. They asked the questions of concerned professionals, men who believed their lives might depend on the information they thought I might be able to provide.

"Will the Americans use chemical weapons?"

"I don't think so. Not unless Iraq uses them first."

"Will the Americans use nuclear weapons?"

"I don't think so. It is just my opinion, but I don't think so."

"When will the ground war begin?"

"I have no idea." I decided to try again. "I'm answering your questions," I said, "please untie my hands."

They spoke among themselves in Arabic and my hands were untied. I took a deep breath, moved my arms around, and went for paydirt. "Can I have a cigarette?" I said.

There was a pause. Then I heard the voice of a man who had clearly learned his English in the United States. "Is Marlboro OK?" he asked.

"Marlboro is fine," I said. They laughed. Someone put a cigarette in my mouth. I could see a flame through my blindfold, and the silhouette of a tall man with a mustache. I took several deep drags, felt a dizzying sense of warm well-being.

There is such an inclination in the Arab world for things to get so personal so quickly that even though this was a formal military procedure, even though I was a blindfolded prisoner, the interrogation was somehow becoming social. In the give and take, it was clear that they knew so little, their channels of information were keeping them so much in the dark, that on several occasions I was on the verge of saying, "Look, don't you guys get it? You're going to get slaughtered. They're going to hit you with the force they put together to take on the Russians. They're in a different league. Don't you understand?" I felt on the verge of saying it, but I didn't and to this day I wonder what would have happened if I had. Maybe nothing at all. Maybe they would have taken it seriously. But they were too far from the border to defect, and the Americans never came near enough to give them a chance.

The atmosphere was so benign that even when the dreaded theme came up it didn't frighten me nearly as much as it should have. "We think you are a CIA man," the head of the panel said, a little laugh in his voice.

"I'm not. I'm a journalist."

"But we don't know that."

"You have my credentials."

"Anyone can get credentials."

"You can check. I'm reasonably well known in the United States."

"Maybe, but not here." They liked that. They always liked that. Even a young soldier who became a friend later on had a wonderful time every time Peter said to him, "Mr. Bob very big man in America," and he would reply, "Yes, but Mr. Bob very little man in Iraq." Peter liked it too.

When I sensed that the interrogation was coming to an end, I made the appeal, the urgent appeal I had been preparing from the start. "We are all nervous and frightened," I said. "Please, let us stay together. It is so important."

"That is not possible."

"But we're together now. Can't we just stay where we are?"

There was a pause and some talk in Arabic, an argument, it seemed. "All right, we will keep you together."

I got up and reached my hand out into the darkness. Someone shook it and I was taken away.

Juan, Roberto, and Peter all came back from their interrogations in high spirits. Peter said they brought up the spy question with him too, but they told him we would be taken to Baghdad soon for a television appearance. That was the best news yet. Whatever paces they put us through on TV, it would let our families know we were alive. It would also mean the Iraqis acknowledged we were in their hands, a giant step toward survival, toward not being "disappeared."

The most critical problem right now was the cold. We had each been given a blanket. We put two on the cement floor to absorb some of the dampness. And then, putting the other two blankets over us, we four lay down together in a corner, pressing against each other for warmth and reassurance. Even Peter's snoring, which might well have been overheard by the pilots soaring overhead, couldn't keep us awake.

CAMP

❧❧

THE bombing woke me several times that night. Once it wasn't the noise that woke me as much as the floor trembling underneath. I wanted to get up, walk to the window, see what was happening, but I couldn't tear myself away from the warmth of Roberto. He was on his side, facing Juan; I was snuggled up against his back, thinking this is how I usually sleep with Françoise. A few times I put my arms around him to draw him even closer, hoping that the move wouldn't startle him. Juan's breathing was congested, sounded like he was getting sick. He had fallen into a rhythm with the bassoon of Peter's snoring. Their nasal chorus drowned out much of the bombing.

I woke up in the morning to see a square, barred sunblock on the floor. I watched it awhile, listened to the birds, and looked at my hands. The swelling was down, but the gash looked infected. My friends were fast asleep. Then I saw round shadows move into my sunblock. I looked up. Three soldiers were peering through the window with huge smiles. One of them held up what looked

63

like a whole-wheat roll. It was feeding time. I got up, took the roll, and said, "Thank you." They seemed to think that was funny. "Sank you, sank you," they mimicked me, laughing, and walked away. I took a bite of the hard roll and walked back inside. "Hey, get up, breakfast is served," I said.

Visitors came by all morning and stood outside our cell, asking questions and offering comments through the bars. The most common question was, "Why you come to my country?" The most frequent comment was a single syllable: the name of our president. It was pronounced "Boosh" and was usually followed by the sound of a thick wad of spittle being fired at the ground. But these were children; they looked like high school boys in uniform, students showing off their English. There was more curiosity than malice in their voices. "What your name? Where you from?" they would ask. And we would go through our routine, always in the same order: "Cuba, Nicaragua, England, New York." I always said "New York." It seemed to carry less of a sting than "America."

Fortunately, they tried out other phrases as well. "You smoke?" we were asked. "Yes," we would say. Roberto, Juan, and I ended up chain-smoking much of that first morning. We began to stockpile cigarettes on the windowsill. We had no idea where we were, but it was clear these soldiers hadn't seen many of our kind before. Word must have gotten around that some very strange people were in one of the cells.

We figured it was lunchtime when the soldiers disappeared. After a while one of them came into our cell with a metal mess tray and one spoon. Pieces of bread were floating in a cloudy liquid. We started taking turns wolfing down the soggy bread. It was cold and tasteless; almost tasteless, but not quite. Peter was convinced someone had urinated in it. Faces, laughing mischievous faces, reappeared at the bars as we sat looking at the floor. We believed Peter.

Our cell was one in a row of ten in a long one-story concrete building. Other, identical buildings, seemed to be barracks. One of them, across a dirt lane from us, was the latrine. We were taken there that first afternoon, one by one, escorted by an armed soldier. There were a dozen sinks, but only one of them worked; it had cold running water during the day. There were two rows of toilets, Middle Eastern toilets, holes in the floor with platforms for your feet. Two of them, the only ones anyone used, had rubber hoses with running water. There was no paper, of course. Middle Easterners generally use water to clean themselves. It's not a bad system when you get the knack. We had definitely come up in the world from Basra.

The back of the latrine faced an empty lot; our mud lot as we came to call it, because for days after it rained, the puddles didn't dry up. The lot was bordered by a bunch of bamboo stalks which stood, tall and graceful, over coils of barbed wire. The complex was dominated by a water tower on the other side of the wire. Beyond it a highway, long and straight and heavily traveled, led we knew not where.

What kind of place was it? We didn't really know. It was an army camp. That much was clear. But it was also a prison, even though it didn't seem to have been built as one, and we were the only prisoners.

We felt safer as the days wore on, but our health was deteriorating quickly. It was cold and dank in the cell. Moisture seeped up from the floor, soaking our blankets. Ominous as the nightly bombing was, I thought pneumonia was far more likely to get us. By the third day Juan was feverish with a deep, rasping cough. I was coughing too. That morning an officer came to our cell. His voice was familiar; it sounded like the genteel interrogator of a few nights ago. Peter asked him if the Ministry of Information had been informed of our situation. He said, "Communications have been sent. Maybe you will leave in a few days." I told him we needed a doctor and Juan coughed on cue. The officer nodded and five minutes later a medic arrived with a dozen ampicillin tablets, cough syrup, aspirin, and vitamin C. I walked to the window because, for the first time since we were captured, I thought I was going to cry. "We're going to make it," I said to myself. "They have antibiotics. We're going to make it."

A few minutes later Juan was baring his ass for a glycerin shot. That evening a little boy—which is how I will always think of him, though he carried an AK-47 and wore an Iraqi uniform—a little boy brought his kerosene stove to our cell. His name was Maher. He would be cold in coming nights. We would be warm.

Our situation improved dramatically after the officer's visit. They started letting us out in the sun in the afternoon. We sat against the cement wall of the latrine—our

66

sunning wall, as we called it. We took the occasional prisoner's stroll around our mud lot; we chatted and we snacked. There was always plenty of bread: brown rolls, baked in the camp. Juan did most of the cooking, toasting the rolls on the fire the guards kept going day and night, piling on great globs of butter. Roberto specialized in blankets and cigarettes, organizing the hanging out of blankets in the morning and the securing of cigarettes whenever possible. I was the orderly, doling out pills and vitamins and stirring up a baroque dietary supplement the medic had given us: strawberry-flavored protein powder which needed to be mixed with water. Naturally, there was considerable overlap in our vocations — except for Peter. He was the only one authorized to make tea, brewing it in a blackened kettle over the fire. He was adamant that our circumstances should in no way compromise his standards. The tea must not be too strong, or too sweet, the way the Arabs like it. When we didn't have tea, Peter made a concoction from orange peels and sugar which we joked about but which wasn't bad at all.

We were in a camp, but sometimes, in our lighter moments, it reminded us of summer camp. Then, to bring us back to reality, we would without explanation be herded back into our cell, a piece of cardboard shoved over our window. There were some things we were not meant to see.

One night the bombing was very close and seemed to be getting closer. Clearly, the allies knew about this army base. Peter and I rushed to the window. Tracers streamed across the black sky. We shouted at a guard sitting by the fire outside to let us out, take us to a bunker. He looked up, ambled over to our door as a bomb exploded just outside the perimeter. He didn't understand. We pointed at the lock, mimicked the motions of opening it. He said, "*Mafish muftah*," no key. We screamed at him, grabbed the bars, shook the door until the noise was louder than the bombs. Peter swung his arms about, pantomimed bombs falling, the cell collapsing. The guard smiled. He had a mouthful of silver teeth. "*Inshallah*," he said. "*Inshallah*."

"It's OK for you, mate," Peter said. "You get hit, you get to go to paradise. We just get dead."

The third or fourth night, Maher brought us coats for Peter and Roberto. He spoke no English, but broke into a warm, ear-to-ear smile when Peter grabbed him by the shoulders and said, "Maher, you are a great man."

We were making other friends too. In fact, before long Peter and I found ourselves reflecting how much more we liked these people than the Saudis. There was a natural softness and kindness here. Compared to them, the Saudis seemed cold and arrogant. These Iraqis had so much less and smiled so much more.

One boy, tall and lanky and laughing, came around one of the first mornings with a cup of tea. He took a sip from it to show me it hadn't been poisoned. Then he passed it through the bars. Hassein was the cook. He became a frequent visitor. He always asked, "What my name? What my name? Tell me my name," and we would pretend not to remember. He spoke enough English to teach me some Arabic. I was learning the words for wall, floor, ceiling, window. I was learning how to say, "I'm hungry, I'm thirsty, I'm cold." But to me, in those first lessons, the most beautiful word in the Arabic language was *"patanya."* I loved the sound, the poetry of it. I let the syllables linger. *"pa-tan-ya."* What lyricism for a household item—a blanket. But blankets were the most beautiful, the most comforting objects in Iraq. That night Maher came by and gave us two more.

One soldier who was around us all the time but kept his distance was Aziz, a fierce-looking, well-built man with an orange mustache and an angry scowl. He must have been our guard. He would stand in the middle of the lane, never putting his weapon down, never coming over for a chat. Sometimes, when he thought we were laughing too much with other soldiers, he would chase them away. Whenever he looked at me, his eyes would narrow and hate would creep in. We never exchanged a word. One afternoon, as the sun was setting, I was standing against the wall outside the cell, waiting to be ordered back in. I was not feeling terrific just then, and it must have shown. Aziz looked at me inquisitively. I said, *"Ana za'alan,"* I'm sad. He walked over, handed me the cigarette he had just lit, and walked away. Aziz became a friend.

One morning I was sitting against the wall in the cell, my blanket wrapped around me like a poncho, waiting for my friends to wake up, when I heard someone pacing back and forth slowly outside, counting, in a low but clearly audible voice. *"Ehad, steim, shalosh,"* he said. He was counting in Hebrew. It was the most threatening sound I had heard in Iraq. Could they have found out? He came to the window, looked inside, caught my eye. "*Ata medaber ivrit?*" he asked. Do you speak Hebrew? I pretended not to understand. He was an older man, seemed to be in his late thirties, and impeccably groomed, clean-shaven, his black hair plastered down and neatly parted, an elegant mustache curled up at the ends. He beckoned me to come to the window. "*Ata medaber ivrit?*" he asked again with a smile. He had one star on his epaulet, the mark of a lieutenant. He seemed quite old to be a lieutenant. He gave off the authority of a much higher rank, and a heavy scent of cologne. "You speak Hebrew?" he asked me in English.

"No," I said, "I don't speak Hebrew." I knew I had to be terribly careful. Any slip here could be fatal. The notion that a Jew based in Israel could be a bona fide American journalist would have been unthinkable to the Iraqis.

"Too bad," he said. "I speak Hebrew good, not good English." He offered me a cigarette, a Rothman. "What your name?" he asked.

"Bob," I said.

"Bob," he repeated with a laugh. "Mr. Bob," he said and walked off.

Lieutenant Abu Jihad was the only officer we got to know. He must have been in charge of us, was always dropping by, rolling cigarettes for us when he ran out of Rothmans. One night when we'd had very little to eat, he showed up with a brown paper bag full of gorgeous, grease-saturated fried fish. He was our "comforter" more than anything else, offering constant reassurance that it would end well, that we would get back to our families.

Our status in the camp was improving because the soldiers were hearing about us on the radio. One morning Hassein told us *very* confidentially: "Radio Monte Carlo say you lost, say you names, say CBS, say you lost."

Precision was of the essence here. "Say we lost or in Iraq?" I asked.

"Lost, you, you four, lost."

"Radio Baghdad?" I asked. "Radio Baghdad say something?"

"No, Monte Carlo. Baghdad say nothing."

So Iraq wasn't acknowledging us yet. Our families must still be walking around with what Peter described as "that empty feeling."

Françoise would know by now. Whatever anyone tried to tell her, she would know that I was either dead or in very serious trouble. I pictured her in a hotel room at the Parker Meridien in New York, surviving on black coffee and cigarettes. I knew she wouldn't be depressed. She would be too busy for that. She would be working the phones around the clock. Actually, I had more faith in her ability to cope with this than with my own. The toughest thing for her would be the television appearances. I knew she'd have to do them, and I knew she would force herself to do them, but my wife is the most private person I have ever known. She loathes melodrama; would hate making a spectacle of her anguish. I suspected she would leave her room only when she had to; that she would turn it into her own private cell to be close to me.

Tanya would also know, of course. When we lived in Saigon and she was a year old, the '72 spring offensive was under way, and I was filing stories from Hue. When they were broadcast by the American military television network, as they were most nights, Tanya would get on all fours and look behind the TV set to see where her father was hiding. When I wasn't on, she would get agitated. In 1975, when we were living in London and I went back to Vietnam to cover the last months of the war, the BBC carried my stories. The first night I didn't appear, Tanya announced to Françoise, "Mommy, Daddy's dead."

Roberto and I tended to wake up earlier than Peter or Juan. It would be dark. We would pace around the room, crisscrossing in silence, occasionally stopping to talk. I called these our "anxiety walks." I didn't voice what was really on my mind; the cell seemed too primitive to be bugged, but I couldn't be sure. Time, I figured, was on the side of my three friends, but working against me. Eventually the Iraqis were bound to find out more about us, if not from interrogations, then from sources outside Iraq. They would find out that Juan, Peter, and Roberto were exactly who they said they were and that I was not. I was not Protestant and I was not based in New York. I did not know if I was more afraid of what this could mean in the long term — death, for example — or in the short term: the possibility of being separated from my friends.

Roberto did not speak about fears of death, at least not then. He was worried about how long we'd be held. It did me good to hear his anxiety stop at the issue of duration. We played a game those nights, Roberto and me, a speculative game: "Choice," we called it. What would we do, we asked, if we could make a deal right now, sign on the dotted line? Choice A: we get out of here safely in three months but not before. Choice B: leave it up to the fates. I would grab the three-month deal, I told him. Roberto wasn't sure.

Juan was sinking further into silence. His health was improving. He smiled his warm smile and said he felt fine whenever he was asked. He was full of affection for the rest of us. But he talked less and less and spent more time sleeping; lying down with his eyes closed, anyway.

Peter and I spent hours debating whose fault it was that we had been captured. We would sit outside, our backs against the wall, those long afternoons, each trying to grab on to the lion's share of blame for everything that had happened. There were a few things we could agree on: that we had always been excited by and gone along with the wilder instincts of the other; that, in this sense, while we had enjoyed each other's company for years, we were really quite bad for each other. The jury was in on that. We also agreed that when we took that stroll we were just doing what we do, what we'd always done, not only in the obvious sense of checking out a story, but in a deeper sense as well. We had always been moved to go where others don't go, to see what they can't see. We were voyeurs at heart, as were so many of our finest colleagues. You took a peek at the forbidden, you undressed an event: you didn't get involved, you just watched, then you told the world what you'd seen. It was the secret credo of the journalist. Peter said it was all he'd ever wanted to do since his boyhood in the north of England, just peer around that corner, then tell your friends.

73

Moving past lines had been the foundation of our friendship from the start. We had met in Beirut in 1983. He was new to the CBS London Bureau, having just left a job with PBS in Washington. I was working out of New York and knew Beirut fairly well. I'd spent three months there during the Israeli invasion a year earlier. The Israelis were gone now; the conflict had reverted to its essence: a civil war between the Christians and the Syrian-backed Muslims, with the Americans caught in between. Peter and I drove into the Shouf mountains, the principal battleground, most days. At night we'd stroll around the city after dinner and watch the battleship *New Jersey* fire over Beirut at Syrian enclaves in the hills.

After one harrowing week, we decided we'd start taking Sundays off, go to the beach. We drove north along the coast, past the ancient walled city of Byblos. We stopped at the many checkpoints, manned by the myriad Lebanese factions, reached into our pockets full of press cards and laissez-passer, hoping we'd pull the right card for the right militia. About twenty miles north of Byblos, we slowed down for a roadblock and saw that it was manned by Syrians. It was too late to turn around. The Syrians were at first amazed that men working for an American outfit had come their way. Then they started laughing. They pointed at the hills, at their positions in the hills just then, being pulverized by American naval gunfire, and they pointed at us and laughed. When they stopped laughing, a few of them came along with us to the beach, joined us for a picnic. On our way back to Beirut that night, we stopped at a restaurant carved into the ruins of Byblos, overlooking the sea. We had fresh shrimps and cold white wine and decided that we'd had a perfectly wonderful day. We went back every Sunday, bringing sandwiches, beer, and newspapers to our Syrian friends. Our first foray beyond the line had gone well.

Years later, in 1988, our incurable curiosity landed us an exclusive which became one of the most controversial stories either one of us had ever covered. It was the height of the *intifada*. I was already based in Israel; Peter was a visiting fireman. For days we heard that a lot was happening in Nablus, the largest and most radical town on the West Bank, but we weren't getting any pictures. Peter and I drove to Nablus on February twenty-fifth. There was certainly a lot happening, but the pictures were familiar, almost ritualistic. Palestinian kids threw rocks at Israeli troops; the soldiers fired back with tear gas canisters and rubber bullets. We'd seen it before. The world had seen it before. Then a group of Palestinian boys climbed partway up the hill overlooking a main road and started stoning cars. A platoon of Israeli soldiers went up after them. We were about to join the chase and then thought better of it. They were all a lot younger and faster than we were, and our cameraman, Moshe Alpert, who makes nature films when he isn't covering riots, always carries a very long lens. He set his tripod up on the road and we looked through the viewfinder. The soldiers caught up with two of the boys and started beating them mercilessly. They picked up large rocks and battered their arms and shoulders, clearly trying to break their arms. We knew this sort of thing went on. We had seen many Palestinians hospitalized with broken bones. But it never happened in front of cameras, and it was only happening now because we were too far away for the soldiers to know we were there. We took turns looking in the viewfinder, took turns peeking at this sadistic show, took turns running around looking for an officer to make it stop. We didn't find one, and the footage we aired that night was broadcast and rebroadcast all over the Americas, Europe, and Asia. The world came down on Israel, and Israel came down on CBS. Alpert, a tough and robust kibbutznik, received so many threats that he needed a bodyguard, was warned not to set foot again on the West Bank. I wound up trying to defend our coverage for months afterward, in dozens of interviews and panel discussions, trying to explain that we were just doing what we do, trying to see what others don't see, and then telling our friends.

Peter and I weren't very demonstrative about our friendship. When I left Beirut in '83 (earlier than planned because my father was dying in America), we didn't say goodbye to each other. We just waved as I got into a car on the dark street in front of the Commodore Hotel.

Now, our backs against the wall, we tried to express to each other what we were both feeling: "I'm sorry you're here, mate, but if I have to be here, thank God you are too."

We were losing weight. I could tell by looking at Peter's face and at the notches on my belt. But it wasn't drastic. The daytime meal was usually soup, served in the metal mess tray. Almost inedible before we got the kerosene lamp, it was OK once we could heat it up. After dinner the kids would assign one of us to take the tray to the latrine for a cold-water wash. In the afternoon, outdoors, we got a couple of eggs once. Another time we got a tomato. At night Hassein dropped by when he could with a little meat.

After one such evening, I woke up long before dawn and walked to the door. Two soldiers in great woolen coats were warming themselves by a fire outside, their Kalashnikovs leaning against the latrine wall. The flames threw out enough light to color the cell walls a pale orange. I could see my friends huddled together, fast asleep. I could still smell the cooked meat we had devoured hours earlier. I could taste the bitter orange from Peter's patented brew. The sound of bombs had woken me up. But it was quiet now. Smoke from the kerosene stove hovered near the ceiling, providing what looked like a white and protective cloud. But there was something else permeating the air of our cell that morning. That dark morning, the only word I could find to describe it was love.

At first light we would stand by our window and receive offerings. The soldiers would pass by and pass through the bars anything they had squirreled away from their breakfast: dates, usually, sometimes a few oranges. Maher walked by quickly once and without stopping or smiling handed me a potato, an unpeeled, boiled potato. I stared at it in wonder for a moment before launching into an unforgettable breakfast.

It was only later, much later, that I realized how naturally, in the space of a few days, I had made the transition from credit card–carrying correspondent to itinerant beggar. It was so quick, and instinctive, really, I didn't even think about it at the time.

We were all articulating that adjustment in different ways. Roberto mentioned how he never thought he would find himself without shampoo or hair conditioner and how, remarkably, life seemed to go on without them. What we all really missed were toothbrushes. I took to pulling twigs off a tree outside the cell to clean my teeth and rub my gums. We asked Maher and Hassein to buy us toothbrushes the next time they went on leave, but even though we offered to pay them, it never happened. Roberto had several hundred dollars which the friskers had missed in one of his pockets. We plotted offering to pay one of our friends to telephone the Al-Rasheed Hotel in Baghdad, get word to our colleagues where we were. But the enterprise seemed too risky. How much could we trust them, after all? Memories of Basra urged caution. We never followed through.

The special irony of our situation — how the makers of stories were becoming the subjects of a story — was never lost on us. Every evening we gave the day a title, the kind of caption we would, in another life, fax to CBS in New York before we satellited an item. Our title for the fourth day, for example, became "We all take a shit, and receive new guests." We were quite proud about our growing proficiency at using the latrine of a common Iraqi soldier, and using it with impeccable hygiene, a process I will not describe but which took some doing. It became an "event" during days which were not always packed with them. On day four, however, we heard a commotion, and saw, from our cell window, two men in flight suits being led to the latrine, blindfolded. Three Iraqis were supporting each of them. It wasn't clear whether they were being propped up because they were in such bad shape or because they were just being closely guarded. But one of them, especially, seemed to be in considerable pain. He wasn't being led as much as dragged along the dirt lane. We weren't meant to see this. When a guard saw our faces in the window, he ordered us to sit down and shoved the cardboard across to block our view. We weren't let out that afternoon. The next morning Hassein told us they were British pilots, shot down in the south. Two days later, three more blindfolded men arrived. They were also British, but not pilots. With a combination of English and sign language our friends told us they were artillery spotters captured in Iraq, a good sign that the ground war was under way.

The next day, in fact, Hassein and Aziz let us know, by making their fingers move like men falling from the sky, that there had been an American paratroop landing in Kuwait. Things were looking good. We knew it was not going to be a long war. It had begun.

When we were let out again, we saw clusters of soldiers gathered outside two other cells along our block, like children at a zoo, peering into a cage. That night, two of our blankets were taken away. We never saw the Brits again. Our window was covered more often now, every time, we supposed, that they were taken to the toilet. They were never let outside with us. They were never allowed to sit in the sun or hang out their blankets. They, apparently, weren't "privileged" the way we were. Word had obviously come down to the camp to give us special treatment. At least that was our fantasy for a while.

I was concentrating on my Arabic as hard as I could, both to focus on something other than our predicament and because there were several "end-game" scenarios I could imagine where a working knowledge of street Arabic would be helpful. I was taking a lesson with Hassein one morning, reviewing words I had learned the previous day, words for things we could see from the mud lot: tree, birds, fence, car. I pointed to the road and asked, "*Shoo?*" What?

"*Tariq,*" he said.

"*Wen tariq?*" I asked, the only way I knew how to ask "the road to where?"

"Baghdad," he said.

"*Kedesh?*" I asked. How far?

"*Hamsa oshreen,*" he said before he realized what was happening and walked away. I felt a tinge of guilt for having tricked someone who had been kind to us, but I rationalized it without too much trouble. What I'd learned could be important. We were twenty-five kilometers from Baghdad.

BAGHDAD BOUND

❖❖

W HEN you're a prisoner things always happen suddenly. You have very little information, you're never part
of any planning, you don't witness any preparations. You
never see the windup; you just feel the punch.

We were having a jog around our mud lot one afternoon
when suddenly a few officers appeared and ordered us
blindfolded and bound. Our friends did the job; Maher
took care not to hurt my hands, which were beginning to
heal, as he tied them behind my back. "Television," he
whispered. "Television."

We were led down the lane past the cellblock and
shoved into a small car, the four of us squeezed together on
the backseat. It was as uncomfortable as it had ever been,
but I didn't care. The war was under way and we were on
our way. I calculated: if we're released tomorrow, I can be
back in Amman the next day and fly to Saudi Arabia the
day after that. I wouldn't miss the war after all. Physically,
I was OK. A couple of cheeseburgers, I thought, and I'll
be back up to scratch. I just hoped the Saudis would give
me a visa. They might be pretty pissed off.

Nothing happened for a while. The front door opened and men got in: the engine started, but the car didn't move. There was a lot of shouting and running about. Everyone was kicking the ball at once. Then soldiers started taping newspapers to the car windows. This made sense; they didn't want us spotted in the streets. Then, just as suddenly, it all stopped. The car doors opened, we were yanked out and taken back to our cell. No one offered any explanation. We were not taken outside any more that day; our friends didn't come around that evening, and we never found out what had happened.

Peter voiced what had become his preferred metaphor for the twists and turns of our fate. "Well," he said, "one more stop on the roller coaster."

The supplies we had accumulated on our windowsill — butter, oranges, and dates — had disappeared. Other than that, we were back to square one. I was still a jailbird. The journalists were in Dhahran.

That night we played the word game "Botticelli" to try to forget the day. It reminded me of the long overnight drives I took when I was in college to go skiing in Vermont. I was lying on the floor next to Peter while we played, and I stayed there when we went to sleep.

The next day, pacing in the lot, our eyes on the ground to avoid the puddles, I told Peter something I had never told him before, something I hardly ever discussed with anyone. I told him how, after being immobilized for several months with my ruptured disc back in '86, I dropped into a deep and debilitating depression. I told him I was a touch worried that it could happen again, but

I didn't really think so; certainly not while we were together.

The days tried to slip by unnoticed while we collected captions to leave our prints on the passage of time. "Peter Gets a Haircut" was one day's headline. The camp barber made the offer; only Peter accepted. The ceremony was performed in a room just a few doors down from us, which actually resembled a barbershop. There were even newspapers on a table. We sat and watched and laughed along with a bunch of amused soldiers, but when I picked up a newspaper, Abu Jihad quickly and unobtrusively took it away.

Another day they offered us the opportunity to wash, and this became "The Cleansing of the CBS Four." They took us, one by one, out to the water tower, where there was an open cold water tap and a bar of soap. There were no towels, so when I was clean and wet and cold, I jumped up and down until I was dry enough to put my dirty clothes back on. The soldiers, peasant boys mainly, had a natural discretion about them. They turned their backs as I did my drying dance in the sun. Hassein gave us a razor that afternoon and we all shaved, except Peter. I'd never done it without a mirror before. I managed not to cut myself too badly, and felt good, running my palm over my smooth skin. Aziz gave us his toothbrush, which we shared.

Evenings, we would review our captions and talk about how one day we would make a movie out of our experience, how we would sit under Peter's great tree, the four of us, and put it all down on paper. Abu Jihad always came by. "You will go home," he would say. "When, I don't know, but, *inshallah*, you will go home." Deep down I didn't believe him; I didn't think he knew anything; I thought he was just saying what he knew we needed to hear. But we all waited for his nightly reassurance sessions and listened, like frightened children, when he told us everything was going to be all right.

It was Abu Jihad who came up to us after we'd been in the camp a week and handed us an Arabic newspaper. I wondered about this change in policy and then looked at the front page and understood. There was a picture of Saddam Hussein and Peter Arnett of CNN. They were both smiling. We got very excited. I had known Arnett since '71 in Saigon when he had been in Vietnam many years with the Associated Press. We had covered the Cyprus war together in '74, and we were now both based in Israel. Clearly, the photo meant that Arnett was pleading our case with Saddam. It probably meant that the entire press corps, including CBS, was back in Baghdad. That would mean daily appeals on our behalf, daily assurances from our colleagues that we were who we said we were.

To me it also suggested that maybe, just maybe, the Iraqis were becoming a little more sophisticated about reporters based in Israel. Of course, Arnett was not a native American and he was not Jewish and he was not a prisoner . . .

That afternoon I was taking the circular prisoners' walk, arm in arm with Abu Jihad. He was at his warmest and most comforting. He was looking at the ground, searching for a word. We walked a few feet past the edge of the latrine building, where the lane came into view. Coming toward us were fifteen soldiers, including our very best friends. They were kicking and beating a tall POW in an Egyptian uniform. Some of them had sticks. They were clobbering him on the head, taking long strokes, as if they were swinging a scythe. He did not fall down because the soldiers did not give him enough room to fall down. I had never seen anyone beaten so badly. When Abu Jihad saw what I was seeing, he hurried me back to the blind spot behind the latrine and walked down the lane toward his troops.

I knew the sound of Abu Jihad's voice when he shouted an order. I also knew the Arabic word for "stop." I did not hear either.

I told my friends, who were sitting and soaking up the rays, "I just saw something I did not want to see," and realized, then and there, how my mind had been blocking out so many awful possibilities, so many things that could happen to us.

Minutes later we were hurried back to our cell and Abu Jihad came by on his rounds. He spoke to us through the bars. He assumed a distraught expression, but was not much of an actor. "He is an Arab," he said, "an Egyptian. He was fighting his brother. Not like American or Englishman. He must die."

I did not question Abu Jihad. I was questioning myself. I had been feeding on Roberto's jaunty optimism, Juan's childlike faith, and Peter's robust cheerfulness for support. My own thoughts, had I permitted them to surface in their plenitude, would have taken me down different and dangerous roads.

That night I woke up from a bad dream. A man was being beaten. He was lying on a green lawn, being kicked and pummeled by an enraged mob. He was surrounded. There was no escape. When I woke up, I realized that the man was me. It had happened twenty years ago, in Belfast. I hadn't thought about it in a long time. It was on the sweeping lawns outside Stormont, the seat of Ulster's government. The Reverend Ian Paisley, firebrand right-wing Protestant, had called on "twenty thousand men of Ulster" to follow him on a protest march. They were denouncing political concessions being offered to the Catholic minority. We'd been covering the demonstration all afternoon. There was considerable sound and fury, but nowhere near the numbers Paisley had called for. When it came time to do my stand-up, we found an unpopulated expanse of green. I took the microphone, and the cameraman started rolling. What I said was innocuous enough: "The Reverend Ian Paisley and some two thousand of his followers came to Stormont today . . ." But I never finished it. I got a fist in the face. Then three men tackled me to the ground. They picked me up again, started punching and kicking me as I saw the mob that had been listening to Paisley turn and start toward me. I could not fall because there was no room to fall. I must have passed out, because the next thing I remembered was being dragged through the crowd by two officers of the Royal Ulster Constabulary who had fought their way in to save me. I thought I'd been attacked because of what I'd said, disputing Paisley's numbers. The cops thought it was because I had "sandy hair," and, therefore, "looked Catholic." The cops said the men of Ulster had gone for me because they thought I was "an Irish spy."

In the morning, when we were alone, I forced myself to ask Peter, "Do you think much about the spy thing?"

"Yeah, well I try not to," he said, "but it's always there, isn't it?"

We never saw the Egyptian again. We knew the two groups of Britons were still with us. We saw regular activity outside their cells. But we never saw the Egyptian again. The soldiers never spoke of him, nor would they answer questions about him. There was no sign of his presence anywhere in the camp.

It seemed as though we weren't going to see much more of Abu Jihad either. He came around one morning looking dejected and didn't appear to be acting this time. He told us he had been ordered to the front. We told him we didn't want him to go, that he should tell his commanders that the CBS Four wanted him to stay. "I must go," he said. "It is my duty."

That afternoon Peter and I were sitting outdoors, watching an officer wash his car, a Toyota, on the other side of the lot. We talked about how when you're a prisoner even the most humdrum domestic scenes look like they're sketched in remarkably tender colors.

Peter is built like a rugby player, but there is something elusive, almost waiflike, about him. I have always thought of him as an Anglo-Saxon version of Le Petit Prince, prancing through his life on tiptoes, hiding behind trees. But sometimes he narrows his eyes, concentrates, and, in a fleeting flash frame, lets you know precisely what's going on. It was such an instant when he said to me: "You know what really keeps me going, don't you? I just want to see how this story is going to end."

Sometimes now I think I knew back then. I remember sitting there against our sunning wall, watching the bamboos bend with the wind and feeling the view being transformed into a photograph in front of my eyes, a photograph I would contemplate with deepening nostalgia. I remember thinking: I am going to recall this scene with longing. It's not that I was happy then. When you're happy somewhere you don't want to leave, and I certainly wanted to get out of that place. But I knew somehow that things were going to get a lot worse, that I would remember this muddy lot with wild weeds, bordered by a latrine on one side and barbed wire on the other, as the golden age of our captivity, and that there were only three other people in the world who would ever understand.

Months later, when I went back to Iraq to shoot a documentary, more than anything else I wanted to return to this place. It was my secret agenda, one which I never discussed with my colleagues from CBS, the producers and cameramen, who came along on the trip. Of course I didn't know exactly where it was or how to identify it and the Iraqis never would have permitted it anyway. But whenever I saw Iraqi soldiers, I would comb the ranks, looking for Maher and Aziz, Hassein and Abu Jihad, expecting to see them somehow, fervently hoping to see them so I could dismiss from my mind the haunting specter that they had perished in the allied onslaught.

It was the ninth day of our stay in the camp. I had just finished washing up in the latrine. I was rounding the corner to the sunning wall and saw Juan, Peter, and Roberto being blindfolded, their hands tied behind their backs. It was time for a trip. But something felt wrong. I knew something was wrong when, after I rushed back to our cell to pocket our pharmaceuticals, after I'd been blindfolded and bound, the soldier leading me down the lane whispered, "This is Aziz, Mr. Bob. I'm sorry, Mr. Bob, I'm so sorry."

Before we were pushed into the car, I felt Peter next to me, and I blurted out, "Hope springs eternal . . ."

"Yeah," he said, but the way he said it let me know he understood. He knew we were not boarding the freedom train. We were not going to Iraqi TV. We were not going to drink sweet tea with the Minister of Information. I managed one more sentence before the guards in the car made us shut up.

"At least we're still together," I said.

THE WHITE SHIP

❖❖

S AMI wanted to do it but he was nervous. We were finishing dinner in a restaurant near the Sheraton Hotel. Sami ordered another cup of coffee. He was a large, solid man in his fifties. He had been through a lot, hated the regime, and took risks every day to help us, but this one made him nervous.

It was the twenty-second of May. I'd been back in Baghdad two days now, working on our documentary, and there was a place I wanted to see: not the camp, another place. Sami was one of our Iraqi contacts; a translator who doubled as a driver. He'd been on and off the CBS payroll for years. "Only bad things happen there," Sami said. "People who live in the neighborhood, when they walk by, they don't even look. Drivers, when they drive past, they keep their eyes straight ahead. Someone may be watching. Everyone afraid."

"Well, what do you think?" I asked.

"OK," he said. "I do it. I just finish my coffee."

I sat next to Sami, in the front of the car. We drove past restaurants and nightclubs, gaudily decorated with strings of Christmas tree lights. There was a lot less bomb damage in Baghdad than I'd expected. Life was returning to normal. We pulled up onto a sidewalk and stopped. It was an outdoor tire shop, illuminated by a couple of naked light bulbs. Men sat on stools, patching up inner tubes. Sami got out of the car, asked them to check his front left tire. It was OK, they told him. He gave them a few dinars; they tried to refuse; he insisted. As we drove out, he waved demonstratively, shouted "Thank you, good-bye," in Arabic, and looked at his watch. "Nine-thirty," he said to me. "They will remember. You remember. We stop here at nine-thirty. That's why we're in area, check tire."

We were in a residential neighborhood now, making many turns. Streetlights were still off all over Baghdad, but the moon was almost full and the night was clear. We turned onto a wide avenue. Sami lit a cigarette. "Passport office will be on left," he said. "You look right." I opened my window, and there it was: a sleek white building, three stories high, heavily damaged, but elegant some-how, clearly designed by Europeans. I saw instantly why it was called the White Ship. It was long and narrow, with rows of small windows on either side, like the portholes on an ocean liner. A round stone turret on the roof could have been the bridge. It looked so different from my experience of it. It looked so modern and mundane; it could have been an office building, a ministry. No one could know, driving by on a moonlit night, what it was like inside, the things that happened there, just around the corner from the Sheraton and the kebab joints. "Remember, you see passport office, not white building," I heard Sami saying. I turned toward him to say thank you. He was trembling.

I was trembling when we arrived there blindfolded that day in January, trembling from the cold. We had been driven right into the building, dumped out in what felt like an underground garage, shoved onto a bench.

"Nationality?" I heard a voice scream. No one said anything. I heard someone spit. A wad hit me in the face and trickled down my cheek. I tried to lift my hands but couldn't. "Nationality?" he screamed again, in my ear this time.

"American," I said, and got bashed in the face.

Another voice screamed, "Nationality?" I didn't reply. I got hit with a closed fist and kicked in the shins. "Nationality?" he screamed again.

I lowered my head and whispered, "American." I got yanked up by my hair. He held on to my hair with one hand and slapped me back and forth with the other. I felt his rough open palm on my right cheek, his knuckles on my left. "Why you come here?" someone else shouted.

"I'm a journalist," I said. Then three or four men started giving me the Basra treatment, but tougher and longer. They asked no more questions; they took no breaks. These were not young thugs; they were professionals. They hit me on the head with sticks, they punched me in the face, they kicked my legs. I started rocking back and forth on the bench. I felt like I was davening, something I'd never done before.

I heard Peter's voice, a hoarse whisper. "Take deep breaths," he said. "Take deep breaths."

"I want to die," I said. "Just let me die, no more of this." But they weren't paying attention to me anymore. They were going for Peter. We were leaning against each other. I could feel his arms tense every time he got hit. We must have been right up against a wall, because I felt him pitch forward and I heard his head bang against something which then steadied him in a forward crouched position. He must have passed out.

"Nationality," I heard them scream again, farther down the line.

"Cuban," I heard Roberto say.

"Oh, Cuban, that good, that very good." Then Roberto started screaming, then Juan, and then we were alone on the bench.

I was yanked to my feet and pulled across a cold, draughty space. My blindfold was ripped off. The four of us were in a small office. An officer with two stars was sitting behind a desk. There were half a dozen other men in the room, some in blue jeans, some in sweat suits. They were cursing us under their breath, studying us, their faces distorted by hatred. Then attention seemed to focus on me. The officer got up from the desk, walked to me, forced my mouth open and spit in it. "*Yahoudi*," he said to the others. "*Yahoudi*." He exposed my gums, turned me around, and said it again. He was showing my teeth to the other men: something about my teeth would show them that he knew what he was talking about. I was Jewish.

We were in the basement of Saddam Hussein's Intelligence Headquarters on 52nd Street in Baghdad. We did not know that at the time. We were never to know it all the time we were there.

But we could see that there was a high level of organization here. We were being put through the paces of a well-established routine. Roberto's videocamera, which we hadn't seen since the first day, was on the desk. So was an envelope which had been taken from him with more than a thousand dollars' cash. We'd never expected to see that again.

One of the guys, wearing a red kefiyah, fingered the camera, looked at us, drew his finger in front of his neck in the classic move. He was going to cut our throats.

They made us empty our pockets on the desk and started putting the contents in plastic bags. They made lists of what they were confiscating. They took away the toothbrush, the vitamin C, and eight packets of the strawberry-protein concoction I had pocketed before leaving the camp. I begged them to let me keep the antibiotics and the cough syrup. One of the young guys in a sweat suit punched me in the face. New place, old lesson. Never ask for anything.

There was background music to all this. A radio on the desk was blaring away, providing bombastic counterpoint to the body searches which were under way. When the music stopped and a stentorian voice came on, the men stopped what they were doing and stared, mesmerized, at the radio. When the news was over, they broke into a raucous cheer, slapped each others' hands, and I knew they weren't going to beat us anymore. "See," the officer said to us, "our soldiers invade Khafji right now. America finished, you see." I saw. The meaning was clear. The Americans had launched the offensive. Radio Baghdad was calling it an Iraqi attack. The ground war was well under way.

I recalled that news broadcast often in weeks to come. I used it as a morale booster and as a platform from which to build elaborate constructs of the war which was raging around us. Everything I built turned out to be wrong, of course, but I took it to mean that I just had to tough it out a little longer. And that wasn't the only encouraging note to come out of that evil office that winter day. Before we were taken away, the officer, the same man who a few moments earlier had cursed me with the most heinous word in his language, told us that we would get our things back when we left the prison, when the war was over. It was so simple and logical to him, as if wars and prisoner releases were the routine, everyday things of life. But I invoked the words of that man many times every day for many weeks. He had communicated, I thought, that they were not planning to kill us; that one day we would be released, and that, one day, this war too would be over.

In May, when the war was over and I was back in Baghdad, that nocturnal drive with Sami turned out to have been unnecessary. A few days later, our last afternoon in Iraq, permission suddenly and surprisingly came through for us to go to the White Ship. They were going to let us shoot a stand-up outside. In the anteroom of the Information Ministry, where foreign journalists congregate every day, waiting for morsels from the regime, I quickly jotted down what I would say. "This is Saddam

Hussein's Intelligence Headquarters," I wrote, "the building where the regime's political prisoners are starved, beaten, tortured, and tried."

We got there just as the sun was setting. We had to shoot it quickly, not just because of the fading light, but because as soon as we arrived four guys in sweat suits, like rats emerging from a wreckage, appeared from nowhere. I recognized one of them. The Information Ministry flack who accompanied us, usually a cool and arrogant man, was sweating profusely, telling us to hurry, that "they" would let us stay only five minutes. The cameraman set up on a tripod and started rolling as the four young men from the Muhabarat stood next to him. Their arms were folded across their chests. They were listening. I was about to begin, but discovered I was trembling. No one else would notice, I thought, but my right hand, dug deep in my pocket, was shaking. I chickened out. I got through the stand-up. The first take was just fine. I didn't stumble or forget my lines. But what I said was, "This is Saddam Hussein's Intelligence Headquarters, the building where the regime's political prisoners are held." I left out the "starved, beaten, tortured, and tried." I would put that in later, in a voice-over I would do in New York.

When we were back in the car, a photographer who was with us, an Arabic speaker, told me he'd asked the guy I recognized whether he recognized me. "Oh sure," the man said in a cocky voice, "he was with us a long time."

I remembered him too. That January in 1991, we were quick-stepped up a dark and creaking stairwell; after two flights, pushed out onto a landing. We were in the middle

96

of a cellblock: a narrow corridor with steel doors on both sides stretched long and far to the left and to the right. Attached to a bar at the bottom of each door was a set of handcuffs. There were light bulbs behind iron grilles on the ceiling, but no electricity. An older man with a gray mustache was sitting at a desk on the landing. He took no notice of our arrival. There was something about him suggesting that this was his permanent habitat, that he was rarely let out for air.

I was gazing at him, trying to get him to look at me, when a hard palm in the small of my back started pushing me down the corridor to the left. I looked over my shoulder to see Juan, Peter, and Roberto still standing there on the landing, looking in my direction. It was too dark to see their faces.

I was thrown into a cell and heard the door slam shut. There was a rush of cold air making it icier than it had been downstairs. I paced the cell, swinging my arms at my chest to keep warm, reciting my mantra. The door opened. It was the old man. He pulled me out of the cell, pointed at some strange-looking piles on the floor at the other end of the corridor. I started walking toward them. He came from behind and kicked me. I started running, but I was running the gauntlet. Other guards appeared from nowhere, kicking and swinging sticks. When I got to the piles, I saw that they were blankets. I picked up one of the piles and ran the course back to my cell. On the door, I saw the number "11." I had four blankets. I opened one on the floor, lay down, and put three over me.

I couldn't have been asleep very long when a steel

window in the door opened with a metallic whine. It was the old man again. He pointed to a plastic basin sitting on a ledge. I brought it to the window. He put in a ladle of food from a plastic garbage pail. It was some sort of bean paste, hot and tasty.

I tried to eat it slowly and before I could finish it, he was back. This time he opened the door, not just the window. He blindfolded me, tightly and well. It wasn't the work of a bumbler; I couldn't see my shoes. He led me back down the stairs and into another room. I felt air and sunlight from an open window. This was not the office where we had been. It seemed astonishing that it was still light out, that the sun was still shining. This day just refused to end. There were three men in the room. One, sitting right next to me, spoke the best English I had yet heard in Iraq. He was the interpreter. The man in charge spoke some English too.

When you are blindfolded, your mind forms instant images and ideas of the people who are talking to you. They can have little to do with reality; they are programmed less by sensory input than by your mind's silent pleading to see what it needs to see. I saw the interpreter as a young university student, thin and slight and serious. He was free-lancing, making a few extra dinars to get his degree. The man in charge was a civilian in his forties; informally but well-dressed in western clothes. The third, quiet man was the stenographer, neat and fastidious. There were no soldiers or sweat suits, blue jeans or kefiyahs, in the room, no sticks or canes.

Today's opening remarks went like this: "You can talk freely or we will use force. It is you to choose."

"I have nothing to hide," I said, and then latched on to a theme Bluff had taught me from his days in Baghdad. "I hope you will treat me with dignity," I said, "because I know how important dignity is to the Iraqi people."

They picked up on this in a flash. "You will be treated with dignity," the interpreter said after some heated Arabic from the chief. "You are our prisoner, but you will be treated with dignity."

The interrogation focused on what we were *really* doing north of the Saudi border, who had *really* sent us on the mission: how far had we *really* intended to go into Kuwait.

The interrogation was interrupted by bombs exploding very close by. "Do you hear that? Do you hear that?" the chief asked.

"Yes."

"What do you hear?"

"I hear bombs," I said. "I hear antiaircraft fire."

"Maybe we will all die now, together," he said.

"Maybe we will," I replied. The movie was not getting any better.

The interrogation ended after twenty minutes. The chief came to my chair and put his hand on my shoulder. It was the first time anything like that had happened. It felt menacing. "We know you are a famous journalist," he said through the interpreter, my friend, the college student. "But you must tell us the real story. What you're telling us is not satisfactory."

"But it's the truth," I said.

"We will talk again."

I asked, "Do the four of us ever get a chance to spend some time together? It is so important."

He laughed. "Oh, that will come later," he said. "First you must tell me who really sent you on your mission."

Minutes after I was put back in my cell, the steel window opened again. It was the old man with more food; beans on rice this time. I had not yet finished the bean paste, so I dumped the leftovers in the toilet and got my basin refilled. "Not-so-bad," I told myself. "This is the most food and the best food we've had yet." It was also the last time we were to see beans or rice. It was the last time I saw that old man. It was the last time the catering service was to offer more than one feeding a day.

MONKS

❧

I SHOT an Easter story soon after we moved to Israel in
1987. Françoise, a camera crew, and I spent four days
living and filming at St. George's, a brilliant turquoise-
blue monastery carved into a sheer white rock mountain in
the Judean desert. There has always been a tradition of
hermitage in the rough hills around this Greek Orthodox
shrine. It is here that, scholars believe, Jesus spent his
forty days and forty nights. The focus of our story became
Brother Gregorius, a fifty-year-old monk who had just
returned to the monastery after living alone in a nearby
cave for twenty-one years. Once a day, the monks put a
little food and water in a basket and sent it up to him on a
pulley.

St. George's was one of the quietest places I had ever
known, but to Brother Gregorius, it was Times Square.
The sound of footsteps, of water bouncing off a pan in the
kitchen, seemed to shock him to the quick, to rattle his
bones. We passed the evenings talking, the monk and I,
sitting on a stone veranda overlooking the Wadi Kelt and
the dark desert hills. He told me he'd had a pretty good

time in his cave. "But," he admitted, "it took ten years before I could really begin to concentrate."

I don't want to make a big deal out of this. I've never been a believer, and this was no spiritual awakening, no epiphany in the desert; just some nice chats on cool clear nights with a guy who had spent twenty-one years in a cave. But memories of the good monk helped me through my solitary confinement. I thought of Brother Gregorius as an explorer. The undiscovered world was solitude, and I was just embarking on that course; a short one, to be sure, and comparatively safe. We're not talking years, I told myself. Even the pessimists believe this war will be over in a couple of months.

I thought the fact that I was an only child would make it easier. I was used to being alone, to filling my world with fantasy. And, I told myself, a little quiet time has never hurt anyone, particularly someone whose fiftieth birthday is just a few months off. . . .

The day before we left St. George's, we took Brother Gregorius back to his cave. He hadn't been there since the day he decided to pack it in, and he could barely control his excitement, he was so happy to be back home. He seemed to miss it terribly.

The Baghdad cell was twelve feet long and eight feet wide. The walls and floor were smooth red bricks. The solid steel door had a narrow steel window which could be opened only from the corridor. It was there so the guards could look in and pass in food and water. There was a light bulb high on the wall behind a metal screen near the door—it looked like an altar—but there was no electricity. Walking three paces down the cell, you came to a shoulder-high, red brick partition. It was a foot wide and I quickly noted that I would be able to sit on the top of it, stretching my legs out, leaning my back against the wall. There were two plastic utensils on the ledge: a green bowl and a blue cup. There was also a bar of soap. On the other side of the partition there were a shower stall with knobs for hot and cold running water and a western-style toilet. But there was no water. More than half of the porcelain had been broken off the toilet, making it unusable even if it had been possible to flush, which it wasn't. Someone had left this cell not very long before my arrival. The toilet was filthy.

But the highlight of the cell, the only thing that mattered, was near the ceiling on the wall above the toilet. What looked like five thick closed wooden venetian blinds, behind a metal grille, let in some air and some light. Sitting on my ledge, I rarely took my eyes away from it during the day. From its brightness and hue, I learned to tell what time of day and what kind of day it was. More important, those dirty blocks of wood became the screen upon which I projected my fantasies and my memories. I called it my reverie screen.

I slept on the floor near the door, my head against the wall. I used my boots for a pillow. I woke up long before dawn that first morning. I was freezing. My feet felt numb. I managed to put my boots back on without removing the blankets, but it didn't help. I got up and paced through the blackness. The feeling in my feet came back and I lay down again. The first thing I saw, after the screen turned a pale yellow, was my breath. It looked like I was smoking. I turned on my side and saw a small black bump in the floor a few inches from my nose. I thought it was a piece of wool from the blankets. Then it moved. It was a cockroach. Very slowly, I reached down under the blankets to take off one of my boots, my eyes pinned to the roach. It started running away as I smashed the boot down on the floor. But I got it. White paste oozed from the flattened black shell. I wanted to chuck it in the toilet, but there was nothing to pick it up with, and it was too cold to get out from under the blankets. After a while, I got up, pushed it to the door with my boots, and tried to kick it through to the other side. But the door hugged the floor. There wasn't enough room even for a dead cockroach. I left it lying by the door.

The screen was a dirty gray now and I could hear muted traffic noise. I paced the cell. I could still see my breath but it was thinner now. I thought of riding up ski lifts in Vermont. The steel window opened. An unkempt-looking man with a four- or five-day growth put his face to the window. "Welcome to Hotel Baghdad," he said. "This is my hotel. Do you like it?"

"I am cold," I said.

"Veddy cold?"

"Yes."

"Veddy, veddy cold?"

"Yes," I said, "I'm very cold."

"Veddy, veddy, veddy cold?"

I turned my back on him and heard the window slam shut.

I had no watch, but figured it got dark at six in the evening and stayed dark, so dark I could not see my hands, for about twelve hours. Once every three days, the steel window would open in the morning and a man with a ledger would ask my name and nationality, check it against his book, and slam the window shut. Then I would press my ear against the door to listen for other question and answer sessions. I heard Peter once or twice but then didn't hear him anymore. I tried not to think about that.

Sometime after noon the window would open again and I would be given food. Water was usually brought in the evening. Aside from these three events, there was no structure to the day, no imposed routine.

After we were freed, Juan told me he spent much of the time praying. Roberto said he invented mind games, talked a lot, and made a little ball out of string from his clothes, which he then bounced against the wall for hours at a time. Peter, the irrepressible country gentleman, repaired his house in Oxfordshire. He became a handyman in absentia, repairing the plumbing, hanging new drapes. He also walked, he calculated, five miles a day.

Every morning I would fold my blankets, put them on the ledge, and hoist myself up. I would sit down, press my back against the wall, wrap my arms around my knees like a schoolboy, and let my mind wander, hour after hour, into reveries of release.

I went to Wiesbaden, to the airport and hospital where hostages are taken for checkups. I had been there a number of times, on the other side of the cameras. My second day in hospital, I would escape for a few hours, wander downtown to the local BMW shop, and buy the biggest bike they had. Françoise would pretend to be horrified. Then she would wrap her arms around me and we would take off for France, for the lush French springtime which we had careened through on a slightly smaller BMW exactly twenty-two years ago.

I went to the beach, to the beach north of Tel Aviv a few blocks from where we live. It is not very Mediterranean at first glance. The sands stretch long and straight without the hint of an inlet or a cove. But it is my beach. I like to think, when I'm walking there at dusk, watching the sun slither down, that this is where the sun is really setting. Everywhere else, it's an illusion. I would be back by summertime, I knew that, and on the screen above my toilet I projected an idyll of Mediterranean life, from the fishermen launching their oversized rowboats before dawn, to the deeply tanned princesses strutting at midday, to my slightly older crowd munching red mullets and pouring down the white wine until the fishermen show up and shame us into going home.

I would see Tanya neither in Israel nor in France, but in her apartment on the Upper West Side of Manhattan, near Columbia. I had never seen it, so I imagined the apartment I rented there when I was a graduate student: shabby and cozy, with movie posters and stacks of unwashed dishes and friends dropping by all the time. We wouldn't do anything dramatic, Tanya and I. We would just lounge around. We hadn't done that for a while. I would sleep on the floor; I was getting so good at that. We would go to a local Chinese joint for hot and sour soup and noodles and I would look at her, tall and blonde and lovely, and not tell her that just the day before yesterday I was carrying her around in a knapsack.

I had to be free by the middle of May. May twenty-eighth was our twenty-fifth wedding anniversary. My birthday was the twenty-ninth. We were planning to celebrate in France. Françoise's family had adopted me over the years, and they'd all be there; sisters- and brothers-in-law, nephews and nieces. The burgundy-soaked lunch would be held in the garden of a country restaurant, just as our wedding party was a quarter of a century ago. Walking the four paces of my cell, I began composing the toast I would deliver. But I never got very far. My mother-in-law would start crying after the second line. I would catch her eye, go to pieces, and that would be that. *Peu importe. Passez le pâté, s'il vous plaît.*

The family lives in Bourg-en-Bresse, a small city between Lyons and Geneva. That's where Françoise and I met when I was on a Fulbright in 1962. It is an unremarkable city in most respects except for "le poulet de Bresse," which forces Michelin to take notice. Aside from a Gothic church there are no sites of any special beauty; very little to enchant or, one would think, inspire reverie. But somehow my mind kept walking back and forth between the apartment owned by Françoise's parents and the one owned by her sister. It was evening. It usually was evening when I took that walk. There were very few people in the street, and they were older women, mostly, hurrying home with full shopping bags. No one noticed me here or paid any attention. I was alone, anonymous, and very deeply at peace. I realized that I had always been at my happiest strolling the dark streets of foreign cities.

I crossed over to China; not to the glorious mad days of May two years ago, but to the China I knew a couple of years earlier when I spent two weeks in a Taoist monastery in Beijing. Those evenings were also passed strolling dark streets; unlike Bourg, streets teeming with humanity, but for me, with just as much anonymity. I spent the days learning t'ai chi and some meditation techniques. I sat by a wonderfully garish flower garden in the monastery, slowly closed my eyes, and tried to retain the imprint of each flower in the darkness. Now, sitting on my ledge, I did the same. I remembered every one of those flowers in that garden in Beijing.

I was cruising into bathos and I knew it but I didn't care. It seemed to be the ride I needed to take and it was keeping my mind quiet, free of anxiety and self-pity. I knew I had to avoid negative thoughts, keep my metabolism low. I decided to meditate three times a day.

I was up on the ledge one afternoon, watching the surf crash against the rocks outside the CBS office in Capetown, when the window opened. "What you do up there?" a guard shouted. I recognized him. It was one of the thugs from downstairs.

I jumped down. "It's warmer up there," I said. "So cold in the cell."

He didn't believe that. He looked like he didn't know what to believe. I guessed he had never seen anyone make use of that facility before. "Stay down," he screamed. "No go up there no more." He lifted a truncheon to the window, waved it a few times. Then the steel slammed shut.

I paced the cell, feeling quite desperate. I had nothing without my ledge. I didn't think I could do without it. I decided to obey orders for a day or two, then try again, very carefully. It would give me something to look forward to.

The next day, when the window opened, I was standing in the middle of the cell. It was a different guard this time, and he had brought his friends. Four men stood in the corridor, their faces in the window, studying me, talking about me. I heard the word "*Ameriki*," the word "*zahafi*." I was the American journalist in a cage. I looked back at them for a while, then turned around and faced the wall. I decided I would never go to a zoo again.

On the third day I saw Peter, Juan, and Roberto for the last time during our solitary confinement. We were marched downstairs and outdoors. The sun on my blindfolded face felt like the warm hand of a lover. Prisoners always talk to themselves, and now I said, "Oh thank you, thank you." I thought it was time for another move or at least for some time against a sunning wall. Wrong again. It was time to get our uniforms. The CBS Four in stripes.

Roberto and Juan looked OK, I thought. When our blindfolds were removed inside the prison office, and I caught his eye, Juan winked at me and threw me a kiss. Peter looked pale, tired, and haggard. But once again he set the standard. When we were asked our names and nationalities, instead of reciting our meek litany, "*zahafi americain, zahafi nicaraguan,*" et al, Peter pulled his shoulders back and, with profound contempt, said, "British."

Peter was not going to take any more shit.

They wanted us to strip down to our underwear, give them our clothes and put on pajamas. But we were becoming more experienced in the profession of prisoner. I handed over my safari jacket (which I'd had since covering Vietnam twenty years ago) and put the pajama top on as quickly as I could, hoping they wouldn't notice that I was still wearing a T-shirt and a sweater underneath. It worked. Then I put Peter's jacket on top. My friends, I saw, were involved in similar sleight-of-hand negotiations. One guard wanted to take our shoes. They settled for our shoelaces. There were no beatings. There was no real abuse this time. But the bottom line seemed clear. There would be no shortcuts. We had our uniforms. We were here for the long haul.

D O G S

❧

W HEN I was a kid growing up in the Bronx, my uncle Simeon had a German shepherd named Rhea. He kept her in his apartment. It was the first dog I knew well and we were good friends. Sometimes I walked home with Simeon after he finished work. When we opened the street door to the white brick walkup on Valentine Avenue, I could hear Rhea bounding back and forth at full sprint along the corridor of the apartment two floors above us. She would jump on us when we opened the door, but would not linger or suggest games. She wanted Simeon to lay out her dinner.

I thought of Rhea when I heard steel windows opening and closing like gunshots along the corridor. I took my plastic bowl and paced up and down, waiting for my window to open, waiting for my bread and soup. Even though this was a good opportunity to put my ear to the door and count the number of windows being slammed shut—the only way to get an idea of how many prisoners were on the floor—I could never muster the discipline. Pavlov was unbeatable. The response was bigger than me.

There were three different guards who delivered the food on different days, and I never saw them do any other kind of work. They always handed over the bread first—and the amount would not vary, not by day, not by guard: two pieces of thin Arab bread. I would stuff them in my jacket pocket and tender my bowl. I knew how much soup to expect when I caught a glimpse of the guards. Two guards often worked together, never looked me in the eye, and seemed somehow overwhelmed by the complexity of their task. They were not hostile, just in a hurry, and appeared to be confused. They always doled out one ladle of soup.

Another guard was vicious: tall and scowling. Even when I would be waiting at the door, bowl in hand, he would get impatient and scream, "*Kelb.*" Dog, the most derogatory word in the language. I was not being singled out. I heard my neighbors getting the same treatment. He would slam the window hard before he left. But he usually handed out as much as three or four ladles. I would stand and watch and every time I saw the ladle head back to the soup, murmur, "Oh yes, oh yes." The dog man was good news.

It was a thin reddish soup. I have no idea what went into it. Once or twice a week I could see small white lumps falling from the ladle to the basin. Those were red letter days. They were pieces of potato.

I am a very slow eater. Françoise often gives me the look at dinner parties, letting me know that everyone else has finished while I'm lumbering on. Come on. Get on with it.

But no matter how hard I tried, I could not make my meal last more than a minute. I drank the soup in seconds and then started tearing pieces of bread out of my pocket. Once or twice, when the dog man had been especially generous, I filled my water cup with soup before I drank from the basin, put the cup on the ledge, and saved it for a bedtime snack. I spent the rest of the afternoon looking forward to what would be a cup of cold soup. And it was good. Fat nodules would form at the top and the sides of the cup, making it seem almost like food.

It wasn't easy making do with one cup and one basin. I was becoming a juggler, a circus act. Once a day a guard would fill the basin with water. It could happen anytime. When I heard the food coming, I would fill the cup from the basin and drink the rest. That left the basin empty for the soup. But it meant I had only one cup of water until the next delivery, a day later. It wasn't enough, but the situation was tolerable unless I had to use the toilet and needed more than one cup of water to clean myself. Fortunately, with the amount of food I was getting, that wasn't a problem very often.

All my working life I did research before covering a story. And now there was none of it. I did not know how long we could survive on two pieces of bread and a little soup a day. Peter and Roberto probably had a reasonable life expectancy, I thought, since they started out a bit chunky. Juan was even thinner than me, and I was cursing my bones and my luck. For five months in Saudi Arabia I had worked hard, exercised daily, and slept very little. I went into jail ten pounds lighter than I'd been since college. I had finally managed to lose that middle-aged spread, finally, when I needed it most.

I was too old for this, I decided. POWs should be in their twenties or thirties, have a lifetime to get over it. A fifty-year-old shouldn't be a prisoner of war. Clearly some-one made a mistake.

In my campaign to close my mind to unsettling sights and thoughts, I managed to avoid looking at my arms and legs. It was dark in the cell and I never took my clothes off. At night, though, when my hands got cold, I would slip them under my pajamas around my stomach. But it was gone. Just two sharp hip bones with nothing in between. When I did a few push-ups in the morning, I could feel the loose skin hanging down.

I was on the prowl for reassuring images. Bobby Sands, the IRA hunger striker, was a good place to start. I had covered his ordeal. It took fifty-two days for him to die. And he had nothing but water. I was getting something, something every day, quite a lot, actually, compared to nothing. We must be talking months, I told myself, months at the very least.

The North Vietnamese helped me out. They came down the Ho Chi Minh trail laden with weapons and ammunition, but very little rice. I used to dream of taking that trip with them, the great uncovered story of the Vietnam War. Diaries I read recently described how they liked to have dinner after the B-52 strikes. Their celebration of survival was one bowl of rice. I'm probably having as much as that, I thought, and I'm not walking through the jungle all day.

And if millions died in the Cultural Revolution, millions more survived. I'd spent several evenings in Beijing last year talking to Dr. Zhou, who'd been transformed by Mao from pediatrician to digger of ditches. Days went by when he had nothing to eat. He smiled as he described how the Red Guards would stuff themselves with rice and force him to watch. His smile, warm, wise, and incredulous, reminded me of a concentration camp survivor I know in Tel Aviv. Whenever he talks about the camps, which is not often, he smiles too. Images from the camps were somehow the most reassuring pictures of all. I wondered whether those images had ever been mobilized for reassurance before. We knew what the camp diet was. We knew what the Jews looked like when the camps were liberated. And we knew that years later there were often few physical signs of what they'd been through.

My paternal grandfather, a wealthy Frankfurt milliner, always insisted he was German, not Jewish. Despite my father's urgings, he refused to leave Germany, ended up paying for his mistake with two months in Dachau in 1938. My father, already an American citizen at the time, arranged the papers necessary for his release. When "Opa" got to New York, the women in the family always said, he weighed 120 pounds and had double pneumonia. That was all before I was born. When he died of a heart attack in 1957, he was eighty, happy, and living in luxury on the Upper East Side.

My mother provided the least dramatic but to me the most important image of all. She'd had a colostomy in 1977, decided after my father died six years later that she did not want to go on living. She pretty much stopped eating. Her friends were always telling me to talk to her because "to you she will listen." She didn't. The staff at the nursing home where she spent her last year told me they didn't understand how she survived on so little. But she did. And if she could make it, so could I. Survival was in our genes.

There wasn't much left of my mother when she died last January of an intestinal blockage. I remember being surprised when, in a boat I had chartered to dispose of her ashes in the Gulf of Mexico, the moment came for me to pour them over the side. I was surprised by how much there was. Left a dark stain on the clear waters.

I was glad my mother was dead. She knew so much worry over the years when I was off covering wars. But she got something out of it too. I was fulfilling many of her own fantasies; of travel, of adventure, of language. My mother had always treasured the written word above all. She began taking me to the library on Saturday afternoons before I could read. And she admired endurance. "I'm made of pretty stern stuff," she told me in the nursing home. But I was glad she was dead. She enjoyed talking about her son the war correspondent, particularly when I was in Vietnam or Israel or Lebanon. But this—Bobby missing in Iraq—this would have been a bit much.

I had a lot of sore throats when I was a kid, was surprised I didn't have one now. Even my cough was gone. I hoped the cold cell was as tough on germs as it was on me. I wasn't going to catch a stomach bug from fresh food because there was no fresh food. I was on a vegetarian diet, with no vegetables. But what about hepatitis? Or a heart attack? I was, after all, middle aged. What would happen if the census man or the dog man opened my window and found me lying on the floor? Would they do anything? Would they bother? Was there a doctor here? Was the death of a prisoner a big deal? I didn't think so. I imagined the guards carrying a body out of a cell and going back to their radio. But they can't want prisoners to die, I told myself. If I get sick, they will take me to a hospital. I had visions of nurses and IVs.

That night I got dysentery. The dog man had given me an unusually large helping of soup. After putting one cup in the bank, I gulped the rest down. The dysentery started thirty minutes later. I was worried. Last April, covering the release of American hostage Robert Polhill in Damascus, I got a bad case, was on antibiotics for several weeks and lost fifteen pounds. If it's something like that again, I thought, I'm in trouble.

After my third round on the toilet, I was convulsed with stomach pains. I went close to the door, sank to my knees, and started screaming. I was in terrible pain but, more important, I was testing the system. Someone in the corridor shouted, "*Shoo? Shoo?*" What? What? My window opened. I recognized the guard. He'd been one of the guys downstairs when we checked in, appeared to have some authority. "Doctor," I said. "Doctor."

"Doctor here tomorrow."

"Medicine, I said."

"Medicine tomorrow."

I had a fallback position. "Pain," I said, pointing to my stomach. "You have tea?"

He laughed. "Sure, tea, coffee, what you want. Give me cup."

I dumped the soup in the toilet and gave him my cup. He came back with lukewarm sweet tea. I sipped it so slowly it lasted a minute. I kept the leaves in the bottom of the cup for days, flavoring my water with magic.

No doctor came the next day. No food came the next day. I guessed it must be Friday, the Muslim holy day, and they were not cooking. This helped me with a quandary. What was I to do? Fast—the best way to get rid of dysentery—or eat, because a day with no food would weaken me too much. One more problem had solved itself.

The next day I ate my bread and drank my soup and held on to it. Two days later a man I had not seen before came to my window. He was thirtyish and thin. He wore a brown suit jacket, but it was the kind of jacket you'd expect to see on a man sleeping underneath a bridge. He dug deep into a trouser pocket and came up with a large white pill which wasn't very white anymore.

"What's that?" I asked.

"Aspirin," he said.

"Are you the doctor?"

"Yes." He was still digging in his pockets.

"It's my stomach," I said, "not my head."

"Moment." He found what he was looking for and handed me a yellow capsule.

"What's that?" I asked.

"Tetracycline. Take it now."

"But if I take it now, I will need more tomorrow."

"Yes," he said.

"Will you come back tomorrow with more?"

"Yes."

"I don't want to die here."

He laughed. "Why die? Most people don't die here. Only some die."

"Is there a hospital here?" I asked.

He laughed again and left. I did not take the tetracycline. He did not come back the next day. I never saw him again. I never fantasized about nurses and IVs again. It appeared that I would have to take care of myself.

I heard the sound of running outside my door more often now. It was usually at night and it was always accompanied by the shouting of guards. It was the corridor-sprint for blankets. More POWs were arriving. That was not all bad, I thought, at least not for us. It meant the war was progressing. (No matter how well the allies were doing, there were bound to be some prisoners.) It meant more comrades for us, ghost comrades perhaps, unseen, but clearly present. It meant we were being surrounded by military men. We would be part of the crowd, POWs just like them. That's what I told myself, anyway.

It also increased the chances of a rescue operation. I had that fantasy drawn in detail. First we'd hear the sirens, then the bombs, then the helicopters, and then the voices shouting, "Any Americans here?" After all, even a grade-B movie can have a happy ending.

One day I heard someone thrown into the cell next to mine. When the door had been slammed shut, I rapped on the wall with my button. Not knowing Morse code, I numbered the letters of the alphabet. One rap was "A." Twenty-six raps meant "Z." There was no response. Not all clichés were operative.

All the blankets were filthy. One was smaller and a little less ragged than the others, so I wrapped it around my neck like a scarf and tucked it inside my jacket. After much thought and many experiments, I figured out an intricate way to fold the other three into a kind of blanket roll which would not come apart when I tossed and turned at night. I trained myself to do this in the dark, a source of some pride. Me, with the manual dexterity of a duck. If I ever get out of here, I thought, I'll be an asset on a camping trip.

I never found a solution to cold feet. I could take them out of my shoes and massage them, which would warm them up for a few minutes. But not for long. Whenever I woke up at night and felt that my feet were cold, I knew that sleep was over.

There was no way I could sleep the twelve hours of total darkness, so I tried to stay awake as long as possible after night fell. I would sit up on the ledge and talk to myself, make speeches, tell jokes. My sense of humor was evaporating, but I had one routine which always worked. I knew it worked because I could feel my facial muscles flex into a smile.

"I'm an American Jew based in Israel," I would say.

"I'm being held prisoner by the Iraqis, who are at war with America and with Israel and who suspect me of being a spy. Now . . . I'd really like to hear about your problems."

I had always been a wise guy. My only hope of surviving now was to go on being me, to stay in touch with myself. If that meant stand-up comedy routines to an audience of red bricks and cockroaches, so be it.

My thinning frame was revealing the outline of a hard core I never knew was inside me before because it had been concealed by layers of comfort. It was a round metal disc, or so I pictured it, and it was nothing but an implacable will to survive. There was a thinly engraved sketch on the surface, the round face of a boy with a leering grin. That was the crux of the matter: a defiant smirk. I was not going to let them wipe that smile off that face.

When Robert Polhill was released, he walked to the microphones and, with immense dignity, apologized for his weak voice. He hadn't used it in a long time, he said. When asked how he kept his mind intact for thirty-five months, he said, "I never let go of my anger. I nursed it all the time."

I nursed my anger in speeches, one in particular, which I delivered regularly. It was addressed to the CIA, the KGB, the Mossad, the Deuxième Bureau, and MI-5. "What are you clowns doing?" I would ask. "What's with your bureaucracies, your big budgets, your fancy buildings? One fat fascist with a mustache is making monkeys of you all. Take him out. Do it. Justify your existence."

Keeping my voice in shape turned out to be problematic. In the middle of the night, the first night, I woke up and it was all quiet. I whispered, "Roberto."

No response.

I tried "Juan," then "Peter."

Silence. I tried again, louder.

Nothing. Then I heard the sound of snoring. There was only one man who snored like that. Peter was there and all right and asleep so I leaned into his music and closed my eyes.

The night after my dysentery I tried again, louder this time. No response.

In the morning, my window opened. It was a guard who took the census sometimes. I had named him Abdul.

"I hear you last night," he said. "I hear you call names. What you think? I don't hear you? I also hear you talk all day. You talk again, first I punish you, then I kill you. You understand? Don't speak anything!"

No more evening speeches. No more nocturnal serenades.

I would always wake up in darkness. But I was getting better at guessing how much time I would have to wait before dawn. For one thing there was always a lot of bombing early in the morning. Most of the time I heard the explosions. Sometimes I felt them.

I tried not to let it worry me. I told myself that Beirut had gotten hit a lot harder in '82. I had survived that. Besides, American bombs now are so much smarter, and they'll never go for a prison.

The worst thing was the sirens themselves. An awful

shriek, fifteen stanzas each time. And there was no point trying to go back to sleep right away. The all-clear was just as piercing.

The first hint of light coming through the screen was always a question mark. Is it the moon? Is it a car? Is it dawn? I would close my eyes, give it ten minutes, and look again. When morning came, I would lie very still and scour the room for cockroaches. There were almost always two or three of them, almost always very close to my blankets. I still killed them, but they were losing their fight. I would hold my boot a few inches off the floor for a moment, give them a chance to run away. "Come on, beat it," I would say under my breath, but they never did. I wanted them to run, show some determination to survive, but they let me down, the fucking roaches. The place must have gotten to them.

I would make the morning linger as long as possible: what a luxury, a sleep-in, I would say, because as soon as I got out of the blanket roll, that slow clock would start ticking for mealtime.

My morning routine never varied. I would refold my blankets and put them on the ledge, ready for reverie time. Then a checkup. Can I still walk? Am I dizzy? Are all systems go? My pulse is normally around sixty when I'm in shape. Without a watch, I couldn't take it accurately now, but it felt much slower. That's good, I thought. We're coasting, saving gas. It's day five, I would say, and I'm OK.

Washtime meant removing my hood for a moment and rubbing my scalp, rinsing my hands if I had any water, and cleaning between my teeth with a fingernail I had bitten off for that purpose. I kept it in my pocket.

Then—the Morning Ceremony—the most important moment of the day. They had taken my safari jacket—my correspondent's uniform—but I had hidden one of the buttons in a pocket of Peter's windbreaker. I kept my bar of soap in the shower stall because it was the driest part of the room. Every morning, with great deliberation, I would take the button and draw a line on the soap to mark another day.

This was my accomplishment. This was what I could do. This was the role I had to play.

I knew that Françoise would be moving the world to get me freed. I knew that my friends inside and outside CBS would be with her.

All I could do was survive. Push day after day, I called it. Every line on that bar of soap was one step closer to the end of the war, to "you'll leave the prison when the war is over," as the Yahoudi-man had put it. That bar of soap was my scorecard and I was winning.

"*Fais un petit effort*," was Françoise's theme song in life. Just make a little effort.

I'm doing what I can, Minou, I'm doing what I can.

CHOCOLATE

❖

W HAT I could no longer control were my food fantasies. Chocolate was the main ingredient. My mind was turning to chocolate.

Back in the lobby of the International Hotel in Dhahran there was a little shop which sold nothing but sweets. Since it was Saudi Arabia, they made nothing of their own. But they had mounds of Swiss chocolate bars; with almonds and hazelnuts, liquid fillings and raisins. Milk chocolate, bittersweet chocolate, white chocolate, M & M's. A whole shelf was devoted to bags of Brach junk sweets: red and black licorice, sugarcoated almonds, hard candies with soft fillings and fudge. By the door was a display of freshly baked pastry: éclairs and fruit tarts, and what had been my favorite since childhood: German Black Forest cherry cake.

What would I go for first? The red licorice, probably, but it was open to debate. I could think about it for hours. Another question became a kind of intellectual game. How much would I pay? What portion of my net worth would I part with to be locked up in that shop overnight? Tens of thousands, obviously. Maybe half of the whole nest egg, maybe more. And how much of that store could I consume? That's where my imagination stopped. I could not conceive of satiety, of saying "OK, that's enough. I'll go now."

Food was invading my fantasies of freedom. When the Red Cross came, when the guards would take me downstairs to see the blond and pleasant man from the IRC, he would ask, "What is your name?" and I would reply, "My name? Forget about my name. Do you have chocolate? What! You're Swiss and you don't have chocolate?"

Or—we would be taken outside and put into buses. We would be driven south, to American lines, certainly in Kuwait by now. People from CBS would be there. We would get in a car, drive toward Dhahran. It would be emotional. My friends would tell me how worried they were, how they missed me. I would reply, "Stop! Stop at that store! I want ice cream and apples, cookies and candy, peanuts and popcorn."

When I got home to our little house by the sea, I would see myself standing by the kitchen stove, making popcorn in one pot, melting chocolate in another. Sometimes I'd pour the chocolate on the popcorn, sometimes the other way around.

Now and then, as a fallback position in my negotiations, I would agree: OK, we won't stop thinking about food. But we will stop thinking about sweets.

Then I would be at home, eating Françoise's chicken wings and spare ribs. I would be in an all-night Tel Aviv restaurant by the market where they bring you grilled goose liver on a skewer and freshly baked Arab bread

126

which you munch while you wait, munching more before a meal than I would eat here in two days. I would be on the terrace of André's in Paris, slicing confit de canard with my fork. But my most regular haunt would be the Carnegie Deli in New York. My choice would never vary. It would be the corned beef–pastrami combo with two Dr. Brown's cream sodas. The pickles are on the table. I suspect that I walked my mind here so often because I could sneak back to sweets. The meal could end with nothing but a gargantuan piece of chocolate fudge cake.

One night, leaving the Carnegie, I heard commotion in the corridor. A man was being beaten. It was a westerner. I knew that. I could hear him trying not to scream. I heard the thumps of kicking—it sounded like he was being kicked in the stomach—and the sound of his pain, a sharp grunt, after each kick. He was exercising superhuman control, I thought, but I couldn't really pay attention. Right then, I was too busy waltzing down Broadway, an ice cream cone in one hand, a bag of popcorn in the other.

Whenever I tugged my mind away from food, it would find its way back. I would, for example, command, "Let's think about Dad," and within seconds we would be at his favorite restaurant, a fish joint on Second Avenue, eating crusty crabmeat au gratin and Nesselrode pie. "Thanks, Dad," I said. "I was never hungry when you were around."

Thinking about his younger brother, my favorite uncle, was even worse. Uncle Peter ran a chocolate factory when I was a kid. I could remember and decode every piece in his "deluxe" assortment. The one with the little circle in the corner was the caramel.

Bourg-en-Bresse was no longer sultry streets at dusk. It was a store called Le Prieure de Brou, with candied oranges and pineapples displayed in its glorious window. I tried to picture the salesgirl's expression when I would ask for ten kilos of *fruits confits*.

Other brands of fantasy were either not accessible or utterly transformed. Usually, I can close my eyes in a plane or in a car, no matter where it is going or why, and summon up images of women I have known and drift off to sleep. But they wouldn't visit me anymore, and when they did, they were different. I would watch them come into my room, gently opening the door, soft and white and lovely as I lay on the floor, but before they could reach me, they would stop, transfixed, and turn into chocolate; life-sized statues of light-brown milk chocolate. Mounds of Venus were stunningly adorned with multicolored sprinkles; glazed cherries were at the tips of their breasts; toenails were thin red sugar shells. I would begin with a love bite to the ankle: and then came the surprise. Nibbling through the thin chocolate crust, I would bite into a marzipan filling. My women had turned into candy stores. This wasn't oral sex. It was gluttony.

"How are you?"

"Cold and hungry." It was my second interrogation here. It was day eight.

When the guard came to my door, I asked, "Where are we going?"

He said, "The manager wants to see you." I had images of an administrator sitting behind a desk. Perhaps it was the man who called himself the hotel owner that first morning. I took the blanket off from around my neck and threw it on the floor with the others. This was my first mistake.

I was blindfolded and led downstairs. Prisoners called these guards the "walking-police."

In the corridor I could make out a very short man, blindfolded, sitting knees up against a wall. I thought it might be one of the artillery spotters from the prison camp. That was a good sign. Military guys were being interrogated today too. I was not being singled out.

I was also told to sit against a wall. But I was freezing; I couldn't control the shakes. I got up and started jumping up and down to keep warm. From the bottom of my blindfold I saw that an Iraqi in uniform was "dancing" with me, laughing. Others were standing by, clapping.

"It's not funny," I said. "Being cold is not funny." I sat down again and was still shivering when they took me to the interrogation room. These were different men. There were two of them. They did not speak English. They had an interpreter. He was sitting close to me.

"You know why you're hungry?" I'm asked.

I did not answer.

"You're hungry because you're bombing."

"I'm not bombing anyone," I said.

"Your name?"

"Robert Simon." I had given up using the name Robert in the fourth grade. A teacher who didn't like me insisted on calling me Robert in a whiny, sarcastic tone, turning the name into an accusation. I told my friends to switch to "Bob." But I didn't want to confuse these guys. I knew my credentials said "Robert," and in any case I was on trial again, wasn't I?

"Are you married?"

"Yes."

"What's your wife's name?"

I wanted to say, "That's none of your business." Instead, I said "Françoise."

"Where is she now?"

"She is in New York." I didn't know where she was by now, but figured they wouldn't know either. This was all too easy. Where were they going?

"Do you have any children?"

"Yes."

"How many?"

"One."

"A boy or a girl?"

"A girl."

"How old is she?"

"Nineteen."

"What is her name?"

"Tanya." The questions were coming so quickly, they could not be writing down the answers. They were not looking for information. What was going on?

"Where is she now?"

"New York."

"Do you ever want to see her again? Do you ever want to see your wife again?"

I did not answer. I was not being cool. I couldn't talk. The shivers started again. I knew I was losing control.

"We do not think you will see them again, because we

have emergency regulations now and we consider you a spy. Do you understand what that means?"

"I'm not a spy. I've never been a spy."

"You were caught on the field of battle. You are a spy." As if the words didn't have enough punch, the interpreter was adding tone, giving a dramatic reading to "field of battle," spitting out "spy."

"I'm a journalist. I told you, I'm a journalist."

"Bazoft said he was a journalist. Do you know who Bazoft was?"

"Yes." I was sounding meek now. I could hear myself. They were winning.

"Do you know what we did to Bazoft? We did it here. Did you know that? We did it right here. We tortured him. Then we killed him. He begged us to kill him. Did you know that?"

"Yes. But I'm a journalist. I've been a journalist for twenty-five years."

"It could be a cover."

"It's not a cover," I blurted out. "It's been my life." I was surprised when I heard myself say that, surprised that from somewhere deep inside my panic I could pull out a nugget of audacity.

"Maybe we will show you what your bombs have done to Baghdad. You can report that to America." They were switching tracks. Maybe there was hope.

"I would do that," I said. A thin shell of composure was returning. "I am not an enemy of the people of Iraq."

The man across from me shot back, "Maybe you are an enemy of the government of Iraq."

Careless of me, I thought. These guys know the doctrine. "I am not an enemy of the government of Iraq," I said. It sounded pretentious when I heard it. Blindfolded, my hands tied around a chair, terrified, I wasn't in a position to be an enemy of anyone. I was pleading for my life, that's what I was doing.

But they were back on the main line again. "How many other CBS crews crossed the border with you? How many other CBS crews are crossing the border now?"

I realized how serious they were. They really thought I was a spy. They were not trying to frame me. They thought I was a spy and they were looking for information about other spies.

"We were alone. I told you we were alone. There was no one else."

There was a pause. The two interrogators were whispering to each other in Arabic. I heard one man get up. I thought they were going to torture me. I clenched my fists behind the chair. "Who sent you on your mission?"

"No one sent us. We just wandered across the border."

"Your answers are not satisfactory. If you ever want to see your wife and daughter again, tell us who sent you on your mission."

"No one sent us," I said. "How can I make you believe me? My answers may not be satisfactory, but they're true."

There was another pause, longer this time. I tilted my head back so I could see from under my blindfold. The man on my right was in uniform. His legs were crossed, his boots were polished. He looked young and sharp. He was not looking at me. The man across from me was in civvies. He had a black and white kefiyah loosely wrapped around his neck. He was also looking away.

These men did not look happy. I could not tell if the pathetic spectacle of a frightened man had shamed them—not very likely, I thought—or if they felt they had failed as interrogators. They had received no new information.

The army man said something in Arabic. The interpreter said, "That is all." I heard the door open. My hands were being untied. I was pulled to my feet. My hands were retied behind my back. The walking-policeman grabbed my arm, started taking me to the door.

I stopped, turned back toward the room. "Are you going to kill me?" I asked.

Silence.

"You must tell me something," I said. "You can't leave me like this."

"We have nothing to tell you. The investigation continues."

In the corridor I see a man with a black sweater sitting against the wall. It could have been Peter. He grunts when I pass.

Back in the cell I start pounding the wall with my fists closed. I hear screaming. I know it is my own. My knuckles are bleeding.

The window opens. It is Abdul. I say, "I want to see the manager again." I want to tell him since they are planning to kill me, I want them to kill me now. I can't take any more time in this cell. Not now. Not now that I know what's waiting for me. Please, please, get it over with.

Abdul says, "The manager is gone for the day."

"Peter, Peter Bluff. Can I see Peter just for a minute? Just let me see him. I won't talk. Just let me see him."

"He is not here."

"Will he come back?"

Abdul smiles. The window slams shut.

I remember something. I rush to the toilet. There is a strip of thin metal coiled around the rubber water pipe. I unwind it a few inches, feel the edge against my thumb. Is it sharp enough? Is it strong enough? I look at my left wrist. It seems thin, the blue veins right up against the skin. I could certainly pierce the skin. Could I get deep enough? It would be messy, but it could work, it could work. Twenty-four hours can go by without anyone looking in. It could work.

I leave the toilet, start screaming, pounding the walls again. The window opens and slams shut. Again and again. A guard is shouting at me, laughing. I am surprised at the energy rushing through me. I didn't know I had that much energy. I have to defecate. Usually it's every three days. I took a shit yesterday, but here it is again. I sit on the toilet.

The window opens. It is the dog man. *"Kelb,"* he shouts.

I stagger to the door with my plastic basin, my pants dragging around my ankles. He puts in three ladles of soup. I start gulping it down. I hear myself saying, "Don't listen to what he says, watch what he does." I'm watching myself. I'm drinking soup. This is not the act of a man bent on suicide.

I pace awhile. I rap my button against the wall. No response.

I sit on my blanket. I try my mantra. "POWs survive." But that doesn't work. I'm not a POW. I'm a spy. I start taking deep breaths. I think of a ditch in the desert. That's what has happened, I say. A ditch has been dug in the desert. Something has pierced my peace of mind. I have to get it back. I have to get sand back in that ditch. I have to make it smooth again. I can't do it right away. I can't even know that I'm doing it. I just have to let my mind loose a bit, let it shovel some sand back into that hole.

I don't make a blanket roll that night. I do not plan to sleep. I don't expect to sleep. When it gets dark, I just throw two blankets over me and lie on my back. But lying on my back hurts. I've lost so much weight that I don't have an ass anymore. I'm lying on my bones. I turn on my side. I face the wall.

When I was a kid and we lived in the Bronx, we spent summers in a bungalow on Whaley Lake in upstate New York. There weren't many kids there and I was alone most of the time. My parents sent me to summer camp when I was eleven, my first time away from home. I broke my arm the second week of camp, couldn't do much with the other boys, so, again, found myself alone. I'd sit for hours on a hill overlooking the mountain lake and think of Lake Whaley. At night, in my bunk, I buried myself in blankets, pushed myself as hard as I could against the wall, and disappeared into the warm darkness.

IRENA

❧

In the summer of '62, I gave myself a trip to Greece. I had just graduated from college. I met Bernie, an old high school buddy, in Paris and we hitchhiked down to Athens. We were joined by two lady friends and went frolicking off to Crete.

Irena was small, blonde, smart, and outspoken. We were sitting in a taverna one evening: a large, brightly lit terrace with waiters in white scurrying about with platters full of meat on skewers, piles of fried fish, and salads laced with feta. The restaurant was crowded, we were the only tourists, and we were being ignored. We'd been on the beach all day, had skipped lunch, and were hungry. We sat for more than an hour. The serenity which usually comes with the bread and the white wine was missing because we were getting neither.

Irena said, "Watch this." She started screaming. Everything at the restaurant stopped. People stopped eating. Waiters stopped moving. Everything stopped except Irena. She kept on screaming. No words. Just a long, high-pitched screech.

Minutes later we had bread and wine. The meat and salad followed. So did the serenity.

That morning after the interrogation I thought about Crete and Irena. She had coached me in the uses of hysteria. It produces results, something every infant knows. But in this setting it had no use at all. There was no audience. No one was listening. So why bother? I felt I had learned a lesson so primal that it had fallen right past my thoughts into a bedrock of instinct. It would alter my behavior. Somehow I knew I wouldn't crack again, and I felt myself getting calmer. My knuckles would heal, the metal strip coiled around the rubber pipe would remain coiled. I thought again how uncannily our system is geared for survival in ways we know nothing about. I remembered the Wordsworth line "thoughts that lie too deep for tears."

Sand was being shoveled into that ditch. The surface was almost smooth again.

I had been interrogated, and interrogators try to scare you. That's all. There was little reason to take the threats seriously, I told myself. Why would they kill me? Hostages are currency. They'll need to take me to the bank sometime. The Iraqis will want to restore relations with the west. They'll want the embargo lifted. They will want, above all, a good image on our television screens. Hadn't Saddam always staged his "guest releases" in front of the cameras?

The talk among journalists in the coffee shop in Saudi Arabia had been of Saddam the executioner, the man who murdered for power or for sport, the man who, according to those who knew him, was indifferent to the sufferings of others. But in my cell, undisturbed by dissonant views, I was inventing another Saddam; the grandstand player, the man who would save my life to score big points on the small screen.

The interrogators might have frightened me. But I had not changed my story. That's why, when I'd shot a glance at them from under my blindfold, they were looking so sullen. It was all so clear.

But the more confident I became of survival, the more I had to face another specter, one that drove me to pace my cell until I had to sit from exhaustion. The war was being waged without me. I was missing the big one. I knew just how big it must be because the sirens wailed in the afternoon, they wailed at night, they pierced the pre-dawn darkness, each time punctuated by the dull thuds of the bombs. The Gulf War had been my story from the beginning. I had stayed in my airport hotel in Saudi Arabia, whiling away weeks in the desert, waiting for the war to begin. I had not dared to take a break, afraid that it would start without me. And here I was in the capital of the journalist's dream, right where it was happening. And it was happening without me.

But the frustration was comforting in a way. It was such a familiar emotion, such a commonplace pain. How many times had I felt it before when I'd been kept from a story by bad roads or bad luck? I must still be OK, I told myself. They haven't broken me. They haven't tampered with my instincts. And if I can be so consumed with missing a story, it must be a sign that, somehow, I know I will survive.

There was another consoling thought. This was not the most desperate situation of my life. I had been through worse, and survived. When I was hospitalized with my back problem in '86, and the doctors told me I would never play tennis or run or ski again, and the depressive darkness began closing in, I lost all hope. I lost all sense of myself. From doctors suggesting that I might not be able to function as a foreign correspondent anymore, I convinced myself that I had nothing left to function with. There's nothing anyone can do to you as bad as what you can do to yourself. The Iraqis hadn't laid a finger on me. The minute they let me go, I'd walk right back to being what I was, doing what I do. That would be my revenge.

There was something else I learned, or thought I had, through that dismal experience: the cunning of the survival instinct. It turned out that the physical lassitude which accompanied my mood drop gave my back time to heal. I saw it now as another smirk on the face of that engraven image, that portrait of the Alfred E. Neumanesque boy. "Leave it to me," he was telling me. "We got you through that one. We'll get you through this too."

But the threats about never seeing Françoise or Tanya again had left their mark. My fantasy life was changing. I no longer imagined being reunited with Françoise in France or in Germany. I didn't think about seeing Tanya on the West Side or anywhere else. It was too tenuous, too risky. I headed toward safer territory, toward the past. Those fuckers can end my future, I thought. They cannot touch my past.

I would spend more time on my back on the blanket

roll in the morning now, less time on the ledge. Perhaps I was losing energy, perhaps it was simply more comfortable. But I could see the reverie screen just as well.

I'd been troubled by what I thought was an increasingly bad memory in recent years. On the news circuit, I was constantly running into old friends and colleagues who would ask me to remember that demonstration we covered in Lisbon or that bar we watched getting bombed in Belfast and I would nod usually but wouldn't have the slightest idea what they were talking about. Now I realized that my mind had just been too cluttered, the pace of my life too fast. Vignettes came floating onto the screen from nowhere, with no apparent sequence or logic, triggered by nothing but the need to fight the hunger and filth and fear with the only weapons I had left, which were quiet thoughts of beauty.

There are things all kids do. One thing Tanya and Tanya alone did was this: When we were living in an apartment in Saigon and she was a year old, and I would come home from the war, she would stomp one foot on the floor. She would come to the door and just stand there, laughing and stomping one foot on the floor until I picked her up.

The first time I took Tanya to the sea (she was three months old and we were vacationing in southern Spain), the first time I carried her into the sea, she did not cry or laugh. (I don't think she could really laugh yet.) As I lowered her legs in slowly, she knit her brow and looked me in the eye as if to say, "I don't quite know what this is, but it feels nice enough." I wondered then if that expression would remain in her repertoire. It did not.

When we left Saigon in 1972, we stopped off for a short vacation in the Seychelles. We were sitting on some concrete stairs on the way down to the beach. Tanya was on my lap. We weren't saying much. A woman—a young, black, beautiful woman—ambled by with a large bunch of bananas on her head. Tanya took one look, pointed right at the bunch, and shouted, "Danane." The woman smiled, tore a banana off the bunch. Tanya looked at me, laughed in triumph, and ripped into her second breakfast.

Another R & R from the Saigon days had taken us to Bali when the airport was still too small for 747s and the island still grew rice and coconuts instead of curio shops. We stayed in a hotel which was not a hotel really, just a collection of thatched huts set amidst the rich green paddies. When we arrived, we dumped our bags in our hut and ran to the beach. Françoise went dancing into the surf before me. She turned around and said, "Oh, I'm so happy."

It had been just as green and she had been just as happy the day our courtship began. It was twenty-nine years ago. We had met at the University of Lyons, where I was studying history and she was studying English. She was also teaching at a girls' boarding school in the country. It was springtime when I bought a map, rented a bicycle, and took off for the hills in search of an elusive village called Trévoux, thirty grueling kilometers away. The school was behind high walls. I rang the bell a long time before a surprised headmistress peered through the cracks in a wooden gate and went off to tell Mlle. Arnaud that *un étranger en vélo* was asking for her. Françoise giggled when she saw me. Gentlemen callers were not an everyday occurrence at Trévoux. We strolled through the garden that afternoon. We sat on a stone bench and drank coffee. We'd been having an affair for several months, but it had been on my turf, in the tawdry hotels catering to students and others between the Rhône and the Saône. That day I knew our courtship had properly begun. I had invaded her life and found that I was welcome. I planned to stay.

If I was taking refuge in the past, I knew that Françoise would be doing just the opposite. She would not permit herself thoughts of our life together. It would be an admission that I was dead. She would be locked in her room with no past and no future, just an eternal present, a never-ending instant of anguish.

Two days before I left Dhahran for that drive to the border, I faxed a form to CBS in New York upping my life insurance to the maximum. At least Françoise would never have to worry about the rent. Tanya could finish her studies. But the thought of Françoise widowed and Tanya fatherless pained me more than thoughts of my own disappearance. These things happen, I tried to tell myself. A cousin died in a car accident last year. His wife and kids are coping. A friend and fellow journalist in Israel had contracted an efficient form of cancer while I'd been in Saudi Arabia, which finished him off in two weeks. But that was different. If I die, I'll be hanged and that photograph will haunt Françoise and Tanya for the rest of their days. That wasn't even the worst possibility. They might just "off" me somewhere. No one will ever know. Françoise and Tanya will never be able to start a new life. They will join the fraternity of families who never laugh, like the families of the missing from Vietnam. I had interviewed many of them and I knew that it is not a fraternity. Everyone is alone.

I had a new mantra now, two lines from a Dylan Thomas poem, lines I had recited to my father again and again when he lay on his deathbed eight years ago.

"Do not go gentle into that good night,
Rage, rage against the dying of the light."

But I could contemplate my execution with equanimity, sometimes even with humor. Most comforting was the faith that some rituals would be observed, even by these clowns. A cup of sweet tea, for example. They're sure to give me a cup of tea. Food perhaps? What could they conjure up for a last meal in wartorn Baghdad? Rice and beans? I'll take it.

If I could buy my way out, how much would I pay? Would I give them everything, start from scratch? Yes, of course I would. How much would I pay for some food? How much more was my life worth than a chocolate bar? Probably not all that much.

If this had happened a long time ago, I thought, I would have regretted going to my grave without having finished reading Proust. What a decline! Now I was sorry that I had missed part three of *The Godfather*.

I wondered who at CBS News had prepared my obit. I

wondered where they would hold the memorial service. I had attended the service for Charles Collingwood at St. Bartholomew's, the last great gathering of the CBS clan. I wondered where these things are held for Jews. Would there be food?

Morley Safer and Charles Kuralt were especially eloquent at the Collingwood affair. I imagined they might find a few words to say at mine. Rather would officiate of course, as he did for Charles. But I was thinking of Rather not so much as a mourner these days. In my increasingly urgent fantasies, he had another role to play.

None of the release scenarios seemed credible anymore. I could no longer play out visions of the flight to Wiesbaden or the drive to American lines. They were interrupted by blocks of logic. Who could arrange it? The Americans had put together the most extraordinary coalition in history. Good for Bush, bad for me. The characters you could usually rely on to intercede — the French, the Syrians, the Egyptians — were all at war with Iraq. And I couldn't forget that Saddam had executed Bazoft long before the war, during a period when he was looking for good relations with the west.

I couldn't even summon up the commando scenario anymore. What I did believe in was the symbiotic relationship between the media and Saddam Hussein. Arnett had been in town. We knew that. The other nets must be lining up to come. Rather had been in Baghdad several times before the shooting started. In fact, he'd gotten the first interview with Saddam after the invasion of Kuwait. He will come back, I told myself. He will come back and the first item on his agenda will be to get his guys out. I could picture Dan at his most grave, earnestly imploring The Leader to let us go. Saddam would have no alternative. He couldn't let Dan leave empty-handed. That wasn't Saddam's style. Go for maximum publicity. Show off your big heart while the Americans are bombing you to bits. That's how he operated. I could picture it all. I saw how we would be led down a dark corridor. No one would have explained anything to us. A door would open and there we would be, back on television, in a room with Saddam and Rather and bright lights and a crew rolling on the reunion.

The other person who could pull it off was Françoise. I figured the families of the American "guests" who'd been freed before the war began must have been in touch with her, and their advice would be, "Go—go to Baghdad, make the appeal." That's what many of them had done. And it had worked. I knew Françoise would do it. She is scared of cats and elevators, but she would come to Baghdad under siege if she thought it could do the trick. But would Saddam let her in? Less in it for him. Dan is a better bet.

"Come on, Dan, come on, Minou," I would say out loud. "Let's get this show on the road."

But another fantasy was coming down the road with increasing frequency. It was a parade, a prisoner parade. The North Vietnamese had done it. Why wouldn't Saddam? Weeks ago, in the prison camp, during a night of intense bombardment, Peter said, "Those bombs must be annoying him a bit by now." He must need to show that he

145

is not just taking punishment but dishing it out as well. We would be taken downtown on flatbed trucks bearing floats, a parody of the Macy's Thanksgiving Day parade. The pilots would be sitting in mock cardboard bombers. I would be chained and standing with a distorted CBS eye over my head. People would throw bags of urine and stones. After all, Saddam's defiance was being called the Iraqi *intifada*.

But what frightened me more than the parade was the idea that I was alone. I had not seen or heard my friends in weeks.

During my first days in solitary, I heard Bluff's voice twice, during the taking of the morning census. I had not heard it since. I figured they might well have released Juan and Roberto by now. It would have been so clear, even to the Iraqis, that these guys were exactly who they said they were. That idea was comforting in a way. Not only would my friends be free, but they would be telling people we were alive and in Baghdad and they would be spurring the campaign for our release. Comforting, perhaps, but deeply troubling as well. I was alone.

Then there was a night of miracles. I heard the steel windows opening and closing and I didn't understand. We had already been fed. I jumped down from my ledge just as my window opened and a guard, a short man I hadn't seen before, was looking at me. The miracle was that he was smiling, a warm smile, the smile of someone who brings good news. He reached deep into his jacket pocket and pulled out three dates. Dates! I cannot describe the rapture with which I ate those dates. This food addict had never experienced such joy. Then I noticed that he had not locked the window. He had closed it but had not secured the latch. I could see a hair of light from the corridor. Was this a trap? I didn't think so. The man looked like a human being, the first I had seen in that corridor. I did not think you could fake a smile like his.

I lay down. I went into my blanket roll. But I did not sleep. I waited a couple of hours. Then I got up, pushed the window open gently with my fingers and, in a loud whisper, said "Peter."

Nothing.

"Roberto."

"Yeah, Bob." The reply was sharp and clear and remarkably matter-of-fact.

"How are you?"

"I'm fine."

"How's Juan?"

"I don't know."

"How's Peter?"

"He's asleep."

"What?"

"Peter is asleep."

"How do you know?" Could they be in the same cell? I wondered.

"I can hear him."

I turned my ear to the open window and, like the sound of distant thunder, I could hear him too. I wished Roberto a good night and coaxed the window closed with my fingertips. I crept into my blanket roll and into a deep and dreamless sleep.

DREAMS AND THINGS

✧✦✧

I WAS worried about my things. I know that sounds crazy, but I was worried about the things I left back in my hotel room in Dhahran. It's not that there was all that much or that they were valuable, but even if they were, think of it. Here I was, locked up, starved, and facing the gallows in the middle of bombed-out Baghdad, and I paced my cell worrying about the cassettes, the clothes, the mementos I had left neatly stacked in some drawers of an airport hotel.

It would have seemed crazy even to me if I hadn't remembered that I had the same fixation during those dying days of Saigon, the weeks before the evacuation in 1975. Every day, we'd drive up the road heading north and every day the drive got shorter as the North Vietnamese came closer. Along with many in the press corps, I was determined to stay to the end. But we had no particularly good reason to believe we'd get out alive. There was an American evacuation plan; we knew that. We knew it would be activated as soon as we heard Bing Crosby sing "I'm Dreaming of a White Christmas" on Armed Forces

148

Radio. But we also knew how well thousands of other American plans had worked during the course of the war. Still, I was worried about my things. I knew if the plan worked, we'd be traveling light: no suitcases on a chopper heading for the South China Sea. I decided now it was another defensive roadblock the mind set up: keep the patient worried about something tangible, something he can deal with, when the road leads somewhere he is afraid to go.

When I jogged out of the Caravelle Hotel that morning after Bing Crosby began to croon, the houseboy ran after me, shouting, "Mushieu Shimon, Mushieu Shimon, you forgot your laundry." My things didn't make it, and I was no longer worried about them then. What I carried with me was all I would need: my portable Olivetti, my notebook, and my pen, a Parker. After we parked the bureau jeep outside the American Embassy, leaving the keys in it, and clambered over the wall, pulled to safety by the Marines; after we watched portly embassy bureaucrats chop down a tree in the embassy parking lot so the Sea Lions could land; after we watched the officials burn boxes stuffed with U.S. dollars; after we heard ground fire and didn't know whether the choppers were getting hit; after we were chased off one chopper by a CIA agent wielding a .45 because he had his own protégés to take care of, we finally took off. It was nighttime.

We were the last ones on board, so were sitting next to the tail gunner, looking out the rear hatch, knowing we were taking our last look at Saigon. The colors were subdued, blending into one another: the gray and dark-red roofs of the city, the black curl of the Mekong, the clouds of black smoke where artillery rounds were landing. We started composing our script: ". . . a city we will never see again; a city which will haunt us for the rest of our days . . ." Then, suddenly, we were over the South China Sea, and we knew we were safe. The pilot dropped down to five hundred feet, and the sea looked like a dark, warm blanket. We settled back, leaned against a rucksack, and started to doze off. Then, suddenly, we were hit by a blast of hot air. We looked out the hatch, and there was a Marine standing at the ready with an M-16. We were yanked out of the chopper and run down a corridor, a gauntlet, formed by two columns of Marines and sailors, all wearing pastel-colored helmets. We glanced toward the sky and saw lights flashing through a veil of smoke, and swarms of helicopters heading in every direction. And then, just as suddenly, we were downstairs in the officers' mess, drinking chocolate milk, and the war was over.

I went up to the deck, unzipped my Olivetti, rolled in a piece of paper, typed the title in caps: THE EMBASSY'S LAST DAY, looked up at my colleague Dick Threlkeld, and said, "You know, it's just another story."

He said, "How can you say that?" and walked away.

I hadn't explained myself. What I meant was: more than fifty-seven thousand Americans had died for nothing, the United States had just lost its first war, Saigon was about to fall, and here I was, setting margins, typing in picture notes, exactly as I would have done after a press conference, a peace protest, or a dog race. It didn't matter what the story was; I would always end up telling it. That's what I did. That's why I was there. That's why I would survive. Even in the middle of the fray, I was apart from it, immune somehow. There were many surprises but no surprises at all. Anything I experienced was destined to wind up on television. I knew then, that night on the *Midway*, that I never really believed I was going to die those last weeks in Saigon. My threadbare safari jacket was my cloak, the protective armor of the chronicler; the Olivetti was my shield; the press card, my badge of invulnerability. Many of my colleagues had been killed over the years. A few had been killed these last months. But we're not talking empirical knowledge here. We're talking instinct, superstition, magic.

I remembered: when I was awakened early that morning of August second and told that Saddam had invaded Kuwait, after the first shock, the first surge of excitement, I knew that within a day or two I would be flying off somewhere, me and my Olivetti, to wind up in some hotel suite, stacked with videotape machines, eating cold cheeseburgers at three in the morning. But now I had fallen through the ice, the thin ice I'd been skating on for twenty-five years. My notebook, my jacket, my pen had been taken from me. I had lost my distance, my observer status. I had become the story; not in the sense of "TV Correspondent Held Hostage," but in a far more basic, a far more dangerous way. I wasn't the storyteller anymore. I was a character, a participant, like any soldier or refugee. I was involved in the war, entrapped by it. The cops had taken me away from the keyhole. They wouldn't let me be a voyeur anymore. I thought back on my enthusiasm at the beginning of the buildup, the animated stand-ups I had done with F-15s scrambling behind me, with more than a little shame.

I decided to write a book about it if I survived. It would be another dimension of my revenge. The Iraqis had captured me, so I would capture the experience, deal the last blow.

I had spent my career scurrying from story to story, never stopping to digest, hopping on the next wagon as soon as the last one started slowing down. I had thought of writing about the fall of Saigon, but didn't feel up to it. It was too big, too overpowering. There were others on that carrier, I felt, far more qualified than I. In fact, a week after we landed at Clark Air Force Base in the Philippines, I was back in Belfast, covering the Irish *intifada*. But no one else could write this one. I had the exclusive, and it was worth putting down. I would get out of here, pick up my Olivetti, and write about what it's like when you go down from the bridge and find yourself surrounded by the boilers and the deafening roar of the engines. I would write about this fall from grace.

The instinct had been there since boyhood. The block I grew up on in the Bronx, equidistant between Yankee Stadium and a public library, between my father and my mother, was half Jewish, half Irish Catholic. I don't think I met a Protestant until we moved to Queens when I was eleven. P.S. 74 was almost all Jewish because the Catholic kids went to Saint Mary's. A couple of my friends were observant. There were strange objects in their homes, secret objects, covered by white cloths with embroidered designs in blue thread. There were books with strange letters. We didn't have these things, but I knew we were religious too. I could tell by the way my mother looked at our bookshelves. I could read the letters on our books and I knew which were the religious ones. I could tell by the thickness and the titles. *For Whom the Bell Tolls. The Divine Comedy. Joseph and His Brothers*. Wednesday afternoons, some women would come over to sit with my mother and they would take one of the books down from the shelves and talk. I knew these were religious meetings because they were so serious. They didn't laugh and tell jokes the way my uncles and aunts did when they came over on Saturdays. They passed the book around very carefully. It looked like they were afraid it would break.

Mr. Friedman, the man who owned the drugstore, was the first in our apartment house on Nelson Avenue to get a television set. Tuesday evenings, after supper, my father and I would take the elevator up to his apartment and watch Milton Berle. Before we left, my mother would say, "I don't understand how people have time to watch this nonsense. There are so many books to read."

The nightmares always began in London. Perhaps twice in a lifetime cannot qualify as a "pattern." But if they concern the two most dangerous experiences of your life, if not the two times you came closest to losing it, it is worth taking notice.

Soon after my release from prison in Iraq, my good

friend Joram sent me a copy of a letter I had written to him in May 1975, two weeks after the fall of Saigon.

I was there six weeks, drove up the road towards Xuan Loc most days, almost got wiped out by artillery or mortar rounds a number of times, but once again, escaped without a scratch—though my ears took quite a hammering. You ask about nightmares. I didn't have any, not during the six weeks in Saigon, not during the five nights I slept on an aircraft carrier after the evacuation, not during the three nights I slept in Hong Kong on my way back. The nightmares began in London. Strangely, they weren't "combat" nightmares. Night after night I dreamt I was on a carrier but I didn't know where it was going and I didn't know if I'd ever get off. I guess it's not all that difficult to figure out. Nightmares are a luxury and in Saigon I couldn't afford it, not when I knew that I'd have to drive back up the road again in the morning. Back at home with Françoise and Tanya, I could let the phantoms out. Françoise tells me I've been screaming in my sleep.

I am not screaming now. There is no reason to scream. I am at the Metropolitan Opera with a dark and beautiful woman in a low-cut black satin gown. Her long black hair is falling lightly over her shoulders. I am in a tuxedo. We are watching *Tosca*, the last act, where Cavaradossi sings of the shining stars and the perfumed earth as he awaits his execution and I am thinking, It's not like that at all, it's just not like that at all. The opera is over. We are walking down the grand staircase under the Chagalls. The woman turns to me and smiles. "Lunch tomorrow?"

"Of course," I say, and wave goodbye. I stop in my tracks. I remember. I can't have lunch with her tomorrow. The guards won't let me.

Tom Bettag, the executive producer of the "CBS Evening News," is on the phone. "Can you do the story for Thursday?" he asks.

"Of course I can." I laugh. "Today is only Tuesday. There's plenty of time."

"Great," he says and hangs up.

"But, one minute, Tom—one minute!" I say into the dead phone. "There's plenty of time but the guards won't let me."

There was another, recurring dream, a death dream but not a nightmare, somehow. My mother, old and ashen-faced, is sitting on the edge of her bed in an attic room. The windows are wide open. It is windy. "Is that all there is, Mom?" I ask.

"What did you expect?" she replies.

I was not getting religion in my cell. A certain curiosity was beginning to taunt me, though. Will I hear voices? Will I see visions? They're bound to come eventually. One image, a beatific fresco, did come and started coming more frequently. My mother and father, young and radiant, are standing in the sky. My mother is extending her hand and smiling, coaxing me to come, the way she did when I was learning how to walk.

Then the sky exploded. Antiaircraft fire, cannons,

automatic weapons. It was the biggest barrage yet. It had not been preceded by sirens or the sound of planes. I could hear men shouting outdoors. From just outside my cell, a pistol was being fired in the air.

I was lying on my bedroll when it began. I propped myself up on my elbows and smiled because I knew what it meant. It meant the war was over.

It was not the first time I witnessed this boisterous Arab celebration, this "fantasia," as it is whimsically called. I'd been there in Beirut, the summer of 1982, the day the PLO pulled out of town. The war was over, the departure was peaceful, programmed by American diplomats. But it turned out to be the most dangerous day of all, more dangerous than the day the Israelis blitzed the city, more dangerous than the day they invaded West Beirut. With the peculiar Arab genius for perceiving defeat as victory, oblivious to the western notion that what goes up must come down, PLO fighters and their Lebanese allies danced through the streets, emptying their weapons into the sky, creating a firestorm of falling cartridges. Hundreds were injured by the falling rounds.

The timing made sense. I'd been a prisoner a month now. In my mind, the ground war had been going on three weeks. We never thought it would last longer than that. What was the interval between the cease-fire and the release of the POWs in Vietnam? A couple of weeks? It was good that the propaganda machines seemed to be working well, that the soldiers were celebrating. They will not want to kill their prisoners.

I tried not to get excited. I tried not to think of

Françoise or Tanya. I set up roadblocks to stop the release fantasies from coming back. But my mood was light. When I drifted off to sleep that night, I remembered that my pillow, my hiking boots, had taken me through the French Alps five years ago. We had hiked and camped and thrown snowballs in the middle of July.

That night there were no sirens, no planes, no bombs.

In the morning I decided to try to get some news from the guards the next time they took the census. I'd never done that before. I never asked them questions because I didn't want to hear the answers. I was better off creating my own world and tucking myself deep inside it.

But the only caller that day was the dog man. His cry of "*kelb*" bounced off me. I was feeling strong. The bread was thinner and grainier than it had been before. They must be running out of wheat, I thought.

My weight loss was making me more supple than I'd been in a long time. I could touch my toes now. Last year I'd barely been able to see them. I lay on my back and swung my legs behind my head. I could reach the floor with my feet.

I didn't seem to smell too bad. Maybe I'd gotten used to it, but considering that I hadn't changed my clothes in a month, that I hadn't washed since that day in the camp, I was surprised that it wasn't more pungent. Once I woke up at night and thought I was in a New York subway. I guessed it was the smell. By now, I reflected, I must have set the world record for time spent by a TV correspondent without looking in a mirror. Actually, I must have set that record within hours of our capture.

That night again, there were no bombs. The guards listened to the radio more than they usually did. They seemed to be having heated discussions. There was much martial music.

The next morning I heard the windows opening and closing. It must be the census. When my window opened, Abdul was there. Next to him was a man carrying the big black ledger.

"Name?"

"Robert Simon."

"Nationality?"

"American." The man next to Abdul was making marks in the ledger.

"Is there news?" I asked. "There are no bombs."

"The war is not over," Abdul said.

"But two days ago I heard men firing guns."

"I know," Abdul said. "Maybe Russia join us now. Maybe we get stronger."

BREAD

❖❖

I T was no longer difficult to stay awake when it got dark. An Arab was being tortured in the corridor. His screams pierced what had been the quiet hours and went on and on, interrupted only by high-pitched shouts of "*Allah Akbar*," God is Great. I did not know a man's voice could last that long. I did not understand why he didn't pass out. I could hear the guards laughing and taunting him. I could hear the sharp thwacks of sticks hitting flesh followed by his shouts of "*La-La-La*." No, No, No. Then more thwacks and more screams.

I caught myself muttering, "He's an Arab, they won't do that to me. He's an Arab, they won't do that to me."

Until now there had been a certain discipline in the prison, a method to the system. The dark, the filth, the hunger, the threats and the curses, were designed to break you down, make you feel helpless and hopeless. But the system protected you as well, from casual cruelty, from soldiers running amok. What was happening now was sport and it was worrisome. Something was veering out of control.

I had other worries. For the first time I seriously considered the possibility that they might keep me here a long time. Many of my Palestinian friends in the occupied territories went into Israeli prisons for six months or a year routinely. But they knew when they would get out, and they were held up by a cause. It was a rite of passage, part of the struggle.

My only struggle was to get out and resume my life. But would I ever fully recover from prolonged starvation? What would it do to my tennis game? I was becoming such a passive creature. How long would it be before I dared ask a waiter in any restaurant for more bread?

The lease on the house we rented near the beach north of Tel Aviv was up in May. Would Françoise renew it? Where would she go? Would CBS assign another correspondent to Israel? They'd have to after a while. And . . . a seemingly trivial but troubling question: how would I keep track of time once my soap bar was full, when there would be no room for any more lines?

I was developing a sense of what day of the week it was. One day was always quieter than the others. There would be fewer guards in the corridor. There would be no census. The food would come later in the day and the bread would be especially stale. That day would be Friday.

It was a Thursday when I heard the windows opening and closing. But there was no clanging of the metal cart which carried the soup. "Shit," I muttered, "only bread today, no soup."

When my window opened, I saw the nice man, the jolly man who had given me the dates. He handed me a sealed plastic bag. It was heavy. Inside were five thick, fluffy pieces of Arab bread. I couldn't believe it. I walked up and down the cell, holding the prize in my palm, feeling the weight of it. There was a design on the bag, a man leading a camel, a palm tree. There was writing in English and in Arabic. It said, "Made in Jordan."

King Hussein had come under heavy fire from the Americans for breaking the embargo against Iraq. I offered a prayer: "Blessed be the breaker of embargoes."

I hadn't opened the bag yet when my window swung open again. The man was back, this time with another two pieces of the same bread. *"Bukra mafish,"* he said. Tomorrow, nothing. And he smiled.

I said, "God bless you." I opened the bag and smelled the bread. It carried the rich, sweet aroma of a bakery before dawn, when the ovens are roaring. I calculated: I can eat two pieces right now and another before I go to sleep and another when I wake up and two more tomorrow whenever I want, and another Saturday morning. I was so deep in rapture that I didn't hear the window open again. It was the dog man with soup.

"Kelb," he shouted.

"Thank you," I said.

I laid my blankets on the ledge and carefully hoisted myself up with the plastic bag and the soup and I said, "I'm going to eat this like a mensch." For the first time I let the meal linger. I leaned against the wall, took a bite of the bread and a loud sip of soup and cast a leisurely glance at the illuminated screen, and actually waited before I did it again. I put my hand on my stomach. It was warm and the skin was tight. When I'd finished, I invited the most tantalizing thoughts to visit me: the candy store in the hotel, the Carnegie Delicatessen.

"I don't need you guys anymore," I said. "I've eaten."

Night had fallen and I was still sitting on the ledge when the window was jerked open again. A guard was looking at me. I'm in trouble, I thought. He's already seen me. I'll get in trouble for being on the ledge. But he seemed to have a different agenda. He was carrying blankets on his shoulder. "How many blankets you have?" he asked.

"Three," I lied. I was wearing a fourth as a scarf under Peter's jacket. What a day, I thought. Another problem about to be solved, the cold problem. He's going to give me another blanket. "One blanket very bad," I said. I wanted to show him the torn and filthy blanket, but I couldn't unravel the right one. "Can I have another?"

"No. We need more blankets. Give me one."

"I only have three," I said. "I'm cold."

He cursed and slammed the window.

I had sensed that the hotel was filling up. I'd been hearing new voices, American, flat, Midwestern voices for the most part. Calm, courteous, and controlled.

"My name is Randy, sir." I heard a conversation from way down the corridor one morning. It sounded like a chat outside a drugstore in some windy town on the Great Plains. I wondered if I was beginning to hear voices.

"What?"

"My name is Randy, sir." He sounded so young, a teenager answering a teacher.

"What kind of name that?"

"It's what my friends call me, sir." I realized I had never called any of the guards "sir." Should I try it out on Abdul? On the dog man? Could I?

"You come America?"

"Yes, sir."

"Why you come here?"

"I didn't ask to come here, sir. They made me come here."

"Why you kill Iraqi women and children?"

"I didn't kill anyone, sir. I'm sorry people are being killed." Randy didn't sound worried. He knew he'd make it.

Late Friday afternoon I sat on my ledge and watched the sun paste three slender fingers of light on the wall opposite the air vent. I thought of Meursault, the hero of Camus' *L'Étranger*, watching the sun rise in his cell the morning of his execution. He said, *"Je me suis ouvert à la tendre indifférence du monde."* I opened myself to the tender indifference of the world.

Never had I been calmer, I thought, except in those vagabond moments I projected on my screen, those strolls down lamplit streets, those sessions on rocks by the sea. My mind, calmed by the solitude of the cell, was reaching back to retrieve those moments from the past, memories which were inaccessible amidst the frenzy of my life as a newsman.

How little time I'd spent here contemplating the big stories, the historic events. I was remembering the little moments, the parentheses tucked away in between. Vietnam was coming back not as the spring offensive of 1972 or the collapse of the South Vietnamese army three years later, but the eve of the evacuation, when I'd hired a cyclo and gone gliding through the dark streets of Saigon. Israel was not the grandiose arrival of Anwar Sadat, but the view from my room at the King David that afternoon, the sun setting on the walls of the old city. Lebanon was with Peter, chucking shrimp shells into the black sea at Byblos.

That's when life had been most intense, at its most serene. Would I remember that if I ever got out of this place?

I wondered whether I'd want to resume the activities which I'd called recreation. Had I really enjoyed tennis? Right now it seemed absurdly competitive, full of fury and frustration. I remembered stomping and cursing when I missed a shot. Even skiing seemed too frenetic, except those last runs of the day, when I wasn't rushing to make the next lift, when I could lean way back on my skis and take long turns through the lengthening shadows of the pines. Skiing and tennis — my father's legacy: for he taught me to do them both.

I'd been jogging almost every day for years and realized now how little pleasure I had gotten out of it. Why was I trying so hard to get into shape? It was beginning to look like I wasn't going to make it to Wimbledon or the Winter Olympics after all. I'd stopped smoking in 1983 and missed it terribly ever since.

I went to Japan then, in the fall of '83, to shoot a series called "The Japanning of America." The head monk of one of the leading Zen Buddhist sects consented to an interview in the shaded garden of his temple in Kyoto. He was in a brilliant orange robe, a tall, stocky man in his seventies, without a hair on his head, a line on his face, or a word of English in his vocabulary. But an American-born monk was there to interpret. While the cameraman was setting up I asked the interpreter to explain to the master that I had just stopped smoking and was having a hard time. Could he offer some advice? The serene master got agitated, made expansive gestures with his long, fleshy arms, declaimed loudly in that atonal, bass way Zen masters have. The interpreter translated: "Why stop? Smoking is fun. Life is short." I looked at the master. He had just lit up a Pall Mall, was offering me one.

The Buddha does not jog.

The Buddha is plump, smiling, and happy.

The Buddha smokes Pall Mall.

When we arrived in Bucharest after that all-night drive from the Yugoslav border, it was the day before Christmas and Bucharest was burning. The window of my room at the Intercontinental had been shattered by machine gun fire. From my balcony I could see dozens of buildings wrapped in flames. We walked around the corner to the Palace Square, where the revolt had begun. It was lined with tank columns now and crowded with curious Rumanians out for a stroll, out to see what was happening to their lives, unaware, it seemed, that the fighting was not over, that every moment or two one of the tanks would open fire on the Securitate, Ceauçescu's private police, who were still sniping from many of the buildings.

On Christmas day the revolution gave us two gifts:

news that Ceauçescu was dead, and the opportunity to shoot even more dramatic footage of the Battle of Bucharest. We had a dynamite story in the can. But to transmit it we had to get to Rumanian TV. It was impossible to drive; cars were being shot up by just about anyone who had a gun, and it was too far to walk. We took the subway, which left us off about 300 yards from the broadcast center. There were six of us from CBS. It was only necessary for one to go: Neville Harris, the technician who would satellite the material, but the rest of us didn't feel right about Neville taking a dangerous walk on his own to get *our* stories on the air. A Rumanian interpreter came with us too. There were no streetlights and we walked single file down a pitch-black, tree-lined avenue. About midway, soldiers shouted at us and opened fire with automatic weapons. We hit the ground and saw bullets ricochet off the pavement a few feet away. We shouted, "American, American," our noses in the gutter, while the translator shouted in Rumanian. After a few long moments the soldiers approached, apologized, and sent us on our way.

The TV building was ringed with armor, and the soldiers there would not let us enter. After protracted pleading and negotiations they agreed to let Neville inside. The rest of us would wait in the cold. We paced up and down in front of a tank, tried to joke with the soldiers, gave them cigarettes. They were peasant boys, had never been to Bucharest, were frightened and confused. Our interpreter told us they had no idea who we were and didn't understand a word of his attempts to explain. The

"CBS Evening News" is on the air at one-thirty in the morning Bucharest time, and when two-thirty rolled by and there was still no sign of Neville, we realized he had either decided to spend the night inside or that the decision had been made for him. But we couldn't walk back to the subway; we'd get shot at again. At three in the morning, a man suddenly appeared from nowhere on the deserted street ten yards behind us. He said something. The soldiers opened fire. I saw him actually fly through the air before he hit the ground. He didn't move.

The soldiers shouted hysterically at us now, ordered us to spread-eagle against the tank, shouted at us not to move, not to turn around. What the man they had just killed was saying before they shot him was, "Don't shoot. I'm a doctor." They had panicked. We had witnessed a murder and they knew it. I had my arms up against the tank, trying not to shiver or sneeze, knowing that the slightest movement or sound would be a cue for them to squeeze the triggers. I snuck one quick glance over my shoulder and saw six soldiers lined up, their rifles pointed at us. It was a firing squad. For the next half hour, before they told us to lower our arms and the tension lessened and our only problem for the rest of the night was the cold, I did a bit of thinking, reached some conclusions, which were startingly similar to what had been going through my mind these weeks of solitary confinement.

It wasn't to change jobs or stay out of harm's way or anything like that. It had more to do with my attitude toward time, with the difference between being and becoming. And the message, when time seemed to be

coming to an end, was exceptionally powerful and difficult to put into words. But the words I found myself
repeating that night against the tank were: "Stop becoming. Start being."

Maybe it was little more than the old carpe diem
formula: "Seize the day." But I'd always thought that
notion carried a good measure of frenzy, and what I
wanted to do was precisely to shut off that frenzy machine,
that engine which generated so much steam that the
moment itself became blurred. Stop trying and preparing
and achieving and sink softly back into the moment.

I wanted more than ever to write things down. If I had a
pad and a pen and this much food every day, I thought, I
could do this forever. I was beginning to understand
Brother Gregorius. I saw how, in solitude, time slipped
into different, deeper planes. The passage itself slowed
down until the counter no longer stopped on days, weeks,
or even months, but on the moment. That's all there was.
Nothing else mattered.

That half hour in Bucharest had been a shock treatment, a quick hit with the electrodes, and it hadn't rattled
my brain enough to produce anything lasting. This was
prolonged therapy, and I had every reason to believe there
would be more of it. Time was moving so slowly through
my dark cell, I had trouble even imagining a sudden
interruption, a brusque movement. But there was a
bright side to the passage of time. They hadn't interrogated me in weeks. The spy business must have been a
ruse. They seemed to have forgotten about me.

QUESTIONS

❧

FOOTSTEPS stopped outside my cell. I stood and waited but the window didn't open. I heard creaking metallic sounds and the door swung open. One of the walking-policemen was standing there with an enormous key ring. He beckoned me to come out. The corridor seemed longer than I remembered it, long and dark. A shaft of daylight drifted through at the other end. I hadn't been out of my cell in seventeen days. I looked at the handcuffs attached to a bar at the bottom of every door. I saw Abdul in the corridor mopping up. The man who wielded so much power over my life also seemed to be a janitor.

The walking-policeman handed me a blindfold. It was large and black but it reminded me of the sleeping shades you get on airplanes. I put it on. He tightened it so I couldn't see anything, not even the floor. He tied my hands behind my back, took me by the elbow, and led me quickly down the hall, to the staircase.

"*Yallah, yallah,*" move, move, he said as I tried to take the stairs slowly. We went down two flights, to the interrogation floor. I didn't hear any voices. No one else was being interrogated. He pushed me down onto a chair. It seemed to be the same room as the last session.

"Name? Rank?" a voice shouted. There must be some mistake, I thought, a bureaucratic error. They wanted someone else.

"I'm not in the military," I said. "I'm a journalist." There was a rustling of papers. Two men were whispering to each other. I heard the word "Israel."

"Our sources tell us you have good relations with the government of Israel," a quieter voice said.

That's it, I thought. The game is up. I found this realization calming in a way. I settled back in my chair. It was all over, but I would go on playing for a while, and was, in fact, ready for this. I had trained in my cell.

"I have worked in Israel," I said.

"When? Dates?" It was the shouter again.

"I covered the *intifada* on the West Bank and in Gaza. I worked there a lot in 1987. I am well known to Mr. Arafat."

"Arafat?" He laughed.

"Yes," I said. "I have also worked in sixty-seven other countries. Would you like me to name them?"

"No," he said. "Our sources tell us you are Jewish."

"I'm not," I lied. "I'm Protestant."

"What does your father do?"

"He's dead," I said. "He worked in a bank." That was a mistake, I thought. I had not anticipated that one.

"All bankers are Jewish," he shot back.

"That's not true," I said. "And my father wasn't a banker. He worked in a bank."

"All the media is Jewish. The media is all owned by Jews," he said. I sensed that he was showing off now, showing off what he took to be his sophistication about Jews and America.

"That's not true," I said. "Some are, some aren't. Most aren't."

"Our sources tell us you work for Al-Mossad."

"What?" I pretended not to understand. I wondered where they had gotten that from.

"Al Mossad—Mossad."

"I've never worked for any government in any country," I said. "I have worked for CBS for twenty-five years."

"Thank you," he said. "We will tell our sources what you said. They will have questions and we will talk to you again." His voice was soft now, friendly. Even though I knew better, I found that comforting. No one moved. A silence lingered in the room.

"When will you talk to me again?" I asked. "Tomorrow?"

"No," he said. "I have to leave Baghdad on a special mission. I will talk to you when I return. Do you have any questions?" he asked.

"Yes," I said. "Is the war almost over?"

"It will be over soon," he said, "because some of our heroes assassinated Bush."

"What?"

"Bush is dead," he said.

The shouter joined in. "We kill him day before yesterday," he said.

I said nothing.

"Also, we kill seventy thousand U.S. soldiers. We use chemical weapons."

I said nothing.

"Do you think Quayle will be a good president?" the quieter man asked.

"I'm not sure," I said.

"Me too." He laughed.

When we got back up to my floor, the guard untied my hands and removed my blindfold. Abdul was wheeling the soup tray through the corridor. It had piles of detergent and soap bars on it. He grinned at me.

I felt safe when I was back in my cell. I had just been handed a death sentence, but I felt good that I hadn't broken down. I was pleased with my performance.

There were two small piles of detergent on my ledge and a new bar of soap. I won't be needing this now, I thought. My stay will be coming to an end. I pictured the show trial. I imagined a large auditorium, a stage. I remembered film clips of Chinese students being tried after Tiananmen square. I wondered whether the Iraqis wore black robes.

How sloppy they were, I thought. What clowns. Did they expect me to believe the Bush business? If they'd told me a thousand Americans had been killed, I would have had to think about it. But seventy thousand? Unthinkable, impossible.

There were two pieces of bread on the ledge by the toilet. I had missed lunch. I ate one piece, put the other in my jacket pocket, and sat down on the floor. My head felt heavy, my mind dull. I didn't think much that afternoon beyond reflecting that the most secular of Jews was about to get killed for being Jewish. I imagined the sweet tea they would serve before they hanged me. I dozed a bit.

I was laying out my blankets in the dark, making the folds sharp and neat, when the first bomb hit. I had heard a plane but there had been no sirens, no antiaircraft fire.

The blast rocked the building and lifted me off the floor. Chunks of concrete were falling on my head. The ceiling was collapsing. I spread my hand over the blanket. It was covered in rubble. My mouth was caked with dust and I could feel the debris in my hair.

I knew there would be a second bomb. I knew I was going to die and I felt a deepening calm seep inside me. It will be quick, I thought. It will be over soon. No more waiting for the executioners. I got down on my hands and knees, tucked my head in, the way ski instructors tell you to do when an avalanche is coming.

The second blast seemed even sharper, like the crack of thunder when the storm is near. I heard the sound of breaking glass. I never knew there was glass in my reverie screen. I got up, walked toward it, but a pile of bricks was in the way. There was no partition anymore. My ledge was gone.

I was not afraid. I was not nervous. I felt alert, excited. This was it, and it was exciting. Something was happening, an adventure. The curtains were falling. Slow time was drawing to a close.

The corridor was suddenly full of human commotion. Those matter-of-fact Midwestern voices were yelling now. Men were banging on their doors.

There was no light, but I knew the room had filled with smoke when my coughing began. I would die from asphyxiation. I realized that all I'd been doing in my cell for twenty-five days was preparing for this. Not for the bombing, for death. The ledge had been my deathbed. I had completed the course and I was ready.

The building shook violently when the third bomb fell. I thought my floor had caved in. I was falling. But then I was sitting down, sprawled in the corner. I reached out. The walls were still there. I remembered that warplanes usually flew in formations of four, but somehow I knew this would be the last bomb. Others seemed to think so too. I went to the door and listened. I could hear shouting, but nothing coherent.

"Peter, are you OK? Can you hear me?" I shouted.

Nothing.

Then, suddenly, the steel window to the corridor opened and Juan was there, standing outside. I put my arms out. He grabbed them and started kissing my hands. I put my arms around him.

I heard Peter's muffled voice shouting from down the hall. "We're not dead yet. We're not dead yet."

Juan was hurt. A wall had collapsed on his foot, but he'd gotten out of his cell. He was alone in the corridor. The guards were gone. There was smoke everywhere. Juan was opening other windows.

"Bob, are you all right?" It was Peter. His voice was gone. It was the hoarse whisper of a man with throat cancer.

"I'm OK, Peter. How are you?"

"I'm fine, Bob. We're not dead yet."

"Where's Roberto?"

"I'm here, Bob, I'm OK."

Windows were open the length of the corridor now. Voices were crisp and clear. Everyone was talking to everyone else. It was an air force reunion.

"Do you know if my pilot got out?" It was an American voice.

"What's his name?"

"Devon Jones."

"He was rescued. He's a hundred percent flying again."

The British were telling war stories. We were back in the movies again. This time it was the Battle of Britain.

"I think it was the fourteenth, Roger, uh, well, I couldn't believe it. I felt my five go and then there was this sixth and I thought, oh, dear no, and then there were flames all around and I simply had to get out."

"What about Graham?"

"Oh, he's dead—never had a chance."

How do they do it? I thought. How do they fucking do it? I tried to join this one. "When were you shot down?"

"On the sixteenth."

"Nine days ago?"

"Yes, that's right, nine days ago."

"What was going on then?"

"Sweet fuck-all," he said.

"What?"

"Nothing. Just bombing. Nothing at all."

So the ground war I thought was over hadn't even begun.

An English voice said, "I'm going to try to get through the window." I thought of the small man I had seen sitting in the corridor on my way to an interrogation. I tried to wedge my head through the window but it was too narrow.

Juan came back. He had keys. He tried to open my door, got one lock undone, but couldn't manage the other. "You know, Doyle's been here," he said. "And Pizzey. They've been trying to get us out." Larry Doyle and Allen Pizzey are CBS people.

"How do you know?"

"I heard them. I heard their voices."

"What?"

"I heard them talking to the guards."

"That's impossible," I said.

"No, I heard them," he said. He was talking fast now, trying to run past my skepticism. "They brought us bread. How do you think we got that bread?"

I thought about that. It was possible that they were in Baghdad. But here? "Tanya's been here too," he said. "I heard her. So has Lana, my sister. I heard her say, 'Juan's here, he's here.'"

"Juan, you've been hallucinating."

"No, no, really, believe me. They're here." Juan went off to try to unlock other doors.

"Hey, mate—you been on TV?"

"Yeah. They had me on twice, must be a star now." It was an Englishman, across from me.

"Are you John Peters?" I asked. I had heard him during the census.

"Yes. Who are you?"

"I'm Bob Simon from CBS News."

"Hey, CBS News is here," I heard an American shout. "Come on, open the doors, get us out of here!"

"Bad news," I said. "I'm in here just like you."

"Shit," he said.

"I think you've got a better chance than us. If you ever get out of here, remember our names. Bluff, Alvarez, Caldera, Simon. Tell 'em you saw us alive."

Peter's voice came through soft and strong. Peter said, "If any of you survive this, please tell Geraldine I love her."

I heard the sound of water now. It seemed to be coming from downstairs. I asked John Peters, "Were you guys trained for this? What have you been doing?"

"No, no training. I've just been sleeping a lot and walking. Walking all the time."

"Are you Simon?" It was an American down the hall, on my side of the corridor.

"Yes."

"I've seen you on TV. I'll pray for you."

"Thank you," I said. "What's your name?"

"Wutzel, Bob Wutzel. I've been praying all the time. I pray, then I sleep, then I pray some more. I've been praying for all of us."

Another American shouted, "We're gonna make it. If we lived through this, we can live through anything. We're gonna make it."

Juan was at my door again. His eyes were wild. "What should I do?" he asked.

"You mean, should you escape?"

"Yes. I can walk a little."

"We don't know where we are, Juan," I said. "I don't think you've got a chance. I think you should go back to your cell and wait."

"I don't have a cell. It's gone."

"Then just go sit where it was. Maybe the guards will come back. Maybe they'll shoot you if they see you in the corridor."

Suddenly I was frightened. "Listen. My door is half open now. Can you close it? They'll kill me if they think I was trying to escape." I was ashamed by the pathetic figure I had become, by my overpowering fear of the guards.

Now Juan was the comforter. "Don't worry, they won't even notice. You should see this place. It's a mess."

"Please, Juan." He tried to close it but couldn't.

I heard Roberto. "I always knew something else was going to happen," he said. "We're going to be OK. We're going to be OK now."

I heard shouting in Arabic. I saw rays from flashlights bouncing off the corridor walls. I backed off from the door. I heard keys churning in the lock. Two guards were there. They were shouting, *"Yallah, yallah."*

As I prepared to leave my rubble-strewn cell, as I grabbed a blanket, threw it over my shoulders, and stepped into the corridor, now reeking with smoke and bedlam, I made one mistake which a professional prisoner should not have made at this stage of his career—a mistake which was to cost me dearly in days to come. I forgot to take my cup.

THE BUS

◆◆

"WHAT names do you remember from that night?" the interrogator asked.

"John Peters, Larry Slade, Bob Wutzel." I was leaning on my elbows. The session had gone on for hours. I was exhausted, numb. "I could use a cup of tea," I said.

"That's all? No other names?"

"Yes. David Eberly, Dale Storr."

The shorter man flinched. "Why didn't you mention them the first time?" he asked.

"Because I didn't hear their names in the prison. I only found out about them later, on the bus."

The shorter man, the American, got up and left the room. It was March third, the day after our release. I was in the Humana Hospital Wellington in London. I was being debriefed by an American from Naval Intelligence and an Englishman from the Ministry of Defence.

None of the POWs had been released or even acknowledged yet by the Iraqis. We were the first to come out with any information about them. My friends were in adjoining rooms on the same floor of this luxury clinic, being debriefed by other intelligence teams. Our families were in a lounge at the end of the floor, getting increasingly annoyed, not understanding the need for so many hours of questioning.

The American had left my room to phone Washington. Until that moment they had assumed air force pilot Dale Storr was dead. A member of his squadron had seen his plane crash in flames in Kuwait. He had not seen a parachute.

Two weeks later Captain Dale Storr phoned me at my home near Tel Aviv to say thank you. He told me his A-10 squadron in Saudi Arabia had held a memorial service a few days after he'd been shot down. His family in Spokane had been told they would never see him again. He said people still looked at him suspiciously, as if they were seeing a ghost.

In June I went down to visit Storr at his base in Louisiana. He was back to flying A-10s, in excellent spirits, enjoying his celebrity status. But that's another story. All I knew about him that day in London was what I'd seen of him that night in the bus. He was very tall and in very bad shape.

I was one of the first prisoners to get to the bus. I had been led downstairs by two guards, down to the basement, then to the garage. It must have been where we had arrived twenty-five days earlier, but it was unrecognizable now. We were wading through a foot of water. There was a stench of gas. The hulks of a few cars were cloaked in debris. We were still inside when suddenly I saw the sky.

A whole section of the roof was gone. I could see the stars and the moon.

We climbed over what was left of a wall. A rush of fresh air filled me with rapture. I stopped. The guards yanked me along, shouting. They kept looking to the sky, but not to see the stars. They seemed worried about more planes. I was having trouble walking through the debris. My feet kept coming out of my boots without laces.

We climbed over another wall and then we were in a street. It was a residential street, lined with white stone houses, untouched by the apocalypse which had swept by a few yards away. It was dark and still, no lights anywhere, no sound except the humming of an engine. The bus was parked a block away, the motor running. The guards shoved me up the stairs and another guard pushed me to the rear. There were no seats in this bus. I was pushed down to the floor, my back against the wall. A short man in a flight suit was sitting to my right. I could not see his face. A guard took the blanket I had wrapped around my shoulders and threw it over my head. I felt a blow from a truncheon. I touched my head to see if there was any blood. I was hit again. This time he got my fingers.

Another man was shoved down to my left. From underneath my blanket I could see that his knees were very high. He was in a flight suit. I whispered, "What's your name?"

"Dale Storr. What's yours?"

"Bob Simon, CBS News."

The truncheon came down on my head again. "Don't

speak anything," the guard shouted. The bus was filling up. I listened for some sign of my friends. I heard nothing but told myself not to worry. Everybody would be put on this bus, wherever it was going.

I heard screams from outside. I knew that voice. It was the Arab, the man they beat every night in the corridor. Then the screams came from inside the bus. He was still being beaten. I lifted my blanket and tilted my head back so I could see. He was middle-aged, half bald, wearing pajama bottoms but nothing else. He was barefoot, bare-chested and flabby. Streams of sweat were pouring down his face. I was shivering under two blankets. I didn't understand how he had kept so much meat on him after our prison diet. I wondered how he had managed to walk through the carnage without shoes. There were welts on his head, blood was trickling from the side of his mouth. His hands were tied behind his back, and two guards were pummeling him with their truncheons as he lay writhing in the aisle.

The heads of three handcuffed prisoners directly across from me were covered by the same blanket. I looked to my left. In the moonlight I could see that Storr had a blood-soaked rag on his head. His cheeks were hollow, his eyes expressionless, focused on some invisible point in the distance. I reached out from under my blanket, put my hand on his knee, and gave it a squeeze.

The guards were roving the aisle, punching their trun-cheons into their palms. One of them, bearded and fat, stopped in front of me. "Nationality?"

"American." He bopped me over the head.

"Pilot?"

"No. *Zahafi*, CBS News." This time he hit me hard, on the forehead. I think I passed out. Later, months later, Storr told me they beat me a lot on the bus, always asking the same questions, always hitting me on the head when I said *"zahafi."* I remember very little of that. I must have been wandering in and out of consciousness.

Another conversation was going on in front of the bus which I heard about later. Alvarez's neighbor asked for his name. When Roberto told him, the man, astonished, said he was Colonel Eberly, reminded Roberto that we had interviewed him in January at his base near Riyadh. Eberly was an F-15 squadron commander. He didn't have to fly, took one run for solidarity's sake the third day of the war, was shot down by a SAM over northern Iraq. Eberly had a compass and a map, walked for three days toward Turkey, was caught at the border.

The sound of prisoners hitting the floor of the bus stopped after a while and we started moving, moving slowly without headlights through dark, narrow streets, a black ship through a black and silent sea. Through the window above the handcuffed men, I could see white houses bathed in moonlight behind iron grilles. There were many portraits of Saddam. He was smiling.

The bus made many sharp turns. Guards up front seemed to be arguing. I wondered if they knew where we were going, or were we driving aimlessly, like the *Pequod*, waiting for dawn or enlightenment. Other guards were sitting on seats in the back, cradling their AK-47s.

I was alive but felt I had left the land of the living. The

hollow-cheeked men in flight suits were dead men and we would be in this bus forever roaming dark streets. The sun would never rise, the bus would never stop, we would not be given food or water but would not get hungry or thirsty. The only sound we would ever hear was the screaming of the mad Arab, the only sight, pale moonlight reflected off ashen concrete walls. I closed my eyes, but the white light became unbearably bright, the screaming louder. I felt a blow to the head, heard myself scream. A hand touched my knee.

When I opened my eyes I thought we were on a highway. We were driving faster. Suddenly I knew where we were going and I was suffused with joy. We were going back to our camp, to our golden age. Where else? It was so logical, why hadn't I thought of it earlier? There can't be many prisons ready to accommodate POWs. It was outside Baghdad and we had just left Baghdad. The pilots couldn't know what I knew, couldn't know that our lives were about to take a wide turn for the better. I wanted to tell Dale Storr but knew that I couldn't. I wondered whether Peter had figured it out. I wondered whether the camp had been alerted, whether our friends would be waiting for us. Would we be put back in the same cell? Would Maher bring us his stove? Would Hassein cook up some meat and potatoes? Abu Jihad, if he was still there, would celebrate our return with some fried fish. We would be back together—Juan, Peter, Roberto, and I—and we would chat our way happily to the end of the war.

The Arab was lying in the aisle in front of me now,

squirming. There was froth on his mouth. His filthy bare foot was reaching toward my face. I pushed it away.

Then the bus made a turn and slowed down. We were inching between high walls. It was a tight squeeze. I could hear Arabs outside shouting, giving directions. This was not our camp. I didn't know where we were, but this was not our camp. The bus stopped. I pushed the blanket back over my eyes. A guard pulled me to my feet, shoved me to the front of the bus, and pushed me down. I knew the man on my left was Peter. "How are you, mate?" he whispered.

"I'm OK, Peter—you?"

"We're not dead yet."

"Roberto? Juan?"

"They're here," Peter said. "Juan's got a bum foot." The four of us were led out of the bus. I looked back; I didn't like being separated from the pilots. Two rows of men, heads bowed, were huddled in the darkness on the sides of the bus. No one moved.

Peter and I were half dragging, half carrying Juan through a moonlit yard. He had his arms around our shoulders, clutching us tightly. Guards with truncheons led us to a large cement building. When we stepped inside, I stopped in my tracks. It was a penitentiary. There were two floors with two long rows of barred cells on each. There was not a sound. We were led up a flight of stairs. The guards made us let go of Juan. More than anything else, I didn't want to be alone again.

"Please—can we stay together?" I said. I felt a crashing

blow to the small of my back. I was shoved inside a cell, the door slammed shut. I was alone. I grabbed on to the bars and tried to see what was happening to my friends, but I could only see straight ahead. I heard a door slamming to my left, then a second, then a third. On the other side of my bars was a narrow aisle, three feet wide. A waist-high bar ran the length of it. The cellblock was rectangular. I could see a row of cells on the same floor opposite me. There was another row downstairs. The building appeared empty. I turned around and took a step into the cell. I fell over a soft body. My fall was broken by another body on the floor next to it. Neither moved. I got up.

"Does anyone speak English?" I asked.

Silence. I took my boots off. I wanted to walk to the end of the cell, tried to tiptoe in between the bodies, but there was no in between. People were lying on their sides. There was no room for them to be on their backs. No one moved. I heard breathing. A man muttered something in a language I'd never heard. I whispered urgently, "Does anyone speak English?"

Silence.

"Français? Italiano?"

Nothing.

I turned around, grabbed on to the bars again, and looked outside. Two guards were standing on the floor below. I was about to shout to them, tell them there was no room in my cell, but decided not to. My back still hurt. I would wait until dawn.

"Come here." It was a deep whisper from the back of the cell.

"What?"

"Shh—come here."

I made my way over the bodies. The cell was much shorter than in Baghdad, seemed narrower too. Feet were pressed up against the wall. "Sit down," he said.

"Where?"

"There, where you are." I could not see a thing. I lowered myself slowly. There seemed to be something soft on the floor, a cushion, perhaps. I sat down. My back was against the end wall. The man must have made room for me by raising his knees.

"You speak English," I said.

"Yes," he said. "I couldn't speak when you came because the guards mustn't hear us."

"Where are you from?" I asked.

"Kuwait."

"Are the other men asleep?"

"No, they are awake."

"How many are in this cell?"

"We were six. Now we are seven."

"Where are the others from?"

"They are Kurds. They speak nothing. Are you hungry?"

"Yes."

"There is a bag attached to the wall. There is bread." I got to my knees, tapped the wall until I felt a plastic bag. It was hanging by a nail. There were three pieces of bread inside.

"Don't you need it?" I asked.

"Eat," he said.

A DAY IN THE LIFE OF
ABU GHRAIB

❖❖

Aʜᴍᴀᴅ al-Ateeqi, fifty-four, Foreign Ministry official and ex–Kuwaiti envoy to Algeria, Syria, Saudi Arabia, and Lebanon, was arrested the day after the Iraqi invasion. He'd been driving near his home in Kuwait City with his fifteen-year-old son and their Filipino maid. He stopped to take some home video of Iraqi troops, just to have some pictures, he said, nothing else. He was arrested and questioned on the spot. The soldiers were correct: no rough stuff—at least not then. They let his son drive home with the maid while they took him downtown. That was more than six months ago. Before coming to this jail, he spent a hundred and ten days in solitary confinement in what he described as a red brick cell with a ledge and a toilet but no running water. It was on the second floor of Iraq's Intelligence Headquarters, a building in a residential neighborhood of Baghdad, designed and built for Saddam Hussein by the Rumanians.

"I just came from there," I said.

"Did you sign a confession?"

"No."

"Then why did they bring you here?"

"The building was bombed."

"When?"

"Tonight, just now."

"Allah karim, Allah karim," he said. God is too good.

The cellblock was full, Ahmad said, six or seven prisoners to a cell. But there was not a sound, not a speck of light, just the voices of two strangers stretching toward each other across the darkness.

I told Ahmad of our pilgrimage from Kuwait to Basra to Baghdad, how they accused me of being a spy. "Everyone is a spy." He laughed. "I'm a spy, these Kurdish boys are spies. They were just following their cows across the border. They say everyone is a spy."

I felt light, lighter than I had in weeks. And Ahmad had a litany of good news. You were fed three times a day here, sweet tea with every meal. There was bread from Jordan. Sometimes you had dates. There was a window in the cell. In fact, I was sitting right underneath it. You could look outdoors. I would see in the morning. You could even talk through the window to men in the next cell. You had to be careful, but you could do it. Sometimes you were taken to a yard outside. You could wash and clean your clothes. They hadn't been taken there in ten days, but maybe tomorrow. Ahmad told me we were in the largest jail in Iraq, maybe in the world. It was called Abu Ghraib and it had two hundred thousand prisoners. We were in the section run by the intelligence service, the toughest section, he said, but it sounded like a five-star hotel to me.

"All they do is beat and shout," Ahmad said.

"Do they interrogate people?"

"Yes, sometimes, but no torture, not like the White Ship."

The building we had come from was called the White Ship by prisoners, Ahmad explained, because that's what it looked like from the street: an ocean liner. I realized I'd never seen it from the outside. There was a torture chamber on the floor where I had been interrogated. It had a black door. Ahmad told me about the water torture, where they lowered you with a crane headfirst into a barrel of freezing water, and the rack, where they stretched you until your bones were yanked out of their sockets. Ahmad had seen the room. He had seen a man on the rack. They had shown him the room before one of his interrogations. Many of the prisoners in our jail had been tortured there, he said. He started telling me how they pumped water into your rectum until your intestines exploded, but I stopped him. I didn't want to hear any more of this tonight.

We had been talking for hours. There was still no hint of light in the room. Ahmad al-Ateeqi was a whisper, a whisper leading me from the dark corner of a cell to a new life. I imagined him tall and elegant, the consummate Arab diplomat.

I had eaten two pieces of bread. I was thirsty. Ahmad got up. I could hear the Kurds mutter as he tried to step between them. He came back with a cup of water, told me there was a bucket of water by the bars. There was another bucket where we urinated. I said I hoped no one ever made a mistake. He said no, they covered the water with a cardboard lid. Twice a day we were taken to a toilet.

Ahmad said he'd been interrogated many times during his hundred and ten days in solitary. I imagined they must have found his tale—a government official simply taking home videos—even less credible than ours. There was a system of justice in the White Ship, Ahmad said, a courtroom on the same floor as the torture chamber. Ahmad had been taken there after his hundred and ten days. There was a judge and a woman stenographer. She was kind, he said, told him not to worry,because they wanted to get rid of their Kuwaiti prisoners, send them home. He was given a confession to sign. It was an accurate account of what he had told his interrogators, so he signed it. That was three months ago.

A young Iraqi, now a prisoner in our jail, refused to sign his confession, Ahmad told me. Instead, he showed the judge the scars on his back from the torture his interrogators had inflicted. He was sent back for more interrogation.

After signing, Ahmad was taken to a large room, the white room, he called it, on the third floor, which he shared with other Arab prisoners. They could talk there and they had better food. But he had not minded his hundred and ten days in the red room. Solitary confinement, he said, is not difficult for a Muslim. Even there, they had rice and beans every day. That was before the war began.

Ahmad knew far more than I did about the progress of the war, not that there was much to know. He knew that the ground war had not begun. The guards listened to the radio all the time, and of course he could understand the news bulletins. Also, he said, there were some Turkish prisoners in another building who had a radio and tuned in to the news from Turkey. Word got around.

The blackness was beginning to loosen its grip. Ahmad thought we'd arrived at midnight, which meant that we'd been talking for six hours. I couldn't see his face yet, but the lines of his profile were emerging from the darkness. With his face framed by the blanket he was wearing over his head, he looked like a monk, a Franciscan. I thought of El Greco's portrait of St. Francis. We were not looking at each other. He was sitting with his back propped against the wall at the end of the cell. I was three feet away, facing his side. It had the feeling of a confessional.

There were morning noises now. My new world was coming to life. Doors slammed, a radio spewed out martial music, guards were shouting from below. Ahmad said, "They must not catch us talking or they will separate us."

I got up, turned around, and poked my head up in front of a thick rag which covered the cell window. I was stunned by the light. The sun had risen some time ago and bounced up at me from the white walls of a building next to ours. Guards with automatic weapons shared the roof with birds, dozens of birds. Two kittens frolicked in an alley in between. I remembered the howls of those wild dogs the night we were beaten in Basra. This seemed to be a gentler place. The prison wall, with a guard tower, was a hundred yards away, and beyond it, a grove of date palms provided a pale green backdrop for a billboard plastered with a portrait of a smiling Saddam. The air was cool and fresh. I drank it in and then tucked my head down and turned back to the cell. It had a grainy look now, like a black and white photograph that's been enlarged too many times. One of the Kurds was propped up on his elbows, talking to a neighbor. The five men were pressed tightly against each other. I remembered how the four of us used to huddle together in the prison camp; many years ago, it seemed. But there it was for warmth. Here there was no room. They were all lying on blankets in alternate directions, head to foot, the way sardines are packed in a can. Ahmad lay on a long piece of foam at the end of the cell. I saw the two buckets by the door. One was filled to the brim. I knew it was not the water.

For the first time Ahmad and I looked at each other. He had dark, piercing eyes, and a wispy gray beard. He was much shorter than I had imagined, no more than five foot four, with a very slight build. His chest was sunken, his cheeks hollow. He looked frail, almost tubercular.

I walked gingerly to the door, saw men grasping the bars of cells opposite and below me. Most had dark beards; all seemed to be wearing dirty striped pajamas. In some cells three or four men crowded together intimately at the doors and gestured to other, unseen prisoners across the divide. I felt overwhelmed, intoxicated by the light, the people, and the noise. So much is happening, I said to myself, I'll never get bored here.

Breakfast was served in stages, a ritual in which everyone participated. It was not waiter service as it had been in the ocean liner, the White Ship. The alert was the sound of a man walking down the aisle, stopping in front of cells, talking to the inmates. Ahmad got to his feet. He was the anointed one. He walked to the cell door and waited. The Kurds fell silent, all eyes on Ahmad and the door. A tall, stocky man carrying a sack stopped in front of our cell. He was a prisoner named Abbas, an Iraqi. He'd been here four years, ever since his brother turned him in for criticizing Saddam. Abbas reached into his sack and counted out pieces of bread, some round, some oblong, one per prisoner, but it was not that simple. This was not Jordan bread, it was thin and brittle, very few of the pieces were whole, so it was a delicate process involving much guesswork and negotiation. Meanwhile the Kurds had moved to their positions around the wall and unfolded a sheet of plastic in the center of the room. This was the dining room table.

Ahmad brought the pile of bread to his place, sat down, and began the division, dealing it out on the plastic like a deck of cards. Then we started hearing doors clanging open and shut. This was the signal for one of the Kurds to pick up two empty plastic washbasins and take up his position, a crouched starting position, by the door. I saw other basin-carrying prisoners run past us in the aisle. A guard stopped in front of our cell, a truncheon in one hand, a ring of keys in the other. Tauntingly, sluggishly, he opened the lock. The Kurd was off, a sprinter starting the hundred-meter dash. We waited. No one spoke. An eternal five minutes later, he was back, bearing a basin of soup and a basin of tea. These were also presented to Ahmad, the divider of the spoils. He used his own cup to measure, doled out two-thirds of a cup to each of the Kurds. Three of them had cups of their own, two shared a small basin. I, of course, had nothing. My cup was on a ledge that didn't exist anymore in a building that had been bombed.

Ahmad gave me his cup before he served himself. The soup was lukewarm and tasty. It had a few large beans in it, a little rice. Ahmad told me prisoners did the cooking and did the best they could. When I'd finished, Ahmad gave himself a slightly smaller portion. Then the cups were rinsed out with water from the pail and tea was served. It was the sweetest tea I had ever tasted. The end of breakfast was marked by a closing ceremony. Ahmad said, *"Allah karim."* The Kurds repeated the phrase and then they all prayed.

Three of the Kurds were brothers from Turkey. Two, also brothers, were from Iran. They were all illiterate peasants, arrested around the time of the invasion, all accused of espionage. Jalal, head of the Turkish clan, was thirty but looked younger. He was the father of seven, had a round face and sparkling eyes which, I thought, radiated such kindness. He'd had a little schooling, and spoke a little Arabic, which is how he communicated with Ahmad. Karim, the senior Iranian, was at least six foot five, had a handlebar mustache and wild, reckless eyes. His bald crown was bordered by a semicircle of long, unruly hair. He looked like a cross between a rebel leader and a mad scientist. He didn't know exactly how old he was, somewhere around forty, he thought. He and his brother slept by the door.

After breakfast I enlisted Ahmad to interpret for me. I wanted to know all about Jalal's village, learned it was high and remote in the mountains of Kurdistan. There was no electricity, you couldn't get there by road but, Jalal said, you could find it on some maps. He and his brothers were shepherds. I imagined Jalal sitting on a rock with his Kurdish headgear, overlooking the family flocks. One of his brothers interrupted, wanted to know how many cows I owned. I told them I would find their village after the war, that I would visit them with my wife and my daughter, that they would prepare a feast and we would all celebrate. Jalal translated for his brothers and there was considerable mirth. I told Ahmad that Jalal had the purest smile I had ever seen, that in bad countries you meet the best people in jail. Ahmad didn't reply.

Instead, he went to the wall, banged on it three times, and then went to the window. He was speaking to a prisoner in the adjoining cell. He motioned for me to come to the window. He said, "Talk. Your friend is there."

"Hello," I said.

"Bob, hello." It was Peter.

"How are you, Peter?"

"Oh, Bob, I'm fine, I'm fine."

"Did you enjoy your tea?"

"It was wonderful."

"How many are you? Does anyone speak English?"

"There are seven. A Kuwaiti speaks some English."

Ahmad had his hand on my elbow. The conversation had lasted long enough. Ahmad told me I might see my friend later when they took us to the toilet.

I felt a boyish surge of happiness. I was just beginning to fathom all the freedoms inside this prison. I walked to the door, looked through the bars. Men standing in their cells on the other side pointed at me, smiled. One man waved. On the floor below I saw a man with light hair, no mustache. He was looking at me, making a drawing in the air with his fingers: a large U, then a K. I replied. I drew a U followed by an S. The door opened. I was yanked out, hit on the head, then in the groin. Two guards were beating me with truncheons, one blow after another. They shoved my face against the wall. When I covered my head, they pummeled my back. When I lowered my arms, they went for my head. They pushed me to the floor, went on swinging.

"Who you talk to? What you say?" I was choking. I couldn't talk.

"Who you talk to?" The guard was standing over me, his club high in the air. He was about to knock me out.

"No one. I was waving, that's all."

"You make signal. We see you." I saw the club come down. That's all I remember.

Then I was being yanked to my feet, pulled along by my shoulders, down some stairs. I saw the light-haired man from the UK sitting outside his cell, his head in his knees. A guard was standing over him. There was a desk in the middle of the open space between the rows of cells. A guard was sitting with his feet on the desk. Two men stood on either side of him. "What you do?" he asked.

"Nothing. I just got here. I'm sorry. I don't know the rules." A truncheon caught me above my right ear. I went down to my knees.

"You do that again, we kill you, you understand?"

I was on my knees, thinking of Ahmad and the safety of my cell. "I won't do it again," I said. "Please, can I go back to my cell?"

"No. We put you in different cell." That's what I had been afraid of since the moment they caught me, much more afraid of that than of the beatings. I looked around. It was much darker down here. The cells looked like dungeons. No one was standing by the doors now. A guard was going from cell to cell, looking inside, asking questions. I knew he was asking how many there were in each cell. He came back to the man at the desk, said something I didn't understand. The man got up, said, "Don't move," and walked away. I stood there and came closest, I think, to praying than I ever had before. I would make any offering, any sacrifice, to be back with Ahmad.

I don't know how much time I stood there. It might have been a half hour, when a guard came, took me by the elbows, and led me upstairs. Three, four, sometimes five men, watched silently from behind the bars of each cell as I was led down the aisle. The guard stopped in front of a cell, opened the door, and pushed me inside. I was home.

Ahmad wiped the dried blood from my face, said he should have warned me. The guards could always see us. We could not always see them. The Englishman, he told me, was a man named Brand. He was an engineer, had been working on government projects in Iraq when Saddam invaded Kuwait, was arrested and accused of espionage. Until our arrival he was the only westerner in the cellblock. I told Ahmad how they had wanted to move me but how, probably because of all the new British and American POWs, there was no room in the cells downstairs. *"Allah karim,"* he said.

The Kurds were staring at me. Karim made beating motions. He was telling me that they'd beaten him too. Then he mimicked a man firing a rifle, looked at me inquisitively. Ahmad said he was asking if I was a soldier. I realized how little of our earlier conversation had registered. Ahmad told them again I was *zahafi*, a journalist. I lifted my sweater, showed them the T-shirt I was wearing. It had the CBS eye, said, CBS NEWS MANILA. I had gotten it while covering the revolution in the Philippines. I hadn't taken it off now in thirty-three days.

I went to the window, needing to look at trees. The Kurds gestured me away, told me to sit down. Ahmad said they were afraid I would bring trouble. I was a marked man now. The guards would be watching closely. "But aren't we allowed to look out the window?" I asked.

"No. Most of the guards will beat you if they see you. All they do is beat and shout. It is better in the evening when they are downstairs."

A radio was blaring, the same wretched music I'd heard in the old prison. What I'd been listening to all these weeks were songs about Saddam. That's all they were, Ahmad said, every one.

"You are the great, the greatest leader of mankind,
You are a gift from God, the greatest man God ever
    created,
You are the sun, you give light to the world."

I had to take a piss. I walked to the bucket, saw through the bars that prisoners were standing at their doors again. I looked down, avoided eye contact, but realized I would have to do it facing the door with the whole jail watching. I tried to urinate from a crouching position, the way I had seen the Kurds do it, but it didn't work. I went down to my knees. They were sore. I had to stop before my bladder was empty because the bucket was about to overflow.

Lunch was the same as breakfast, with an extra portion of bickering. The Kurds were unhappy about the division. The three with cups claimed they got less soup than the two sharing a basin, and they all thought I'd gotten too much. Ahmad told me that before he'd arrived in the cell, they could never agree among themselves, that meals usually became fistfights. They asked him to be the peacemaker, take charge of the distribution, but they were never satisfied.

Françoise had always told me I was hopelessly romantic about peasants, that I saw them through the innocent eyes of an American city boy. She knew better. She was French. Calculating, mean-spirited cheats. That was the view from the rue Voltaire in Bourg-en-Bresse. I asked Ahmad what would happen if the guards ever moved him to another cell.

"They will fight again," he said. "The only thing they will agree about is not to give you anything."

The argument did not stop with the end of the meal. The Kurds kept rekindling it most of the afternoon, gesturing angrily with their cups and the basin, casting evil eyes at Ahmad and at me. It only ended when Ahmad got to his feet; the Kurds did the same, and they all prayed, together.

Before dusk fell, the clanging of doors and the hurried passage of prisoners in front of our cell marked the beginning of another pilgrimage, the trek to the toilet. We went cell by cell, but sometimes the last to leave one cell would overlap with the first to leave the adjacent one. That way, Ahmad suggested, I might be able to see Peter. Being the last to leave wouldn't be a problem. The Kurds were already in their starting positions by the door. I was getting to my feet when Juan passed by in the aisle. He was limping, had a rag wrapped around one foot, was being helped by one of his cellmates. He saw me, smiled, and gave the thumbs-up sign. A few minutes later, another group rushed by, and there was Roberto. He seemed to have springs in his soles. He caught my eye and said, "Hey, Bob, not bad here, great food, huh?"

When our door opened, Karim picked up the urine bucket, and the Kurds were off. Ahmad followed and I trailed behind. My legs felt heavy, there seemed to be something wrong with my right knee, but I was relieved that I could walk at all. Outside the toilet, around the corner from our cell, Abbas was scooping water from a large vat, filling up small plastic pitchers with long spouts and handing them to prisoners. This was the toilet paper, another vast improvement from my former residence. There were three stalls in the room, with the usual holes in the floor. There were no doors. Peter was in one of the stalls. When I spotted him I quickly turned around. Karim was pouring the urine into a long sink where other prisoners were washing. There were faucets there, but they didn't seem to work. One prisoner was pouring water from a pitcher onto the hands of another. A window overlooked a yard and a beautiful oak tree.

Prisoners were wandering about aimlessly outside, crossing each others' paths, not looking up. No one was talking, no one was acknowledging anyone else's existence. Some men were doing laundry. Others sat and stared. It struck me as a cross between a gulag and an asylum. If there had been a basketball court, it could have been a scene from *One Flew over the Cuckoo's Nest.* Three guards stood laughing in the shade of the tree, their AKs slung lazily over their shoulders. I heard Peter's voice behind me. "Don't turn around," he said. "They got you pretty bad, matey, you OK?"

"I'm OK," I said. "There's a great man in my cell, a Kuwaiti, Ahmad."

"I heard about him from my guys," Peter said. "They say he's some sort of saint."

Back in the cell, Saint Ahmad gave me a piece of his foam to use as a pillow. At dinner that night he slipped me some of his bread, quickly, so the Kurds wouldn't see what he was doing. He told me he was sure I would see Françoise and Tanya again soon, that the war couldn't last too much longer, that they would free us all when it was over.

I lay back on my lovely foam pillow and thought about a book I read many years ago, a book by an American writer, Dan Greenberg, called *How to Be a Jewish Mother.* Greenberg's thesis was that you don't have to be Jewish or a mother to qualify for the role. An Italian barber can do the job. So can a Japanese karate instructor. But an Arab diplomat? A devout Muslim, pilgrim to Mecca, and scholar of the Koran? This was something I would never be able to tell Ahmad al-Ateeqi. But there was no doubt about it. He was the Jewish mother I'd been looking for even before the Iraqis lent an urgency to the search.

SONGS

❖❖

D AYS after Saddam's invasion last August, I went to Cairo to cover the emergency Arab summit. I did a story there satirizing the Kuwaitis, the Rolex refugees, as I called them, who'd fled at the first distant sound of gunfire and were now struggling for survival in the royal suites, casinos, and discotheques of the Egyptian capital. The Kuwaiti government-in-exile in Taif was one of the few sources of amusement for the press corps in Saudi Arabia. The only substantive decision they took during the months I kept tabs on them was to hire Hill & Knowlton, the American public relations firm, to polish up their tacky image.

But now Kuwaitis were helping us all. Juan was being looked after by the manager of Kuwait's international airport. The only English speakers in Peter's cell were two Kuwaitis, who guided him through the house rules of Abu Ghraib much as Ahmad guided me. The commandante of Roberto's cell was a wealthy Kuwaiti businessman who'd been subjected to the worst torture the White Ship had to offer, hung upside down on the rack, interrogated for days at a time, sometimes with a broken Coke bottle in his rectum.

But the real operator chez Roberto was Youssef, an Egyptian who owned a bar in Basra which sounded like the Gulf branch of Rick's café. Everyone went to Youssef's place, and Youssef trafficked in everything. He got drunk one night, criticized Sadaam, and had been here ever since. That was a couple of years ago. He'd had the time and the promises to get in tight with the guards, which brought extra food and cigarettes for all.

Four of Roberto's cellmates had jobs in the prison, two of them in the kitchen. That was the best break for Roberto. It meant that during the day he had to share the wide-open spaces of his cell with only two others. It also meant as much bread as they could eat and, occasionally, whole bowls of rice. The days of Roberto's starvation diet were over.

It was a pretty tony neighborhood, our block: diplomats, businessmen, restaurateurs. Ahmad pointed them out to me as they passed by in their filthy pajamas on the way to the toilet: Ahmad, a fifty-four-year-old man-of-the-world in a perpetual state of astonishment. "They arrested him for complaining about the price of bread. Would you believe? Look at that boy. They accused him of trying to kill Saddam. Look at his face. Would you believe?"

Journalists who'd covered Baghdad before the war told me that Iraqis were more open with them than with members of their own families. Saddam had created a population of informers. The system penetrated to the home, to the kitchen table, just as it did in Nazi Germany. Ahmad said it would require a generation of cleansing.

All our neighbors were political prisoners. Criminals were in other buildings. They'd been tried and convicted and didn't have it too bad, Ahmad said: family visits, decent food, books and television. Our block, run by the intelligence service, was reserved for men awaiting trial or charges or the whim of Saddam. Some of the Iraqis here, in fact, were ex–intelligence officers who'd been arrested when Saddam installed his half-brother as head of the service six months earlier. They were the short-timers. One of Peter's cellmates had been here fourteen years. He was twenty-five years old now but looked forty. Families — or embassies — were never informed. The White Ship took you on short, painful trips. This place was for the endless voyage.

My relations with the Kurds were not improving. The problem was my missing cup. When I arrived, they had their cups hanging on nails in the wall. When I was thirsty, I'd ask to use one, and permission would be granted, however grudgingly. Ahmad's cup was cracked, serviceable for soup but not for water. Now the Kurds had taken their cups down from the wall, hidden them in their blankets. Whenever I wanted a drink, prolonged negotiations would ensue. Did I really need one? How long had it been since my last drink? Whose cup had I used the last time?

Some mornings there was no soup for breakfast, only bread and tea. This was good news actually. It meant we would get solid food for lunch, usually rice. After one comparatively generous serving, I decided to save some of my bread for an afternoon snack, put it in the plastic bag on the wall. When I returned from the toilet a few hours later, it was gone.

It had been a long time since I'd been robbed. It was something I worried about a lot; coming back from a trip and finding things missing from my home. But having my bread stolen by Kurdish peasants had never made it onto my anxiety list. I would not visit them in their picturesque mountain village. There would be no feast, no celebration.

I looked at the Kurds suspiciously, but they did not return my stare. They were engrossed, or pretended to be, in their perpetual search for fleas. The little buggers were everywhere, in the pajamas, in the blankets, in your hair, in little welts under your skin. The Kurds waged a day-long, if losing, battle, combing their clothes inch by inch, picking at each others' scalps. They also kept busy rolling cigarettes. They took tea leaves from the basin after breakfast, dried them out on the windowsill, and rolled them into pieces of cardboard which Abbas gave them. The intricate part was tying the cigarettes with thin pieces of string they pulled from their pajamas. In the afternoon they celebrated, lighting one after the other, generating thick clouds of acrid smoke.

While they rolled and smoked, Ahmad gave me Arabic lessons. I had forgotten much of what I'd learned in the prison camp and it seemed wise to catch up. The war could end in many ways. If Saddam were overthrown, we might be able to escape. We could end up in the streets somewhere needing help. I learned how to say "We need food and clothes. Where is the road to Jordan?" Stuff like that.

Of all the paradoxes in our situation, nothing, I thought, compared to the triple play of ironies we had just lived through. The Iraqis had threatened to kill us, but the Americans had almost succeeded. But. . . the bombings had saved my life. Saddam's intelligence people would never have believed that a Jew based in Israel, caught in army gear at the border, could be anything but a spy. That's how they jumped to the Mossad question. For them it was a given. But now their system had been disrupted, their files most probably destroyed. Prospects were brightening. But another question lingered. How could the Americans have bombed us? Could they not have known, or at least suspected, that their POWs were in the building? Could American intelligence have been that incompetent? Wouldn't a prison inside Intelligence Headquarters be a logical place to keep captured pilots?

There were other reminders of the White Ship. The Arab was screaming again. The shrieks seemed to be coming from another building and another world. Here they started beating him in the afternoon and, as in Intelligence Headquarters, kept it up for hours. Ahmad heard through the prison vine that he was an Iraqi teacher who had lost his mind after weeks of torture.

Several times a day the guards yanked prisoners from their cells in our building and beat them in the aisles. Here, the sound was not muffled by thick steel doors: there was no escape. We would stand near the door and cast furtive glances through the bars to see who was getting the treatment. "The guards are scared of each other," Ahmad told me. "They beat to prove themselves. That's all they can do, beat and scream."

One man had immunity, or seemed to. He was sixty or seventy, he was very tall, and he was blind. Every day I watched him being led to the toilet by his cellmates. He was a comedian by trade, Ahmad told me, was arrested for satirizing Saddam. Late in the evening, sometimes, we would hear laughter coming from his cell across the hall. Ahmad laughed too. The blind man was imitating the voice of the head guard.

I was getting better at keeping a low profile, cowering in back of the cell most of the day. When I heard guards coming, I made sure to be sitting down and looking down. I'd spent twenty-five years in a job where eye contact was an instinct, eye contact with an interview subject or with a camera. I had lost it in a few weeks.

Some of Ahmad's more extravagant promises were not coming true. There were no dates anymore, no Jordan bread, no trips to the yard. But there was a reason for it now. The ground war had finally begun.

We knew it Tuesday morning when we woke up to martial music. News broadcasts proclaimed that the heroic Iraqi forces had repelled a ferocious attack. We heard the voice of Saddam, calling on his army to resist. The moment of salvation, he said, had come.

The guards were quiet that day, the prison was quiet. When the news came on, you could hear the silence. I would study Ahmad's face, scrutinize every twitch of an eyebrow, until the news was over and he would say, "No, nothing new, nothing new." The guards walked by often, punching their truncheons in their palms, looking in the cell, saying nothing. When the allied victory came, would they take it out on the prisoners? On the Americans? We still had time, of course. The ground war would last two weeks. That was the program.

The lights went out that evening. A power station must have been hit. The guards built a bonfire on the ground floor. Tongues of orange light flickered on our ceiling. Suddenly a voice came floating through the bars, a lyric tenor, as melodious a voice as I'd ever heard at the Met. It seemed to be coming from the adjoining cell, Peter's cell, but it swept through the entire building. It was the first music I had heard in five weeks. I looked at Ahmad. His eyes were closed, his lips moving as if in prayer. It sounded like an aria, an aria with many variations on a few melodic themes. It was the reading of the Koran. I leaned back against the wall and hoped it would never end. I knew exactly what he looked like, the tenor. He was tall and imposing, like Franco Corelli. He had the cherubic face of the young Giuseppe di Stefano, fresh and ingenuous.

Ahmad pointed him out in the toilet the next day. He was a Palestinian who looked like a high school student, pale and wan, with a bold mustache far too big for such a thin face. I wondered how that charmed voice had come from that slight, malnourished frame. I wondered whether a Palestinian and a Jew had ever been political prisoners in the same jail before.

Later, Peter told me all the Palestinian with the golden voice ever talked about was his dream of getting out of here one day and killing Israelis.

WAR

✖✖

I woke up early the next morning. I looked out the window and saw guards on the roof in full combat gear, helmets, flak jackets and all, manning machine gun nests. The Iraqis had repelled the infidel invaders, the radio reported. They had sent enemy coffins streaming in long convoys. Still, these Iraqis seemed to be expecting visitors.

Prison life was curiously unaffected by the mother of all battles. The tea was sweet that morning, the Kurds were querulous, and the guards were screaming and beating neither more nor less than on any other workday. Now and then the whoosh of cruise missiles passing overhead seemed to suck the air from our cell. We heard many planes. Five bombs exploded nearby, cutting hairline cracks in the plaster of our wall.

There were many power failures that afternoon. The lights went off and news bulletins were interrupted. But word from the front continued to be inspiring; for the Iraqis, not for us. After lunch the radio reported there had been a fierce battle overnight, with the Iraqi Third Corps pushing the enemy back from all the positions it had attacked.

Peter was behind me as we walked to the toilet that afternoon. "You know, it's all happening," I said.

"Mmm," he hummed. "You know something else, chum?" he said. "It's my birthday next Thursday. I'll be forty-seven." I turned around. Peter, in a rare moment of self-indulgence, was smiling sadly, feeling a bit sorry for himself.

"Oh no," I said. "Happy birthday."

I was curious whether the POWs knew what was going on. I realized that I hadn't seen any of them since we left the bus. That was strange, I thought. I hoped they were still in the building. I'd have to check with Ahmad.

I also needed to check with Ahmad about Ramadan. It was less than two weeks away. I remembered because back in Saudi Arabia we used to wonder how it would affect the course of the war. How would starving soldiers fight? Muslims fast all day during the month-long observance. They make up for it with a meal bordering on a feast every evening. Would they make us fast too? I supposed they would. This was, after all, a Muslim institution, our jail. Getting through thirty days without breakfast or lunch was considerably more than I cared to contemplate.

I sat up with Ahmad most of that night. He hadn't told me at first, but he'd had a heart attack a couple of months before his imprisonment. Now he woke up often in the night and had trouble breathing. He had medicine for that, in Kuwait, of course, not here. I was startled out of my sleep by the sound of his gasping. I tapped him on the back until his breathing came easier, then put my arm around him. It was the first physical contact we'd had.

We didn't talk much about war or prison that night. We traded dreams, like boys trading baseball cards. I hadn't decided yet whether I wanted to get that motorcycle and go rumbling through France, or just go home to Israel, walk on my beach, and spend long quiet evenings in our garden, talking to friends. I wasn't telling Ahmad about Israel or my Jewishness. I wasn't sure how he'd react, and even if he reacted well, as I suspected he would, I didn't want to burden him with that knowledge. It would be a heavy package to conceal if they interrogated him again. I stuck to France and the bike.

I told him about the last time Françoise and I took that kind of trip, how we had rolled into Chartres one spring afternoon, tired and hungry, headed straight for a *restaurant-en-terrasse*, devoured oysters and *choucroute* and a bottle of cold white wine, and emerged a little drunk and giddy with well-being, and I said, "Hey, let's be the first tourists to get in and out of Chartres without even looking at their damn cathedral." We had both been there many times, Chartres was our favorite cathedral, so the idea was thrillingly perverse and we didn't go through with it. We spent the afternoon in church.

Ahmad was widely traveled, and his favorite place in the world was Singapore, which I found disarming. He would join his family (he thought they would be waiting for him in Damascus because his wife was Syrian) and he would take them all to Singapore. We talked about meeting there and eating Chinese food. I liked duck. He liked lobster. We'd work it out.

I tried to imagine Ahmad *en famille* in one of Singapore's five-star hotels. I saw him in his spotless white *dishdash*, leading a retinue of well-dressed, impeccably behaved children down to breakfast. Mrs. al-Ateeqi would be considerably larger than her husband. Every hair would be in place and she would be wearing a variety of rather large jewels. I had covered the Middle East for many years, I thought, but had never really socialized with Arabs in Asia or in Europe.

We dozed a bit. I was sharing Ahmad's foam pad now. When I woke up, he was sitting in his corner, deep in concentration. "What's going on?" I asked.

"Shh." He was listening to the radio downstairs. I could barely hear it. "They're withdrawing," he said, "Wait."

"Is it Saddam on the radio?" I asked.

"No, no, not Saddam."

The broadcast ended with *"Allah Akbar, Allah Akbar, Allah Akbar,"* and slid into one of the songs to Saddam. "They won a big battle and now they're withdrawing," Ahmad said. "They're asking for a cease-fire."

It was happening so much faster than we had ever expected. I wondered whether the Pentagon had been conning us all those months, talking about the tough battles they expected, especially with the Republican Guards. They must have known. The Iraqis were a bush-league team.

We talked about what must really be happening if this

much was being admitted. Ahmad thought it was good that Saddam was declaring a victory. It meant that the war was over, and he was telling his people that face had been saved. He had won a fight, scored some points.

If they'd been routed so quickly, there must be chaos in Kuwait. There must be whole divisions in disarray, tens of thousands scrambling for the border. I remembered how the South Vietnamese army had fallen apart, turned into throngs of refugees, while the northerners chased them to Saigon. Would Schwarzkopf stalk the Iraqis all the way to us?

After breakfast there were three knocks on our wall. The Kuwaitis next door wanted to talk. Ahmad went to the window, came back with a rumor our neighbors had picked up. A civil war had begun. The army was turning on Saddam.

If Saddam were overthrown, the rebels would probably sue for peace and release us, we agreed. But we didn't want a revolution, not now. There could be anarchy, enraged mobs. We wanted stability. We wanted to be released in an orderly fashion. We wanted to see those Swiss in suits and ties drive up with big red crosses on their cars.

"Do you think the guards will turn on us?" I asked.

Ahmad didn't know, but he was thinking about it too. He had spent months, so much more time than I had, waiting for the war to end. Now that it seemed imminent, we both understood the perils of victory.

The pace kept quickening. There were new developments every hour. At noon Saddam's voice—I could recognize it now—was back on the air. The jail fell silent. Saddam said the withdrawal could be completed by night-fall. Ahmad said, "Would you believe? Three days." Saddam said, "Iraq is victorious." He warned the Allies not to attack his retreating army.

After lunch it suddenly got dark in the cell. I got up, looked out the window, and thought that I had finally lost my mind. It wasn't lunch we'd just finished. It must have been supper, for night had fallen. But there was no moon, no stars. I couldn't see the palm grove or the Saddam poster. I could barely see the building next door. Could it be a solar eclipse? I didn't know; I'd never seen one. I thought of the movie *Ivanhoe,* the scene where Merlin takes credit for the darkness caused by the moon passing in front of the sun. I whispered urgently to Ahmad, "Come to the window. Look, it's night." We stood there like two children, on tiptoes, transfixed by the mysteries of the universe. It gradually dawned on us that the retreat-ing Iraqis must have set Kuwait's oil fields on fire, that the black clouds had traveled all the way to Baghdad, to the capital of darkness.

It was at least an hour before the first hint of light returned. But we saw no more of the sun that day. A dismal grayness covered our world like a shroud, driven by a shrieking wind.

The Kurds weren't rolling many cigarettes now. They sat wide-eyed against the wall, following Ahmad's and my every move. We were the providers of information. *"Helas harp?"* Karim would ask. Is the war over? *"La, la,"* I would say, no it's not. Then he would mimic a man firing a rifle to ask if I was a soldier. *"La,"* I would say. *"Zahafi."* No, I'm a journalist. I had no idea what he might have thought I was talking about.

The next night Ahmad heard about an allied landing in a town called Nasiriya. He also heard that a group of Kurdish prisoners, told they were being freed, were taken away in a van, then brought back. But to balance that grim news, he told me that our neighbors had been on an outing that day. They'd been taken to the yard. The Kuwaitis told him that Peter just stood in the sun for more than an hour, kept walking backwards to keep his face in the sun as the afternoon wore on. When it was gone, they gave him soap to wash his hair. I felt a little jealous and very pleased.

I slept fitfully Friday night. I didn't want to sleep, really. I wanted to listen for bombs. I heard nothing; no bombs, no planes, no cruise missiles, just the chirping of crickets, a reassuring reminder that there was still life outside our cell on this cloud-darkened planet.

Ahmad and I began to memorize the telephone numbers of our families in case one of us would be released before the other. I had no idea where Françoise was by now, so I gave him the number of the CBS News Foreign Desk in New York, which is manned around the clock. There's always the possibility that some intern will pick up the phone, hear a weak, heavily accented voice, and hang up. The desk is saturated with legends like that.

On January 13, 1990, I got a call from the desk. It was a girl whose name I didn't recognize. She told me that a nursing home in Florida had called, said that my mother had been taken to a hospital, that I should be informed. I phoned the hospital. The nurses on my mother's floor wouldn't tell me anything, said I should talk to the doctor. It took them awhile to find him. He told me my mother had been admitted with an intestinal blockage, was having cardiac arrests. Her chances were poor. She'd been calling my name. Why hadn't I phoned earlier? She'd been in the hospital more than twenty-four hours. I called the desk, talked to the same girl. She told me she called me once the previous afternoon and my phone didn't answer and then she went home. By the time I got to Florida all I could do was stand in the back parking lot of a place called "Johnson's," wedged between a Wendy's and a stereo outlet on U.S. 41, and watch two awkward teenagers — high school students, I thought, with part-time jobs — carry a cardboard box from the mortuary to the crematorium. Then my mother and I took a boat ride. She liked boat rides on sunny afternoons. I flew right back to Israel. I didn't stop in New York on that trip even though there were some friends of my mother's I wanted to see. There was a girl in New York whose name I now knew, whose throat I wanted to throttle.

The desk was fraught with disaster. But I couldn't think of anything else. Ahmad gave me a number in Kuwait and another number in Damascus. We spent the morning testing each others' memories. By noon it was official. The radio said all Iraqi troops had been ordered to cease fire. But there was bad news too. Ahmad told me the POWs were not in our building, never had been. They had a cellblock to themselves somewhere else in the complex. I had visions of those Red Cross cars pulling up and pulling out, leaving us behind.

I met Peter in the toilet that afternoon. "Sounds like it's all over," I said.

"Yeah, but we could be here for a year," he said. "There's no one to let us out." I turned around. He looked more bitter than I'd ever seen him. "I'm sorry," he said. "I'm just feeling a bit down today."

Please, Peter, I wanted to say. Be strong. I don't think I can take it if you fold. Instead I told him the bad news about the POWs, how our cellblock did not seem to be on the fast track.

The day kept going downhill. Back in the cell, a furious battle was raging over lunch. The Kurds accused Ahmad of serving them first, from the top of the soup pail, of saving most of the rice at the bottom for himself and for me. The accusation was false, and Ahmad pointed this out patiently, but the Kurds would not be placated. Jalal, his face contorted in rancor, kept the tirade going. The invective was directed at Ahmad, but all eyes were on me. I was the pariah, the foreigner, guilty as accused of taking space and food which rightfully belonged to them. Karim stared at me angrily, a steady stream of Kurdish coming from under his breath.

"Will you guys leave me alone?" I cried out. "Will you let me eat my fucking lunch?"

Then they pointed at the urine bucket. This was another issue. I hadn't carried it to the toilet yet. Even Ahmad was getting impatient with them now. He told them my turn was tomorrow, but they couldn't be convinced. I sat in my corner, chewed on my bread, and said to myself, I don't know how much more of this I can stomach. But they wouldn't let go. I felt soft and spoiled, not up to dealing with these very tough men. I was still the coddled kid from New York. Prison hadn't hardened me yet. Ahmad was ignoring them now as they carried on, gesturing toward the pail of piss, waving their cups in the air. I knew I wouldn't be getting any water that afternoon.

I realized then that this might never end. The POWs would go home to ticker-tape parades and I would stay here with the Kurds until they moved me to another cellblock, a block reserved for long-timers. I would speak fluent Arabic soon, days would become weeks, weeks would become years, and I would be hanging my laundry in the yard in the late afternoon and my former life would appear to me as a mauve-colored dream.

"Ahmad, talk to me," I said.

"Yes, Mr. Bob, don't worry, Mr. Bob."

"I don't think they're going to let me out," I said. "They'll let the military guys out. That's why they're in another building."

Ahmad asked, "What did they tell you in the White Ship, Mr. Bob? Did they say you were a prisoner of war?" He was looking at me with an intensity I hadn't seen since that first morning.

I said, "No. I told you, they said I'm not a prisoner of war. I'm a spy." I realized then that I hadn't really taken my captors seriously. Somewhere I still believed that this was another adventure, a game which, after a few difficult moves, I was destined to win. Their words hadn't been important. They were all for show. Ahmad was suggesting otherwise.

"Well, Mr. Bob," he said, "what did you expect?"

I didn't move much the rest of that afternoon. I didn't look out the window to see how my date palms were doing. I just sat in my corner, thinking about how much time we waste being anxious about things that never happen while the real dangers lurk unannounced. I'd put in my time worrying about cancer and failure and poverty. But ending my days in an Iraqi jail? This had never been part of the file.

The war was definitely over now, but it seemed to have ended with a whimper. The lead story on the news Saturday evening concerned a pro-Iraqi demonstration in Khartoum. This is how the world ends, with a bunch of screaming Sudanese students.

That night I dream I'm on a plane, flying first class. I have the cabin to myself. I ask the steward where we're going. He says only the pilot knows. I realize I'm wearing a kefiyah. The crew is eyeing me suspiciously. They're all Hassids. I try to take it off but it's stuck. The captain announces, "Fasten your seat belts, we're landing in Baghdad." I say to the steward, "Do we have to go to Baghdad?" He says, "What did you expect?" I close my eyes. The steward is tugging me. "Wake up, wake up." I say, "Leave me alone, I want to sleep." He says, "Wake up, wake up, Mr. Bob, something is happening." I turn around, face the wall. I want to disappear. I hear voices in the corridor. I hear Ahmad get up. He is walking toward the door. I hear a guard say, *"Ameriki?"* I hear Ahmad say, *"Aywah, aywah."* Ahmad is shaking me now. He says, "Get up, Mr. Bob, come, come." I grab my blanket, walk toward the door. I trip over a Kurd. The cell door is open. Two guards are standing in the corridor. Ahmad says, "Go, Go." My boots are by the door. I bend down, start putting them on. Ahmad hands me my coat, Peter's coat. A guard says, "The President orders you free. You are going home."

THE VAN

⚜

Peter was standing in the aisle to my right. He was rocking back and forth on his heels, his hands folded behind his back, waiting to be handcuffed. He looked dazed. To my left, Roberto was bending down, putting on his shoes. Two guards were leading Juan out of his cell. He said, "Don't shoot me, man, please don't shoot me."

They took us downstairs, told us to sit on a bench near a pile of glowing embers, the remnants of their nightly bonfire. I felt warm. The orange light illuminated Peter's face. He had dark lines under his eyes, looked ill. I thought about a time when I was in first grade and felt sick and was told to sit on a bench outside the principal's office while they called my mother to come and take me home. I felt privileged sitting there so close to this powerful man while the other kids were still in class.

One of the guards was the guy who had beaten me up my first day there. Another wore a red kefiyah. He was the guard who had threatened to cut our throats in the White Ship. They were drinking tea. Peter said to me, "A cup of tea would be nice." The guards didn't react. Apparently we were allowed to talk.

"Any chance of a cup of tea?" I asked.

"No tea," he said and walked away. He came back with a piece of bread, regular western bread, gave it to me.

"Where are we going?" I asked.

"They will tell you," he said.

The bread was hard, but I managed to bite off a chunk. I passed it along. The guard pointed to a toilet, told us to go. I didn't have to, but wouldn't miss this special treat, an extra trip. We all went. Juan was shivering. "Do you think they're going to kill us?" he asked.

"I don't think so. I think we're OK," I said.

Peter said he didn't think they had the imagination to tell us we were free if we weren't. They weren't free enough for that, he said. I couldn't tell if he believed it.

They took us outside, to a delivery van. A guard grabbed my shoulder, said, "Leave the blanket." They put us in the back of the van and slammed the door shut. We could hear it being locked. It was freezing inside, there were no windows, and there was no place to sit except the metal floor. But I felt giddy: not because we were about to be free. I was far from sure about that, and in any case I wasn't ready to think about it. I felt giddy because we were all together. We were about to take a trip and we were neither handcuffed nor blindfolded. We were VIPs.

We sat in the quiet darkness for what seemed a very long time. Then the guards got in the van and turned on the ignition, which seemed to all of us the most joyful sound we had ever heard. Roberto said, "We're on our way, we're on our way," and we all started talking. We were all talking at the same time, so no one could really hear what anyone else was saying, but it didn't really matter.

There was a slit high up on the wall between the back of the van and the driver's seat. When I got on my knees I could see a sliver of the outdoors through the windshield in front. We were on a dark road and our headlights were off. I could see trees. I provided a running commentary for my friends, who held me by the shoulders until my knees gave out and Peter took my place. Juan asked, "Do you think they're taking us to the border?" and I started playing Cassandra. I didn't think they were planning to kill us, I said, but I thought they might screw up. Their capacity for that seemed infinite. I told him how some Kurds had been taken away in a van, probably this very same van, and were then brought back because something had gone wrong.

We slowed down, seemed to be swinging between barriers. Peter said we were on a makeshift bridge. He could see the river. It must be the Euphrates, he said. We were heading toward Baghdad.

We stopped and started a lot and our hopes went up and down with the motion of the van. So did our conversation. When we were on the move, we were chatterboxes. When we were stalled, we seemed to retreat into those spaces we had created for ourselves over forty days, spaces where there was no room for anyone's voice except one's own.

I tried to prepare myself for a return to my cell. It won't be the end of the world, my voice said. This will still have been a good omen. Next time it will be for real. I imagined it step by step, how I would tell Ahmad about our trip, how he would tell me not to lose hope. I had trouble facing the idea of the Kurds again. I would, after all, have missed my turn as piss carrier. They were sure to carry on about that.

I didn't even try to prepare myself for freedom: not necessary, freedom will be easy. At least that's what I thought that night.

I was back by the slit, taking my turn as tour guide. My restraint fell to pieces when we drove under a large green sign hanging over the road. It said, DOWNTOWN. Now I heard myself say, "We're on our way."

Roberto said, "Yeah," as if we'd just scored a point in a doubles match.

Peter said, "Let's not get our hopes up too high. We're not anywhere yet."

There were soldiers everywhere, bundled up against the cold, kefiyahs wrapped tightly around their faces. We drove past a long column of tanks, on a wide, tree-lined avenue. Soldiers were sitting in the turrets. It reminded me of Lisbon the night of the revolution. We stopped at a roadblock and the guards seemed to be asking for directions. Then we made a few turns and parked. The lights went on in front. The guards were looking at a map. At least that's what I thought they were doing. The four of us could really see each other for the first time. We were a pretty disheveled bunch. I wondered out loud how Françoise would like me with a thick black beard. Peter told me I was in for a rude shock if I thought my beard was black.

The guards left the van and we fell silent. I was now sure

something had gone wrong, surer with every passing moment. We started slapping each other on the back to keep warm, and Peter said, "We're back on the roller coaster." When the guards returned about a half hour later, and the van started up again, we made a U-turn, and I knew we were going back to jail. We drove through narrow streets in a residential neighborhood, retracing our steps, I thought, turning all the time. Peter looked through the slit but said nothing. He didn't know where we were. We parked again, the guards left, came back a few moments later and unlocked our door. They led us along a dark path to a dark house: it could have been a suburban family house most anywhere in the world. Two men were sitting in upholstered armchairs in an otherwise empty living room. A kerosene lamp was on a table. One of the men had a ledger, very much like the ledger from the White Ship. In fact, I thought, it could well be the same one. For the last time we were asked our names and nationalities. For the last time we asked where were we going.

"We take you to the Ministry of Information," said a man in uniform who seemed to be in charge. He was quite plump and in a very good mood. The war didn't seem to have been too rough on him. "The Minister is waiting for you there," he said. "But first we take you to our office and we give you back your things."

"Your office, our things?" I asked.

"Where you used to stay before we were bombed." He laughed.

"Oh no,no,no, that won't be necessary," I said. "Let's forget about our things."

"But you have many things there. You have your camera there."

"Oh, we don't need the camera. Right, Roberto? You don't want that camera, you'll get a new one, right?"

"Oh, yeah, sure," Roberto said. "No problem."

"You must be very rich." He laughed again. "OK—if you say so." He apologized for not offering us tea. The power had been off for days, he said with a sad smile, looking me in the eye, looking for sympathy. The other man went off and brought back four glasses of water, but we turned them down as graciously as we could. Our inhibitions were coming back. We had drunk their water for six weeks. Why risk it one last time if we really were going home?

Back in the van the guards seemed to know where they were going. So did Peter. He was on his knees, calling out landmarks. We went over another bridge, the Tigris, he said.

Then, in a thick whisper: "We're here, we're here. This is the back end of the ministry." Peter quickly sat back down next to me, against the wall. The van stopped and the guards got out.

When I think back on those forty days now, if my worst moment was that interrogation in the bowels of the White Ship, when they first formally accused me of being a spy, this was a close second. The guards didn't come back. How could they? There was no one in the ministry at this hour. Peter knew that. He knew the system. That story about the Minister waiting for us was another fable from *A Thousand and One Nights*. Here, at what I thought was the end, I had forgotten the first lesson from the beginning: Never believe anything they tell you.

We were all shivering now, but there was no more backslapping. I didn't try to psych myself up for the return to Abu Ghraib. I didn't know how to begin. I felt my mind retreating, retreating from the van, retreating to a warm dark corner where I wanted to stay forever. When the guards did come back after more than an hour, they were muttering. One of them actually spoke to us for the first time. He told us what we already knew. "No one here," he said. The van started with a lurch. We didn't say anything. We were all leaning against the walls. Peter and I faced Juan and Roberto, but we were all looking at the floor.

Peter said, "I think we're going to the Rasheed Hotel."

"What?"

"If we make a left in two hundred yards, we're going to the Rasheed."

Peter was on his knees now. The van was picking up speed, plowing straight ahead. Then it swerved to the left. We were turning.

"If we're going to the Rasheed," Peter said, "we'll be making a right turn right away."

I didn't know what "right away" meant. I wanted to ask Peter, but I couldn't talk. The van made a sharp turn. To the right.

We stopped. The guards got out. Peter described the parking lot where he thought we were. The door slid open. As I got to my feet, I saw a fat Iraqi standing there on the pavement, his arms outstretched. "Mr. Simon," he said, "we were so worried about you."

EXITS

❧❧

THE fat Iraqi was Sadoun al-Janabi, a Ministry of Information factotum. He led us into the lobby of the Al-Rasheed Hotel, which, vast, dark, and empty at four in the morning, had the feel of a mausoleum about it. We filled out forms at the front desk like any itinerant businessmen. The registration clerk actually asked to see my passport. I looked at him.

There was no electricity. Carrying a candle which flickered in the draught, like the butler in a horror film leading the way through a haunted house, Sadoun steered us up a stairwell which reminded me of the White Ship. I was brimming over with excitement, but the energy did not extend to my legs. By the time we got to the fourth floor, I was gasping for breath. Sadoun didn't seem to be doing much better.

While he banged at the door of CBS News vice president Don DeCesare, while we waited impatiently in the darkness, he reassured us that Don was definitely there. DeCesare had come to Baghdad, he said, to work our case; other CBS people were in the hotel as well; friends of ours

230

who were here covering the news: producer Larry Doyle, correspondent Betsy Aaron, cameraman Sami Awad.

I never could have imagined that the sight of a CBS News executive in his underwear would carry an aura of the sublime. But when he opened the door, Don DeCesare seemed to be wearing a halo. We embraced, but only briefly. Sadoun's candle threw out enough light for me to see that sitting inconspicuously on the desk a few feet away, trying hard to hide in the shadows, were three Cadbury chocolate bars. Fruit and Nuts. I didn't excuse myself. I didn't explain. I made for them with the alacrity of a defensive end pouncing on a quarterback. I barely managed to get the wrapping off before devouring one in three bites; then, glancing warily over my shoulder to see my friends still laughing and chatting with Don in the doorway, I tore into another. Don told me he had more in his desk. Peter told me later I consumed six in twenty minutes.

Then in came Larry Doyle, a Falstaffian figure in normal times; big, fun-loving, bearded, and brilliant, he now loomed larger than life. Doyle and I had done Cambodia, South Africa, and the Philippines together. This was one of the first times I ever saw him without a can of beer. It was the very first time I saw him cry.

Doyle led us up another flight of stairs to the CBS office on the fifth floor, the office we had fantasized about that first night in the bunker. There was more food here: bags of nuts and potato chips, cans of Coke and Sprite. DeCesare started filling us in. He told us he had been in charge of our case from the week we disappeared, that they had reason to believe we were alive only close to a month later, when Arnett said that he'd heard it from a good source in Baghdad. He described everything that happened on his end, but I couldn't pay attention. I was concentrating too hard on the food. There was little room in my mind for anything but the food. I picked up that the Iraqis never admitted they had us, that the Russians were instrumental in getting us sprung, that Françoise was not in New York or France or Israel. She was in Amman and would come to the border to meet us.

But first we had to make a decision. It was our decision to make, DeCesare said, even though CBS had views on the matter. The Iraqis were giving us a choice. They would provide the papers we needed to leave the country. Or they would accredit us and let us remain in Baghdad to cover the news. We four ex-cons looked at each other and laughed in disbelief. We would pass this one up. De-Cesare seemed relieved.

There was another problem. The hotel was packed with our colleagues: dozens of reporters from virtually every major news organization in the world. No one knew we were out. DeCesare said no one should find out. This was not a time to embarrass the Iraqis, he said, and they didn't want a carnival here. We should go to our rooms and stay there until the documents were ready for us to head for Jordan. Meanwhile Betsy Aaron and Sami Awad would film the four of us making short statements and that would be pooled and distributed to all the media. We would be snuck out of the hotel.

We felt strange about that; the idea of being quarantined from our friends, of trying to escape "the press" like some officious officials or rock stars. We hadn't realized we were such a big story. I thought we would be an obscure footnote in a best-selling war novel. But I knew it's difficult to have a clear view of these things when you're arguing over a piece of bread with a bunch of Kurds. We came to a compromise: we would go, obediently, to our rooms—as long as they wouldn't be single rooms: we didn't want to be alone—but we wouldn't sneak out of the hotel. We would walk out the front door like human beings and say a few words to our colleagues. (It turned out to be academic. With our extraordinary talent for subterfuge, Peter and I had used our real names when we registered downstairs. All the journalists in the hotel knew we were there minutes after they got up in the morning.)

I remember little about the next eight hours. Juan and Roberto shared a room. Peter and I shared another. We were exhausted, of course, but sleep was out of the question. I took my filthy pants and sweater off for the first time in weeks. Now—in a clean hotel room, my usual habitat—I could tell just how foul they smelled. There was no running water, so a shower would have to wait. The bed was soft, unbelievably soft. I got under the blankets in my underwear and Manila T-shirt and, from six in the morning until two in the afternoon, Peter and I lay on our backs and talked. Several times Peter asked me, "Am I talking too much?" And I'd reply, "No, that's not possible." Then I would ask Peter the same question and he would offer the same reply. We both thought we were talking too much because we didn't know what we were saying, so we just kept on talking to get out the few things we knew we wanted to say.

I remember Peter telling me that when he was in solitary confinement in the White Ship, he took his bar of soap and drew a picture of his tree on the wall. It was the last thing he touched when he was taken out of the cell after we were bombed.

I remember him telling me how, when he was in the country two years ago and there was a violent storm at night, he went out to the garden in his pajamas and prayed for his tree. It just swayed there gently, he said, the branches moving around like an athlete stretching himself before a race.

I remember Peter saying, "I feel like me. We've been through forty days of hell, and how do I end up feeling? I feel like me." I wasn't sure how I felt.

Don't get me wrong. We weren't just talking. We had brought cookies, crackers, more nuts and potato chips down from the office. We also had bottles of mineral water. We talked between bites, often—yes, it's painful to admit—with our mouths full. When dawn broke, I struggled out of bed for a glance out the window. I caught myself looking over my shoulder to see if a guard was watching. Postwar Baghdad looked unbelievably modern, and, from this perspective, untouched. A broad boulevard wound to a traffic circle a few blocks away. There were quite a few cars on the road. It could have been anywhere, in the gray morning light. The White Ship was a mile or two away, in another world.

I went to the bathroom, looked in the mirror, and recoiled. I looked like a bum, like an old, demented street person. Peter said I looked like a rabbi.

He felt strange, he said, that he didn't want to throw his hat up in the air. "Aren't I supposed to feel jubilation?" he asked. I said I thought we were in for many surprises. Anyway, there's no way anyone is supposed to feel. Ever.

At noon DeCesare came in with clothes they had picked up in the market. I tried on a pair of jeans with a thirty-four-inch waist, my normal size. They wouldn't stay up. Fortunately there was some rope in the office. I made a belt. Don told us he had made one call on the satellite phone to New York; just a one-liner to the foreign editor to tell him we were out. Françoise and Tanya would know by now.

An hour later the whole CBS team trooped in to film our statements. There was a lot of hugging and kissing and a few tears, but I felt strangely unresponsive. I knew there was a lot more emotion coming at me than I was giving back. That was just a quick preview of things to come.

The four of us sat next to each other on a bed as Betsy passed along the microphone. Peter thanked everyone who'd worked on our behalf and apologized to Geraldine and his mother because, he said, "I think my table manners have suffered in the last six weeks."

Juan said he wanted to tell his mother that he loved her. Roberto broke down as he apologized to his family for what they went through. I offered a similar apology and concluded, "I thank God that the four of us are alive." I don't know what made me say that, but it didn't go down well in Bourg-en-Bresse. Françoise's mother, an inveterate Mitterrand socialist, was on the phone to her daughter within hours inquiring nervously whether her son-in-law had gone religious.

I remembered: when I lived on the Upper West Side, near where Tanya now rents an apartment, I went to the movies in the afternoon, saw a long, slow, black and white Bergman film, and when it was over and I went out into the street, was blinded by the light, overwhelmed by the crowds, the traffic, the honking of horns, and wanted to go back inside, but the theater was closed.

It was two in the afternoon. We walked out of the Al-Rasheed hotel and I stopped. Not so much because there were a dozen camera crews and dozens more reporters standing outside the door. That would have been reason enough. I felt paralyzed, dazed, shocked. I hadn't been confronted with so many people, so much noise and light, in forty days. What's more, I was called upon to perform and I'd lost the habit. I stood in front of a bed of microphones, came out with a few barely coherent lines, and started walking forward. There was no going back, and I knew a car must be out there somewhere. People were shouting. To my left a camera crew was walking alongside me, the lens a few inches from my face. To my right I saw Peter in a mad embrace with Fifi, his favorite French photographer. I heard a voice yelling, "Mr. Simon, you were treated with dignity, weren't you, Mr. Simon?" That rang a distant bell, but I didn't know from where. We were ushered into two cars and we were off, a cavalcade of journalists driving behind us.

You never get something for nothing in the Middle East, and the Iraqi price for our freedom was a Ministry of Information–sponsored tour of bomb damage in Baghdad. Then we would be allowed to take off for the border. The motorcade lurched to a stop on a busy downtown street and I was surprised they had asked for the tour because what I saw was an example of precision bombing at its finest. In a row of high-rise attached buildings, one was missing, but the buildings next to it were untouched. As I got out of the car, as I was meant to do so I could be photographed surveying the damage, an official explained that this had been the Central Communications Office, and that because of the attack, the phones were out all over the city and would remain out for several months. A young American I didn't recognize came up, introduced himself, told me he was from CNN and was glad I was OK. "Where's Arnett?" I asked.

"He's in town but he had to cover another story. He sends his regards."

"Tell him I want to see him," I said. "Tell him thank you and just tell him I want to see him."

"Mr. Simon, you were treated with dignity, weren't you?" It was that same voice. "You know who I am, Mr. Simon? You don't recognize me, do you?" He laughed. It was a clean-cut guy in his thirties, an Arab. Our other tour guides were in suits and ties, but he was wearing a windbreaker and a pair of slacks. He was clean-shaven, the first Iraqi I had seen without a mustache.

"No, I don't," I said, "but I recognize your voice."

"But you don't recognize me. How could you?" he asked. "I was the interpreter at your first interrogation in Baghdad. Remember? You asked to be treated with dignity. You were treated with dignity, weren't you?"

So this was the man I had pictured as the serious young college student. I didn't answer his question. It was not the time or the place for polemics.

When we were back in the car, heading out of town, I realized that he had just given me a piece of the puzzle. We were taken to Intelligence Headquarters two days after we'd seen the newspaper picture of Arnett with Saddam. When Arnett pleaded our case with Saddam, as I figured he must have, Saddam probably knew nothing about us. I pictured him turning his head slowly to one of his aides after Arnett left the room, saying, "Find out who these jokers are." That's when the order came down to take us to the White Ship, the place where Saddam's questions are answered.

Peter and I sat in the back of the car. DeCesare sat in front with the driver. He told us there had been major changes at CBS during our absence, that there was a new bunch running the evening news, that my friend Tom Bettag, the executive producer, was out and that several of his associates, also friends of mine, were gone as well. I thought of a French movie I had seen about POWs returning home after the second world war to find their farms sold, their wives remarried. How time has been telescoped! You can't even be gone forty days now. I realized how I'd been counting on the world being frozen during my captivity. I wanted everything exactly the same. I didn't want to deal with change. I was feeling agitated, feisty. "Who did the obit, Don?" I asked. "I want to know who wrote my obit."

"There was no obit, Bob."

"Come on, Don. You must have had an obit ready. Who did it?"

"No obit. We always knew we'd get you out."

"Bullshit," I said, and left it.

We were passing through a town. Drunk with power, I asked the driver to stop. I was hungry. Both cars pulled over. Roberto, Juan, and I walked amidst the street vendors, smiling at each other, at the smell of kebab roasting on open fires. Peter stayed in the car. He beckoned me over. He told me he was more frightened sitting there in that town than he had ever been in the last forty days. "Some of these guys must be back from the front," he said. "They must be pretty pissed off." We bought a bunch of meat sandwiches, a few dozen pieces of Arab bread, and headed off.

We were making time now, racing against the clock. The border closed at nine in the evening. If we didn't make it by then, we'd have to wait in the car for dawn. We'd never been on this road before. In fact we'd never driven anywhere in Iraq before without blindfolds. But the landscape was familiar; it was the same rugged desolation we had come to know so well in Saudi Arabia. There was no sand here, no dramatic dunes; just a flat, rocky wasteland which could only turn into something different or better far beyond the limits of imagination.

We made only one more stop before the border. Juan and Roberto's car had a flat tire. We pulled over to the side of the road. Night had fallen, but the horizon was aglow, stained with an extraterrestrial light. It looked like the scene in the sci-fi flick before the spaceship lands. Then we saw the first halo of the rising moon. We stood there, the four of us, and for the first time that day I felt an inkling of what I can only describe as "free." I remembered a night five years ago when my back was healing and the black mist was beginning to lift from my mind. It was stormy and I was walking alone near our home in Maryland. I stopped to watch a cluster of pine trees shudder in the wind against a cloud-shrouded sky. I wondered then whether my months of unhappiness were the price I'd had to pay for that vision. Now, for the first time in my life, I was watching a full moon rise over the desert. I felt a distinct sadness that this was the last time the four of us would be alone and undisturbed before the world took over. We wouldn't be seeing this, I knew, we wouldn't be standing here at the edge of the universe, if we hadn't lived through Basra, the White Ship, Abu Ghraib. At that moment I felt so deeply at peace that I wondered if it might not have been worth it. Not that, ultimately, I had any choice in the matter. Then or now.

OF CAT SCANS
AND KINGS

❖

L ESS than twenty-four hours after I had pleaded with a prison guard for a cup of tea, I was talking to the King. That transition seemed as seamless, as natural, as my metamorphosis from broadcaster to beggar forty days earlier. Our tragic tale was turning picaresque. We were involved in the planning of our lives again; we were back in the world where anticipation runs ahead of reality, where climaxes are almost doomed to be anticlimactic.

We arrived at the border just before nine. We paced and joked nervously outside the Iraqi immigration hall as our ministry escort took care of the paperwork. I could see a few cars parked with their lights on a hundred yards away, on the other side of a couple of fences. I hoped I was up to this.

After a half hour we got back in our cars for the last hundred-yard sprint. I had baggage now: a pillowcase I had robbed from the Al-Rasheed packed with icons: my prison pajamas, my blue sweater, my CBS News Manila

T-shirt. The driver handed it to me as I got out of the car, and there was Françoise. She was in blue jeans and a tweed jacket; a little makeup didn't mask the black rings under her eyes. She looked gaunt, exhausted. I knew she would have been trying to envision this moment with precision; not the mind-bending fact of my return, my safe return, our reunion; but the detail of it, the exact how and where, what we would say. The only thing Françoise fears more than elevators and cats are public displays of emotion. We embraced, and the CBS camera crew, there to record the event, was discreet enough not to roll. In my arms, Françoise felt thin and frail. I told her I'd never leave her again.

Correspondent Allen Pizzey and Doug Sefton, a producer out of London and an old friend, were there. So was what seemed like a battalion of Jordanian soldiers. We got into cars; Françoise gave me a boxed lunch she had brought from Amman and started telling me about her day as I tucked into dinner. Sam Roberts, the CBS executive running our case from New York, had woken her at eight with the news: "They're in the Al-Rasheed Hotel," he said. "We have them." Françoise wanted to know how we were. Roberts said, "Fair to good, no marks." Françoise asked whether Tanya knew. Roberts said, "Are you kidding? She's right next to me."

Roberts told her they should leave for the border right away. Françoise, as always, her feet planted firmly on the ground, pointed out that this was silly, that they'd get there a half day before us. But the CBS wagon was already on the roll, so they got to the border and sat there waiting in cold cars for six hours. After forty days, CBS News still hadn't learned that Françoise is always right.

King Hussein had sent his helicopter to the border to save us the four-hour drive back to Amman. Our disappearance apparently had attracted more attention than I'd imagined. When we landed in the military section of Amman's airport, the chief of the Jordanian air force, who came out to greet us, told me that the King was on the phone, wanted a word. We were led into the ops room, where a black phone was off the hook. The King told me how concerned he had been about our situation, how relieved he was that it had ended happily. I thanked him for the chopper and for the Jordan bread which had given us such a good day and he laughed. I kept glancing at my friends, sitting on a bench in the room, remembering another bench the four of us had sat on not all that long ago.

There was something else on my mind, something I had to do before we took off, and the executive jet CBS had chartered was revved up, ready to go. I asked Sefton, who was staying in Amman, to go back to the hotel and phone two numbers I gave him and tell whoever answered that Ahmad al-Ateeqi was alive and well and living in a prison near Baghdad.

We may have been instant celebrities, but the star, or, rather, the starlet on that flight to London was Marione, a shapely young Brazilian who was on board to take care of us. Marione was the doctor. We were impressed that CBS had hired a physician when we were just a few hours away from a hospital. We wondered which of our friends had been involved in the choice of Marione. Roberto told her that if she'd be there every time, he'd make sure to get captured again real soon. There was a lot of horsing around among the four of us on that plane. I felt badly for Françoise, who wasn't really part of it. She hadn't been sewn into the invisible web of our relations; she didn't speak the language. In fact, she felt like an outsider to me just then; even, to be painfully honest, like a bit of an intruder. It would take time.

A wonderful dinner was served and then, for the first time since we'd been released, I felt sleepy. I pushed my chair back to a reclining position and tried to doze off, but couldn't. I knew what was wrong. I lay down in the aisle.

Geraldine was at the Beggin Hill Airport outside London, where we landed at four in the morning. That was no surprise. The surprise was in the small waiting room. Dan Rather was there. He'd stopped off on his way home from Saudi Arabia just to greet us. Jack Smith, an ex–Washington bureau chief, was there too and I cracked when I saw him. During the months I'd been out of work with my bad back and my ravaged mind, Jack sent me a care package every week: candy, cookies, cheerful notes. "You're always there, Jack," I cried, kissing his rough neck. "You're always there when I need you."

John Peters, a lovely London cameraman I had known for twenty-two years, was there to work, to cover our arrival. But he appeared utterly paralyzed; he stood there, the Sony on his shoulder, not knowing whether to roll tape or join the fray.

Dan shared a limo with Françoise and me on the way to

the hospital. He told me he was speaking on behalf of the front office when he said that I could go wherever I wanted to go when I was ready to go back to work. London, Paris, New York. Anywhere. And I could take my time to decide. I told him I didn't need time, that I just wanted to get back to Israel. My beach was waiting for me.

When I was based in London, one slow week in 1974 I shot a story about a luxury hospital which had recently opened to considerable fanfare. It was called The Wellington Clinic and it featured cordon bleu cuisine, wine lists longer than the medical charts, and 'round-the-clock room service. The punch line was that only Arabs could afford to be treated there, while many of the doctors were Jews.

We checked into the clinic, now called the Humana Hospital Wellington, at six in the morning that day. We had adjacent rooms on the fourth floor. Françoise and I had a two-room suite. Tanya was in the air, I was told, on her way from New York. Initial checkups suggested that there was little wrong with us aside from severe malnutrition and Juan's fractured foot. I had lost thirty-five pounds, and my cholesterol level was that of a long-distance runner. An X ray showed what the doctor described as "an unusual amount of debris" in my stomach. He asked if I had been eating heavily over the last twenty-four hours.

At the top of my agenda was a shave. I asked for a razor and some cream, went to my bathroom, and was preparing to do the deed when the doctor came in and said he wanted to take me down for a brain scan. I told him it wasn't necessary, that I wasn't having headaches, that my brain was neither better nor worse than it had been for forty-nine years. He told me I had no choice, that since we'd been beaten over the head, he had to do the scan because if he didn't, we could turn around and sue him in six months. We were back in the west, back in the world of litigation and liability.

I had a thermometer in my mouth and a blood pressure belt around my arm and an orthopedist was examining my knees when I thought I heard Tanya's voice in the corridor. I rushed out, but no one was there, just the nurses. I wandered down to the end of the corridor, heard voices coming from a room, opened the door, and there she was, but she wasn't alone. Tanya was surrounded by pillars of the CBS power structure who had flown into London to see us. I tore Tanya away, took her outside, and held her for I have no idea how long. I don't think I said anything. All I remember her saying was, "Dad, get rid of that beard."

Tanya went to see her mother and I went back to the room to say hello to my bosses. Weeks ago, when we were in the camp, Peter and I reflected that, underneath it all, they must be pretty pissed off at us. If they were, it didn't show, not then, not later. I sat down on the bed, and without really planning or meaning to, launched into a detailed narrative of what we'd been through.

In 1969, when I was being transferred from New York to London, to my first post as a foreign correspondent, the foreign editor told me my debut would be covering the investiture of Prince Charles at Caernarvon Castle in Wales. He advised me to have a chat with a Welsh kid who had just started with CBS as a researcher, so I took Howard Stringer to lunch at a cheap French restaurant. Now he was president of CBS, sitting a few inches from me on the bed. Eric Ober, the president of the News Division, news executive Sam Roberts, and Tom Goodman, the publicity director, were in the room, too. But Stringer was the only one I knew well, and for what he later told me was more than two hours, I talked to him and for the first time since we'd known each other, he did not interrupt me with his razor-edged wit.

I was still in solitary confinement when Ed Bradley came in. He told me he had come to London to do a "60 Minutes" story on us, that cameramen were setting up in a room downstairs at that very moment. Ancient TV News technique, Confucius might have said: get them when they're wired, before they get any sleep, when their defenses are so far down they don't even know where to look for them. I had used it many times myself.

It went on for a long time, the interview. I would have had no idea how long if I hadn't been aware that the cameramen changed cassettes several times and that cassettes last thirty minutes. Once again the four of us were sitting next to each other; once again we were under interrogation, bearded, unwashed, still wearing our Baghdad gear. All the CBS execs were in the room, front-row seats behind the cameras. Tanya was there too. Most of the questions were coming at me. But I was barely aware of my surroundings or my audience. I just wanted to talk. I could have gone on for hours. During one short break for a cassette change, Peter leaned over and said, "Watch it, Bob, they'll bleed you dry." But I didn't know what he was talking about. I wouldn't find out until much later.

What I came to realize fairly quickly, though, was that I'd have to watch my sense of humor. People were listening to me differently now. They seemed to be taking me seriously. I'd have to be careful. The "60 Minutes" story book ended our captivity in a humorous sort of way. After the interview I had a cup of coffee with Bradley and told him that the night before we were captured, when we checked into a fleabag of a hotel in Hafr el-Baten, I phoned the CBS bureau in Dhahran to tell them we would be spending the night up north. Mike Rosenbaum, the bureau chief, said that was too bad because he had hoped to get us on "60 Minutes" that night. He was sure they would take a story from us on the buildup. That made me pause. It would be nice to get on "60 Minutes." I told Mike we would head back to Dhahran to do the piece. While I stayed on the phone, he called "60 Minutes" in New York on another line. He came back to tell me they couldn't commit to it; they hadn't decided yet on the shape of their broadcast that evening. I wasn't going to drive all the way back to Dhahran for a maybe, so I told Mike we would stay up north, as planned. Now I told Bradley to tell Don Hewitt, the executive producer of "60 Minutes," that it was his fault we were captured; that if he had agreed to take our story that night, it never would have happened. Bradley flew back to New York, and the next day a very serious Hewitt was on the phone. "It's not my fault, Bob," he said. "Honest. Don't blame me." He told me I hadn't "sold" the story hard enough. Maybe I hadn't then, but now I'd have to start being careful.

Françoise and I were coming from different directions. I had been passive for forty days; being a prisoner is above all a passive experience. She had been hyperactive. I reacted to my freedom with frenzy. It was the beginning of my new life. She reacted by falling into a nervous torpor. It was the end of her campaign. She came down with bronchitis and a migraine, her first since my capture: she was asleep much of the time. Meanwhile I took calls. When I wasn't receiving doctors and debriefers, I was working the phones. Aside from friends and colleagues, there were lecture agents, literary agents, editors, publishers, Hollywood producers. They all sounded warm and solicitous, concerned about my well-being, and caring.

A released prisoner with any notoriety should be kept away from phones for at least a month; until he can start seeing the world again with some lucidity.

The letters started pouring in too; by the sackful. Many asked for autographs. Many more were addressed to "Paul Simon." There were reams of yellow ribbons, piles of POW bracelets, miniature Bibles, religious artifacts, valentine cards. Very few of the letters were written to me, to Bob. How could they have been? I had, unwittingly, become a symbol. To the left, I was the personification of the fight for freedom of the press, the struggle against the Pentagon's mendacity machine, and not just a poor schmuck who got caught with his pants down. The right blasted me with all the venom it had left after emptying its guns on Arnett. Doctors and lawyers were especially prolific here. "You were primarily looking for some way to discredit American motives," wrote Dr. J. R. Feild, from Memphis. "Serves you right."

Others thought I hadn't suffered nearly enough. "I am very sorry to hear that while you were in the hands of the Iraqis you were not administered the bastinado," wrote Attorney Patrick W. O'Reilly from Phoenix. "The bastinado is a persuasion performed by hauling the gentleman up by his feet and then thrashing the soles of the feet with a split cane lash. . ."

And if Françoise's mother was concerned about my thanking God when we were released, Coni Prez of Connecticut believed it had not been sufficient. "I am sure your wife is grateful that you gave her so much credit," she wrote. "All I am humbly asking is that you give God equal time."

A cousin in New York complained bitterly that she'd had to learn about it all on television, that I hadn't found the time to call. What sense of family did I have, anyway?

But there were others. In fact, the overwhelming majority were so moving and heartfelt, it was difficult to know how to respond. "Please don't get lost again," wrote Eugenia Gelman from California. "I am a little old lady and my heart could not take it."

And my all-time favorite, from Russell Carlton of

Sherwood, Oregon: "My housemate is a 100% service connected vet in a wheelchair. His philosophy is: 'Forget the past with love, look to the future with hope.' On the other hand, I am a Marine. I never fucking forget."

Many letters came from journalism students, from young men and women starting out in the craft. They were so fulsome with praise of my prowess as a correspondent that I began to worry: what's going to happen when I get out of here and start filing stories again and it turns out to be just me? There was a whole new range of expectations out there. I wasn't only fresh out of prison. I was on parole.

The four ex-cons met mainly in the corridor these days. Most of the time we were closeted with our families. Roberto's parents and his girlfriend came in from Miami. CBS flew in Juan's folks too. Jack Smith reported later that, walking past Juan's half-open door one day, he saw Juan's mother holding her sleeping son so tenderly that it made him think of Michelangelo's *Pietà*. Geraldine told Peter that his fantasies of fixing up their country house would never be realized. She had done the work herself while he was gone, believing that if she made the house just right, he would come back to it.

We were back in the movies, but this time it wasn't our imagination. Camera crews followed us wherever we went. Our second day in the hospital we gave four press conferences. We sat up on a stage in the employee cafeteria, converted into a briefing room with a backdrop of blue curtains and a CBS eye. We were introduced by the lead doctor who, decked out in a worsted double-breasted suit, was perfectly cast to play himself. The questions were friendly, information-seeking mainly, aside from a woman from the *Jewish Chronicle* who wanted to know why my one-sheet bio, put out by CBS, didn't mention that I was based in Israel. Goodman fielded that one.

Between performances we were taken backstage for a lunch break. Ober and Goodman began proudly unpacking cartons full of mile-high corned-beef-and-pastrami sandwiches, basins of chopped liver, coleslaw, potato salad, pickles, bottles of Dr. Brown's cream soda, boxes of chocolate fudge cake. It appeared that during my account of our captivity to the CBS execs, I had mentioned my food fantasies, notably my craving for the cuisine of the Carnegie Deli. Ober had placed the order. It came in by Concorde.

The movie was taking a turn for the surrealistic. English technicians stood around as if they were witnessing some arcane tribal rite, waiting for the extras to show up in war paint. I discovered I was being filmed with my mouth so full of pastrami, I couldn't swallow fast enough to ask the cameraman to get his lens out of my face. I felt a bit like a circus performer, waiting for the ringmaster to announce, "AND NOW, AFTER FIVE POUNDS OF CHOPPED LIVER, THE STARVED PRISONERS TACKLE THE COLESLAW."

The day we checked out of the hospital, CBS organized a session for us at Trumper's, the London barbershop frequented by Prince Charles, a softly lit world of red velvet, porcelain, lotions, warm towels, and soft brushes; the last private preserve of the English gentleman, now invaded by Klieg lights and hand-held cameras. When my barber came at me with a long blade, I remembered how a guy with a red kefiyah had threatened to use that very instrument not very long ago. I winced, and with good reason. He nicked my cheek a few minutes later. The Shaving of the CBS Four was recorded for posterity and for a satellite feed that night. It was getting to be a bit much. The party was almost over and it was just as well.

In my mail sack a few days later was a letter from one Godfrey Daniels of Philadelphia. "Grow the beard back," he wrote. "You used to look distinguished. Now you look like a dork."

We checked into the Hyde Park Hotel in Knightsbridge and, now that we were out of the hospital, I discovered that there was something wrong: my eyesight. Françoise and I were walking up Brompton Road, a street I know by heart. When we were less than a block from Harrods, I found that I couldn't read the sign. We ducked into an optometrist's shop; I was tested and the optician concurred: I needed glasses; in fact, I was very nearsighted. I told him that was strange; I'd never had that problem before. He inquired whether by any chance I might be a photographer. Why did he want to know? Because photographers' eyesight often deteriorates suddenly, he said, after they spend long stretches in a darkroom. That night Peter phoned me from his house in the country. "Guess what! I need new specs," he said. "My doc says it's because of all the darkness."

The time had come for farewells. Tanya was heading back to New York, to finish the semester at Columbia.

Françoise was still feeling poorly, so I took my kid to our favorite Szechuan restaurant in Soho. The doctors had advised me to try not to gorge myself, to eat in small quantities, so we ordered only eight or nine dishes. Tanya told me she had been pretty mad at me; that I had forced her to confront a whole host of problems, notably the death of a father, which she had hoped not to face for many years. She'd felt like she was descending a stairway with no bannister. But what angered her even more, I think, was the situation of her mother. Françoise had hooked her life to mine so irreversibly that she really had no place to go, no home to call home if I disappeared. It seemed to me that Tanya was coming out of this determined not to make the same mistake. But it's hard to explain how, with this heaviness, we had a delightful evening, but we did. The restaurant was noisy, the food was excellent, the wine was fine, and my little daughter and I downed two bottles. We'd never had any trouble talking to each other, and what she wanted to talk about even more than her anger was her career. There was little doubt in her mind a year ago and there was even less now. She wanted to be a journalist, a foreign correspondent.

Many weeks later our good friend Gloria Emerson told me that soon after I was captured Tanya had spent hours with her hardly saying a word, and finally asked, "Do you think they're beating my father?"

The next evening Françoise and I went to dinner at the home of David Green, a close friend and a cameraman I have been working with since 1969. He was in Saudi Arabia when I was captured and, in fact, we were plotting to make it to Kuwait together, ahead of the ground forces, which he ended up doing without me. Aside from being a great cameraman, David is a master impresario and a merchant of joy. We have had more outrageously good times together in more places than either one of us will ever choose to remember.

We've crossed some borders together too. In 1974, when the military overthrew the Portuguese dictatorship, it closed the airports and sealed the borders. David and I flew to Spain, rented a car, bought a surveyor's map, made our way along dirt roads, crossed fields and farms and a couple of brooks, and eventually found ourselves on a paved road which wasn't on our map. When the first car passed and we looked at the plates, we exploded with delight. We were in Portugal. We had a day's jump on the story.

But now David was sitting at his kitchen table crying like a baby. He told me he was sure I had been killed. Most of my friends had come to believe I was either dead or alive through an intuition which they could not possibly explain. David had reached his conclusion with characteristically cold logic. He knew that everyone and everything in Iraq ends up in Baghdad and that we would therefore be taken there. He also knew that the allied air forces were bombing everything that moved on that road. While he cried, I sat there at his kitchen table utterly unable to respond. I watched him, I understood what he was saying, why he was crying, but I felt frozen in some arctic space of my mind. I couldn't show any emotion; I could barely feel any emotion. It preoccupied me for days.

The only way I could explain it to myself was that I had shut off the taps so tightly that they couldn't be reopened right away. It would take time.

The four freed men had their last dinner together at a trendy trattoria on Brompton Road. There were lots of other people at the table, so the tight knot of fear I felt at the prospect of our separation in the morning was loosened somewhat by the small talk, the white lights, and the white wine. I embraced Roberto and Juan and we told each other to take care and stay away from borders and the rest of it. We said, "See you soon," which is something else you say, though I wasn't at all sure of it. I didn't wait for Peter to make the offer this time. "I'd really like to keep the jacket," I said.

"It's yours," he said. We didn't say goodbye, just waved to each other on the dark London street before we got into our cars.

ISRAELIS

❧❧

A MAN I didn't know dropped off a cord of firewood the first day. He said he heard that I'd been cold. The people who deliver our newspapers came over with a chocolate cake. The "60 Minutes" interview had been broadcast on Israeli television. Not surprisingly, the part which received the most attention, which, in fact, was re-transmitted several times, was my account of how that Iraqi officer had spit at me and slapped me around for being a "Yahoudi." If I had left Israel a member of that tainted crowd of western correspondents, as something of a pariah, I was returning as a native son. People stopped me on the street, on the beach; our house was flooded with flowers, newspaper photographers lurked in the hedges. We were invited to so many establishment dinner parties those first weeks, I found myself in the same room with Defense Minister Moshe Arens so many times that, after a while, "So, we meet again" was all we could come up with as a limp greeting.

Former Defense Minister Ezer Weizman sent over a

note. "I wanted to come and fish you out myself," he wrote, "but the assholes wouldn't let me."

The press corps' favorite Israeli politician, Jerusalem mayor Teddy Kollek, wrote, "You look much too thin. Let me invite you for a nice, fattening lunch. . . ." Which he did, and which was.

There were some surprises. The chief military censor, a man I had wrangled with many times, had been approached by a colleague while I was in prison, I learned, and asked to censor any references to my Jewishness or to my residence in Israel. "It's not my job," he replied, "but I'll do it."

A spokesperson for the settlers' movement telephoned. This was a woman who had never thought of me as a particularly sympathetic ear, certainly not as a friend. "You're welcome in our house anytime now, Bob," she said. "You're a prisoner of Zion." *A prisoner of Zion?*

I had suffered because I was a Jew. At least that was the perception, and it colored my reception. But that wasn't the whole story. Israel is a country with uncertain borders and very rough edges. Its citizens are notoriously assertive, aggressive, and unschooled in the Queensberry rules. Negotiating a line in a supermarket or at a bus stop here requires vigilance, sharp elbows and, ideally, commando training. But so many Israelis have been through so much trauma that there is an instinctive understanding of how to deal with someone who's been through a bad patch. "Time-out" is declared. "We'll leave you alone. Rest, recover, recuperate. When you're back up to scratch, watch out, we'll be back."

There was another radiator warming up my reception. While I was still in London, Israel's president, Chaim Herzog, wrote to me: "We all look forward to seeing you back in Israel in due course, perhaps with a more acute understanding of the security fears which motivate us." He was the only one who articulated it, but I sensed the same question in the eyes of many Israelis. "Do you get it now? Do you see who these guys are? You, who thought you could stand in the middle. Will you go easy on us now?"

Some of my Palestinian friends also believed I would move off the middle ground now; now that I had been a prisoner, detained without trial, beaten and abused; now that I knew what it was to be a Palestinian, now that, in their eyes, I had been one. Two of my closest contacts were especially warm in their greetings. Sari Nusseibeh, the Oxford-educated tutor of the *intifada*, and Taher Shriteh, the CBS stringer in Gaza, had been in Israeli jails all the time I was in Iraq.

But my relations with many Palestinians were a bit awkward at first. They had worked hard for my release, sending petitions to Saddam pointing out that I was a bona fide journalist, and a fair one. But now they felt uneasy, I sensed, because they knew I knew how enthusiastic their support had been for Iraq. Many called it the "Iraqi *intifada*." There was something else as well. While they had always known I was Jewish, it was something which, in a Middle Eastern sort of way, never came up. Now it was on the table, out in the open. What's more, I had declared in a most unguarded moment on "60 Minutes" that I would have killed that Iraqi officer if I'd had the chance, and would have felt no more remorse than I did when I stamped out the cockroaches in my cell. Those were pretty strong words for my Palestinian colleagues to digest on the patio of the American Colony Hotel in East Jerusalem. One long afternoon there, after what I felt were too many insinuating questions about my thoughts and my feelings, I said, in a voice that was out of proportion to the size of the table, "Look, if you're asking me if I hate Arabs, the answer is no." In a Middle Eastern sort of way, the subject never came up again.

It is so simple, but it is so impossible to explain to Israelis or to Palestinians or to anyone else who is party to a conflict. You tell a story with words and pictures and you use the best words and pictures you can find and everything else is bullshit.

With the exception of Egypt, you can't phone Arab countries from Israel. So every so often I would go through the CBS switchboard in New York and call Mrs. al-Ateeqi in Damascus. She'd heard nothing, but she always sounded glad to hear from me. She was terribly worried about Ahmad's health, told me his heart condition was worse than he'd let on.

The day after I got back, General Giora Rom, the deputy commander of the Israeli air force, invited me out to dinner. I knew Giora socially. I also knew he had been a POW in Egypt, so I figured he wanted to hear about my experience. And he did, up to a point, but what he really wanted was to talk about his own. I sat there transfixed, as my pasta got cold, realizing that this need to talk is not a short-term thing: Giora was shot down in 1969. And that wasn't the only revelation. Giora was telling me about feelings and thoughts which I not only shared but which I was convinced were idiosyncratic, quirkily "me." When he wasn't lost in food fantasies, this ace pilot who'd shot down five MiGs in the Six-Day War daydreamed about his past; only the good times, of course. He was badly wounded when he was captured, was on his back in a body cast, interrogated and beaten from the very first day. But he quickly discovered, to his astonishment, that getting beaten up is not a big deal. Unpleasant, but not a big deal. What frightened him most during his three months in a Cairo cell were not the interrogations or the death threats, but the sound of dogs barking in the distance. . . .

I had, apparently, joined a fraternity I didn't even know existed: an old boys' club with free lifetime membership. The dues had already been paid.

The exterminator came to our house a few days later. We'd had a rat problem for a long time. Whenever Françoise heard them scampering around in the attic, she'd call a real estate agent and I'd call the exterminator. The rats were back now and he was too. He is a large, strong man in his forties; a man of few words. We'd never really spoken before, but now he asked if I had time for a cup of coffee, which I did. We sat in our garden and he told me that he was captured on top of Mount Hermon in the Golan Heights the second day of the Yom Kippur War, spent eight months in a Syrian prison, all of them in solitary confinement. He was beaten with bamboo canes several times a day every day, but quickly discovered that

261

"it's nothing. After the first time, it's nothing." They took out his fingernails. He put his large hands on our garden table to show me how he would offer them to his interrogators, saying, "You want to take, take." Does he talk about it a lot? "No," he said. "Only sometimes when I meet another prisoner. With others, it's too difficult to explain."

I was contacted by another ex-con. Yitzhak Shamir phoned, invited me up to Jerusalem to trade prison stories. Shamir, the military chief of the Stern Gang in the pre-State days, had spent fourteen months in British jails in the 1940s, detained without trial, very much the way Palestinians are today. I had been to the Prime Minister's office many times. Now, for the first time, I was not searched at the door. Shamir sat buried in his oversized armchair and talked about how civil the British had been. "You can't compare it," he said. "The British are civilized people." He spoke of it with humor, a humor I'd never seen in him before, but what I noticed were his eyes. Even when he laughed, they didn't move. I saw that if the British had wanted to break him, they would have had a very tough time. Solitary confinement was no problem for him, he said. He always liked being alone and in fact misses it sometimes.

Our tennis club threw a party for us. I met a lawyer, the husband of one of the best players. He asked me how much light there was in my cell, whether I could tell the difference between day and night, exactly when they took my watch from me. "Hey, these are insider questions," I said. "Have you been a prisoner?" No, he hadn't been a prisoner, he told me. But when he does reserve duty in the Israeli army, he works as an interrogator, in Gaza. I was out of my cell and back in the Middle East, the Holy Land of Inquisitions.

The lawyer was shocked to hear that I'd been blind-folded during interrogations. "You have to look your prisoner in the eye," he said. "That's how you know if he's lying." He thought the Iraqis had been sloppy in other ways too. It was his opinion as a professional. He was like a dentist, shaking his head at the last guy's work. "We know their torture techniques," he said. "They must have been ordered not to torture you. And they don't know anything else. That's why they didn't get anything out of you. If they can't torture, they're helpless." He told me that he'd been pessimistic about my chances. He thought that, as an American, I wouldn't be able to put up with the dirt, the dirt which, he said, all Middle Eastern regimes use to dehumanize, take away your dignity, your sense of yourself. I told him I must not be much of an American. The dirt had been the least of my problems.

I took Natan Scharansky to lunch. Scharansky, the preeminent Prisoner of Zion, had spent nine years in Soviet jails before emigrating to Israel in 1986. "Life was clear and deep," he said as he wandered through the long menu of an Italian restaurant. "You didn't waste time with trivial decisions, like what to order for lunch." When he wasn't playing chess games in his head—he is a chess master, and another advantage of solitary confinement, he pointed out, was that he always won—he also retreated to his past, but not in the sentimental way I did. He remembered what his friends and co-conspirators were doing before he was arrested and he imagined them doing the same things, living in the same apartments, involved in the same work. It was his way of convincing himself that the struggle was alive.

We not only belonged to the same old boys' network, we discovered; we had something else in common. Gorbachev was instrumental in releasing us both. The difference was that I wrote a thank-you note to the Soviet leader. Scharansky did not.

He told me that he identifies now with people a lot younger than himself. He was born forty-three years ago, he said, but his nine years in prison don't count. They were spent on another planet. His friends are almost all in their thirties.

After he was released, he found that he had to write about it. It was the only way to overcome his obsession with the prison, with the past. When he finished his book, he felt that he was free for the first time, free to live in the present.

I was writing every day. I started taking notes my second day in London, when I woke up from a nightmare, and I wanted to get it all down quickly. I wasn't worried so much about forgetting. I was worried about revisionism, that as I re-entered the world, my mind would begin casting the experience in different lights.

By the time I left London, I was ridiculously overcommitted. I had agreed to give a dozen lectures, to participate in at least as many panels, to accept an award, and deliver a speech at the annual Overseas Press Club dinner in New York. I had also agreed to write a long article and was talking to a publisher about a short book.

I spent mornings locked up with my old Olivetti. Afternoons, I walked on the beach and took notes. It came gushing out more naturally than anything I'd ever done before. In fact, I only got blocked once. I couldn't write for a couple of days and I didn't understand why. I mentioned it to a friend and he asked, "Well, what are you up to?" I was up to the day they accused me of being a spy, the day I went to pieces, I told him, and we both laughed. I wrote it the next day.

But while the process felt cathartic, the pressures of the publishing industry did not. I was, apparently, more fragile than I realized. When some minor problems arose with the magazine which had commissioned the article, I got terribly upset and backed out of it. I agreed to write the book. Within days, I was getting phone calls from a persistent editor: "How much have you written? When will I see it? Let's talk about a title. When will you finish?" Although I understood deadlines well enough, I couldn't deal with this, not now.

I started dreaming of my cell again. But they weren't nightmares, I noted with alarm. They were quite pleasant, almost dreams of longing. When I spoke of my imprisonment, which I was called on to do all the time, I noticed a tone of nostalgia creeping in.

Giora Rom provided some context. He told me that shortly after his release, when he had to face flying again, he began thinking of his cell with yearning. Ever since peace with Egypt was declared, he has been trying to get there, not to see the Sphinx or the pyramids, just to see his jail. Because of his position in the air force, the Egyptians wouldn't permit it.

Scharansky told me that a friend of his went to the Soviet Union recently, brought back photographs of his friends and — of his camp in Siberia. That's the picture he finds himself going back to all the time, he said. He would like to put it on the desk in his office, but hasn't because people wouldn't understand. He looks at it when he is alone at home.

Friends were worried that I was heading for a nervous collapse. After one sleepless night, I grabbed Françoise, took her to the beach, and told her I wanted to cancel everything: the book, the lectures, the speeches, the whole lot. She agreed.

I felt relieved for a few days, but then a maddening sense of failure set in. I had never backed out of anything before and didn't like the idea of starting now.

A friend arranged a meeting with Colonel Itamar Barnea, the chief psychologist of the Israeli air force, an ex–fighter pilot. He'd been shot down over Syria in 1973, had a lung removed in a Damascus hospital, and spent eight months there as a POW. What drove him crazy during his imprisonment was not the harsh Syrian treatment or his injuries or the knowledge that he'd never fly again. What haunted him was the conviction that he had failed. He, an ace warrior, had done something dumb in the air. He'd made a stupid mistake and brought this disgrace upon himself. The trauma for me was also the failure. It wasn't the event, but the reaction to the event. I wasn't coping anymore.

Making matters worse, I couldn't talk to Peter these days. He was off on a long vacation to Italy and southern France. I pictured him with his feet up in a bathrobe on a veranda overlooking the sea. Geraldine was pouring the chianti. Once again, Peter had known exactly what to do. I was the idiot, the overachiever from the Bronx, inflicting punishment on himself more effectively than the Iraqis could have imagined. I knew what date Peter was due back in England. That afternoon, when Françoise told me he was on the phone, I rushed in from the garden and, I'm sure, shouted into the receiver: "Peter. How are you?"

There was a little hesitation, followed by an extremely meek little voice. "Not so great," he said.

"Thank God," I replied.

I spoke to Roberto regularly. He said he was feeling good, but I was suspicious. He had signed up with a self-help group called Life Spring. He said that made all the difference. From his description of it, though, it sounded a bit cultish, a touch authoritarian. I heard echoes of Scientology. He advised me to see if there was a chapter in Tel Aviv. He sent me the literature. I told him I'd think about it.

Juan was impossible to reach. He was in Nicaragua with his mother.

Françoise and I had lunch with friends, a married couple, Israelis, both psychologists. We went to our favorite restaurant in Herzylia, where the food is bad but where you can see nothing but the sea. They didn't buy my story. They didn't think what was going on had very much to do with the book. It would have happened anyway. What I was experiencing now was the flip side of that hard metal disc I had discovered in prison. It was the outgoing box of the survival mechanism. All the anxiety I had kept bottled up in my cell had to come out sooner or later. And it was good that it was pouring out now. They said that if I were as happy as I thought I should be, they would be worried. It would mean that I was condemned to break down in a year or two.

There was one patch of light in the darkening sky. The CBS foreign desk called one afternoon to read me a cable they had received from one Ghiass Arabi, an Arab-American, whose name I did not recognize. "My brother-in-law," the cable read, "Mr. Ahmad al-Ateeqi, was released from Iraqi captivity yesterday and is now in Saudi Arabia."

I had him on the phone within a few days. He was buoyant. He would not be a companion-in-misery to Peter and me. I asked penetrating questions; mainly "How are you?" a dozen or more times. And each time he replied, "I'm fine, Mr. Bob, how are you?" When I let on that I was not feeling great, he laughed and said, "Mr. Bob, how many times I tell you? I believe in God, Mr. Bob; that's the difference. Everything that happened was meant to be."

Françoise and I decided to drive down to Taba on the Red Sea, do what we should have done at the very beginning, spend a few days on the beach, far from phones and well-wishers. I found I was driving a lot slower these days than I had before my imprisonment. I had long believed that irony was the guiding principle of the universe and I could picture the headline: SURVIVOR OF SADDAM'S GULAG KILLED IN CAR CRASH ON NEGEV HIGHWAY.

Technically, Taba is part of Egypt. But it is a kind of no-man's land between Israel and Egypt, a two-hundred-yard-long sliver of coastline south of the Israeli seaport of Eilat. Conquered along with the rest of Sinai in the 1967 war, the Israelis gave it back to Egypt after protracted negotiations in 1989, long after it had relinquished the rest of the peninsula. And Taba has not been wholly integrated. The resort hotel—all there is on Taba—still accepts Israeli currency. Israelis, who generally shun the Sinai now, still go to Taba.

It was off-season and Françoise and I found ourselves among the only vacationers in the cavernous breakfast hall. We were just finishing our coffee the first morning when a bearded Israeli in his thirties walked over to our table, looked me intensely in the eye, said, "Thank you," and walked off.

I walked over to the hotel's diving club to look into renting some gear. The Egyptian who ran the place, a middle-aged, muscular man in a black wet suit, said, "Good morning, Mr. Simon." I hadn't expected to be recognized down here, thought I was getting away from all that. I must have looked a bit surprised because he said, "Of course I recognize you. Everybody recognizes you." But he said it with more bitterness than warmth.

Then he told me that he'd been captured by the Israelis in the Six-Day War, had been held for three months, treated pretty rough. There was simply no escape from prisoners in these parts. They were endemic to the region, along with the cactus and the barbed wire. How was it after he'd been released? "Bad," he said, as he gave me a mask to try on. "For a year I slept badly. I lived badly."

I took a stroll on the beach, looked at the mirror-smooth cobalt-blue surface of the sea come up against the stark desert hills in the distance. "A year," I said to myself. "A whole year?" I walked past the Israeli who approached me at breakfast. I couldn't resist. "Why did you say thank you?" I asked.

"Because the war was so impersonal," he said, "so difficult to understand. Just this massive machine, this space age technology. There was nothing human about it. It had no face." He told me he would sit in his sealed room in Tel Aviv when there was a Scud alert, and couldn't relate to what was going on. "You gave the war a human face," he said. "I could follow your fate and relate to it on a personal level. It was something I could understand, or try to. It made it possible for me to feel something about the war."

Apparently I had done better as a prisoner than I ever had as a reporter. I said, "Thank you."

I continued my stroll, walking on water's edge along the whole two hundred yards of Taba coastline, skirted a fence marking the Egyptian border which protruded two or three yards into the water, and meandered on into Egypt. I used to come down here quite often when the

Sinai was Israeli, went diving with friends, camping on the beach. Of all the places I knew, I thought of these mountains and this gulf and the way they came together, as the most spectacular scenery in the world. And it had lost none of its luster. I had climbed Mount Sinai, or Mount Moses as the Israelis call it, a few years back and remembered thinking, I believe it. If God ever decided to break his silence, this is where he would have done it.

Now I walked past an Egyptian army camp, Quonset huts staggered along the beach. I waved at a couple of Egyptian soldiers in a guard tower. They waved back. I turned around and walked back to Taba. The Israeli was waiting on the other side of the fence, shaking his head. "I just wanted to see if Bob Simon was going to walk across another border," he said. I hadn't even realized I was crossing a border. I was just taking a stroll. So much for learning from experience.

PARTIES TO THE
CONFLICT

✧✦

BEFORE we went to Taba, the day I shed six months of commitments, Françoise urged me not to cancel my appearance at the Overseas Press Club. It was an honor, she said, not an obligation. I was being feted by my colleagues, and the award would reflect well on CBS, which had worked so hard for my release.

On the twenty-third of April, we walked into the Grand Hyatt ballroom in New York, Françoise in a smashing black evening suit, Tanya a knockout in a black chiffon gown, me in a baggy tuxedo. We walked into a room packed with publicists and other strangers. There was a pay bar charging ten bucks for a double scotch. I searched for a familiar face, caught a glimpse of my old buddy Peter Arnett, but he was in the tow of his literary agent on the other side of the room. A photographer took some pictures, I was slapped on the back a lot, and I kept remembering Scharansky's account of his first trip to the States after his release. He was celebrated in the halls of

Congress. Every senator, every congressman wanted to have a picture taken with him, and he recalled how to his amazement almost every one of them came up with the same three lines as they smiled at the cameras. "Nice to see you. You are an inspiration to us. Have a nice day." In prison, every word had meaning, he said. In America, there was no meaning; only words. Only selling and buying and photo opportunities.

I had worked hard on my speech and, as we were marched single file to the dais, felt silly to have put in so much effort. But then I saw that Rather and Cronkite, Tom Brokaw and Howard Stringer were there, so the silliness began turning into stage fright. I could talk to a camera anytime, anywhere. But to this crowd? This was another story. To increase my distress, the first speaker was Ted Turner, and he was terrific, hilarious, a tough act to follow. Then I was introduced as "that veteran CBS correspondent, winner of three previous OPC awards. We're so glad to welcome back from Iraq . . . Bob Smith."

I laughed it off, stumbled to the podium, told a few jokes; explained how my years at CBS had prepared me for the ordeal; how covering stories in Tokyo on a CBS meal allowance taught me how to cope with hunger; how covering the State Department taught me how to deal with confinement. I said that we journalists are at our worst behind podiums making speeches about freedom of the press and then proceeded to do just that. I talked about the pool system in Saudi Arabia, how it had been designed precisely to keep us away from the war; how if there had been pools in Vietnam, a number of stories would have gone uncovered: the Tet offensive, for example, My Lai. And I warmed up as I discovered that I actually believed what I was saying.

During my time in prison I never really analyzed the issues involved in what we'd been doing that day at the border. But now, looking at Cronkite, who, more powerfully than anyone else, had called the administration's bluff in Vietnam, I started getting worked up about the Gulf War, as I had before my capture.

Ever since Vietnam we'd been kept away from the action. I'd missed Panama, where a press pool was kept in a hangar until the fighting was over, but I was one of the reporters who covered the invasion of Grenada from Barbados because the Pentagon kept us off the island where it was waging war with, it turned out, only limited success, against one of the world's smallest countries.

They couldn't keep us out of Saudi Arabia and they didn't want to, not if they could turn us into a chorus line for the command, which is what they tried to do. Whenever I visited a unit in the field, the troops were glad to see us, as their fathers and uncles had always been in Vietnam. The division commanders usually were not. It was a rematch of old protagonists, guys who couldn't dance as fast now but who were a lot smarter. They knew each others' moves and came into the ring warily. The cub reporters had acquired larger titles and midriffs. The eager young captains were colonels and generals. But we were the same guys. I ran into several officers I knew from Vietnam. "So you're back again, huh," was the customary greeting. "Are you going to lose it for us again this time?"

They really believed that. They really believed they lost Vietnam because they lost control of the images. And they weren't going to let it happen again.

Their weapons were the pools, the military escorts, the censors. Their guiding wisdom was the insight that no news organization would have the guts to tell them to take their system and shove it, because no organization would risk going it alone, coming away with nothing and getting clobbered by the competition.

They made several assumptions based on Vietnam: that we were against the war and that we wanted to discredit American motives. But this was not true. I couldn't take a poll, obviously, and had no reason to, but the mood in the coffee shop—the press gallery of the International Hotel—was decidedly hawkish. The journalists based in the Middle East, in particular, felt strongly that Saddam had to be eliminated. I believed that as strongly as I'd ever believed anything.

The high command claimed security was the rationale, but this was disingenuous. Security considerations can be handled with the judicious use of embargoes, as they were in Vietnam, where despite the tension between the Pentagon and the press, there were no security violations of any consequence. No, the motivation was political. The war was to appear clean, safe, and sanitary; no blood, no pain, no body bags. The administration wanted handsome young men to come into American living rooms, pilots giving the thumbs-up sign to the deck crews of carriers before taking off. They wanted amplifiers to overmodulate the thrilling roar of afterburners. Cut to video shot by camera in nose of missile honing in on target; see smokestack; cut to hash. "Hey, don't you guys ever miss?" a colleague asked at one of the last press briefings I covered in Saudi Arabia.

Of course they missed, but they were pretty damn good. I knew that. I'd been inside one of their targets. And I was curious about how we'd gotten onto the hit list. Did the command know, or even suspect, that some two dozen American and British POWs were inside Saddam's Intelligence Headquarters? Was the target so important that the loss of these lives was a necessary risk?

After my release I talked to three American pilots who were in the White Ship with me that night. They came from different units and had been briefed separately, but they'd all been told the same thing. It had been an intelligence failure. Not only did the command not know we were there; it had received intelligence that we were all in another building in Baghdad, another intelligence compound which, of course, was not bombed.

But something didn't make sense here. Arnett had broadcast on CNN that the CBS crew was inside the White Ship. On three occasions CBS executives spoke to the Pentagon to make sure the information had been digested. But it seemed they decided to go for it anyway. And why shouldn't they? Just to safeguard a few rebellious reporters who had flouted their rules? This did not surprise or upset me. But if this was where the regime was incarcerating journalists, wouldn't it be prudent to surmise that the POWs might be there as well? Wouldn't Intelligence Headquarters be a logical place to keep pilots whom the Iraqis would want to interrogate repeatedly whenever new questions arose?

I phoned Pete Williams, the Pentagon spokesman. We'd never met but he was extremely affable on the phone, told me how he admired my work, how, in fact, he used tapes of some of my stories from the Gulf as teaching aids in lectures he gave to new information officers. I asked him my question. He said it was a fair question, that he would look into it and get back to me. He never did.

I had something else on my mind now. CBS wanted to know if I would be interested in going back to the Gulf to shoot a documentary. "After the Storm" it would be called.

I walked to the CBS News building the morning after my speech. For more than twenty years now, the twin pillars of stability in my wayward life had been Françoise and this red brick building on 57th Street between Tenth and Eleventh avenues. Whenever I came back from wherever it was, they would both be there. I pushed my way through the revolving door and stopped in my tracks. Standing on an easel in the lobby was a large poster with two portraits of me. A pastel sketch of the smiling, clean-shaven reporter was superimposed on a larger profile of the bearded prisoner. *Welcome Home Bob* was inscribed at the bottom. I saw that dozens of people had signed their names along the edges. I felt overwhelmed. I didn't know how to deal with this, how to react, what to do. I turned around, walked out of the building, and into a restaurant across the street to have a cup of coffee and regroup.

I tried a second take. I went back in, walked quickly past the poster, pretending not to notice, then down a narrow corridor and into the newsroom. Joel Bernstein, my oldest friend at CBS and a cuddly bear of a guy, walked toward me, smiling. Bernstein and I started together in 1967. I worked the overnight shift on the television desk. He worked radio. We used to stand by the wire machines with our Styrofoam coffees and reflect that when we were old and gray, we would be back here, working the overnight by the wires. Now he was Rather's producer and he came at me with a black cassette box. "Here, Bobby, here's your obit. I wrote it." A fellow worshiper at the shrine of irony, he told me he came in to work a few days after we disappeared and, without telling any executives, decided to do the obit knowing that if he took the time to write it, I would not be dead. Murphy's law. Every effort is wasted.

I walked into the conference room, where I had an appointment to chat about the documentary idea. I must have been late. Already seated around a long table were two vice presidents, an executive producer, three producers, a director, some researchers, and our Middle East maven, Fouad Ajami. Apparently, a little planning had already been in the works. Fouad offered some pungent observations on the postwar scene and I sat there thinking I didn't really feel up for this. I'd never done a documentary and I knew that my powers of concentration weren't nearly what they should be. But I'd never said no to CBS. It wasn't in my catalogue of responses. Besides, there were some very talented people in the room; I'd have lots of help; and the only scary part, aside from the project itself, was the plan to apply for Iraqi visas. But I knew they wouldn't be approved; we'd shoot the show in Saudi Arabia, Kuwait, and Israel.

The visas came through in a week. "After the Storm" was scrapped as a title and changed to "Bob Simon: Back to Baghdad" and I was in the Intercontinental Hotel in Amman, waiting for the rest of the crew to show up, waiting to drive to Baghdad the next morning. I felt numb.

I was lying on my bed, reading some clips, listening to the BBC. At three in the afternoon the news came on and the lead item was from Iraq. Douglas Brand, the British engineer jailed by Saddam during the roundup of foreigners last August, had been sentenced to life in prison for espionage. I couldn't believe my ears. I couldn't believe I was hearing this today. I felt a truncheon come down on my head the way it had after I waved to Brand that dismal morning in Abu Ghraib. I saw him sitting on the floor outside his cell, his hands on his head, pleading with the guards to stop beating him. Life in prison? He was going to spend the rest of his life in prison? And I was going back to Iraq tomorrow? I bolted out of my room, ran down the stairs and out the front door of the hotel. I ran up the street, not thinking, not trying to think, knowing I couldn't even begin to think until I'd run past my panic. When people came toward me I avoided their eyes, swung my arms, pretended I was out for a jog.

After I'd stopped running, I came to a small hotel with an outdoor terrace. It was in the sun. There was no one there. I sat down and ordered a glass of tea. I didn't know what the more difficult move was just then, steeling myself up and going to Iraq or steeling myself up and backing out of it. The rest of the team would be arriving in a few hours. I'd have to decide. I knew they wouldn't argue with me if I told them I couldn't go through with it, but I also knew how I'd feel. I'd already backed out of enough things, and CBS had already invested a big bundle in the project. I found I was going through my mantra act again. "They won't arrest me. They won't arrest me," I muttered. "They won't do it again. They won't do it again. They won't do it again." I remembered Giora Rom telling me that going back to flying after his time in prison was the most difficult thing he had ever done. When he flew close to the Egyptian border the first time, he discovered that his hands were shaking. He couldn't handle it. He returned to base and offered to resign from the air force. The command talked him out of it.

Giora also told me he never flew as well again as he did before his capture. Then, he would dive through anti-aircraft fire as if it were fireworks. The scenery didn't look real to him. Others could get shot down, but it couldn't happen to him. He was invulnerable. That never came back. That never can come back after you've taken a dive.

This fear was new to me; this fear which blocked my instinct to lunge ahead, which created pause, reflection, paralysis. I had never felt it before; not in Vietnam, not in Lebanon, nowhere. The Iraqis had taken something from me after all. They had taken away the charm, the magical confidence. And I'd never get it back.

I slept most of the way to Baghdad. We had left before

dawn; there were no problems at the border; I would wake up now and then, take one look at the bleak landscape, and go back to sleep. Once, when I opened my eyes, I looked out the driver's window and saw some lovely light-green palm trees. They were framing a billboard, a large poster of a smiling Saddam. I knew. Slowly, I turned my head to the right and there it was: the prison of Abu Ghraib, a massive complex of gray concrete buildings and barbed wire. A soldier was leaning out of a guard tower, smoking. I tried to locate my cell but I didn't have time and I didn't want to tell the driver to stop. Douglas Brand was still in there somewhere. I wondered about Abbas and the Palestinian with the golden voice, the blind mimic and the Kurds, whom I had finally forgiven for being such assholes.

The Al-Rasheed was bustling with activity now. It was hard to relate the brightly lit busy lobby to the pre-dawn purgatory of two months ago. Our reservations were in order, and once I had checked in, gone up to my room and unpacked my Olivetti, I wasn't afraid anymore. It was just another story. I'd be all right.

Some of my journalist friends thought the Information Ministry would give me an especially hard time. Others believed I was in for special treatment. They were all wrong. As soon as we registered in the ministry's press-room, it was clear that, to the regime's foot soldiers, there was no history. I was another hack. I would spend hours, along with the rest of the pack, sitting around, drinking too much coffee, waiting for permission to go out and shoot street scenes or take some shots of the market. It would be like treading water again in the American pools.

Peter's would-be savior, Latif Jassim, was not the Minister anymore. He had been demoted in the last palace putsch. Apparently Saddam didn't believe he was getting a good enough press.

A colleague pointed out the assistant savior, Naji al-Hadithi, as he walked out of the building, pale and portly, in his tennis gear. It was difficult even to remember how much hope I had invested in this slightly ridiculous and totally inconsequential figure.

The man running the press operation was a suave, cosmopolitan ex-diplomat named Odai. He once worked in Iraq's Paris Embassy, was expelled from France, suspected of espionage. He spoke a fluent French, suffered from a worse case of Francophilia than I did, and was the only official who referred to my checkered past. He asked me why I had complained about my treatment. Because it was pretty rough, I replied. "You must accept what happened," he said, "you must accept what happened." So the Iraqis were still giving me orders. If that was a little hard to swallow, something else was going on that I liked. They still called me "Mr. Bob."

We gave Odai a list of things we wanted to do, places we wanted to visit: the Shiite South, universities, reconstruction sites; a list which climaxed with a request for an interview with the President. "You are forbidden even to dream about it," he said.

The guy I really wanted to see was my ex-interpreter, the man who sat in on my first White Ship interrogation and who asked me whether I had been treated with respect. I knew now that his job at the Information Ministry was a cover; that he had worked for Intelligence all along. I also knew that he had been Arnett's source for the CNN report that we were alive and in Baghdad. I had some questions for him and I asked Odai whether I could meet him. "Yes, certainly, maybe tomorrow," he said. I knew what that meant and when tomorrow came around, Odai told me that it wouldn't be possible right away because he had been hospitalized with a broken arm. Maybe he'd be available before we left. A few days later I learned from people who'd seen him in the hospital that he had been shot eight times shortly after our release, that he was still in serious condition. Maybe the leak hadn't been authorized after all. Maybe it had forced Saddam to admit that he had us, which was something he never planned to do. Or maybe it was something completely unrelated, a minor misdemeanor in the officially sanctioned underworld of the Iraqi regime.

What surprised me most those first few days was how quickly life was returning to normal; how hard people were working to get their lives back on track. Baghdad exuded energy. There were no telephones and there were massive traffic jams because two of the main bridges over the Tigris had been bombed, but reconstruction was proceeding twenty-four hours a day. At night, the bridges and the telephone exchanges were illuminated with floodlights so work could continue. The market was as boisterous as any souk in the Arab world. Classes had resumed in the universities; in fact, the week we were there, students were taking their midterm exams. We went to the racetrack one afternoon, where, if it hadn't been for a bombed-out building in the distance, I would have defied anyone to notice that a war had just been fought and lost. Surprises make good stories. I liked working here.

What's more, I liked the people. They were friendly, fun-loving, and remarkably free of rancor, even when they learned I was American. They were also decidedly secular and western, in their dress, in their demeanor, in the way the punters yelled at their horses, in the way the blue-jeaned students, boys and girls, strolled together on campus. No segregation of the sexes. No masked women. They were so much more like us than our allies in the war we had just won.

There was something else I enjoyed about working here. People didn't recognize me. This was the one country where the CBS Four had not been on television. I didn't have to answer questions or thank anyone or talk about how great it was to be free. I could relax when I wasn't worried about our shooting schedule. I could drink beer with David Green, one of the cameramen on the team, and do what I'd always done.

I also felt a natural kinship with many of the Iraqis I met. These people had suffered during the war, as I had, but were determined to put it past them. We spent a day with Faiz Hanoudi, the master builder of Baghdad, a top engineer in the Ministry of Works, now renamed the Ministry of Reconstruction. He had been involved in the planning of much of modern Baghdad, had seen his life's work destroyed, but kept going to his office during the war, making blueprints for reconstruction while the bombs were still falling. We interviewed Dr. Anjaf, a biochemistry professor, in her lab at the university. She spoke fluent English and broke down when she spoke of her relatives in Michigan. "Of course I miss them," she said, "but they know I'm all right, and they know we'll rebuild better than it was before." I found these encounters frankly inspirational at a time when I was in the market for a little inspiration. I felt far more comfortable here than I later did in Saudi Arabia, where people had suffered little and learned less, or in Kuwait, which was afflicted with a massive case of paralysis, where people seemed to be sitting on their hands, waiting for someone to come around and rebuild their lives, the way the Bangladeshis swept their streets.

People asked me, then and later, what it was like going back to Baghdad. I made up answers after a while because the truth was, it didn't feel like anything at all. I hadn't gone Back to Baghdad. That was a title for a television show. I'd never been to Baghdad; I'd been in a cell on another planet. I would have felt closer if I'd been in a prison in China. I hadn't returned to the same place: war was a different place. The only places are places of mind.

We drove down to Karbala, Iraq's holiest city, fifty miles south of Baghdad and the capital of the Shiite revolt. The city derives its religious importance from the battle which was fought here in the seventh century between the Sunni and Shi'a sects. Hussein ibn-Ali, the grandson of Mohammed, was killed here, and his tomb remains one of the greatest shrines in Islam. It had been damaged in the fighting but was one of the few buildings still standing at all in the downtown district. It was surrounded by a wasteland, by blocks of rubble. An entire neighborhood had been leveled, as if by the scheme of a mad urban planner. No one would talk to us here. No one had seen or heard anything, aside from the soldiers who were now camped inside the shrine. They told us about Shiite atrocities against Ba'athist officials. They showed us a room with nooses hanging from the ceiling and blood splattered on the walls, the room where those officials had been executed. This was when and where Saddam came in with tanks and heavy artillery and crushed the revolt and the city which came with it. This was when and where the Bush administration was faced with its crucial decision. Support the revolt and witness the downfall of Saddam, either at the hands of the Shi'a or by his own restive officers. Or give Saddam the green light to do what he had to do to stay in power. The administration voted for Saddam.

The worst part of television news is how much you learn that you can't get onto the little screen. Things you see at night, people you talk to who can't risk being identified. It is one thing for a newspaper reporter to quote someone without naming him. What's in a name? But how do you do it on television? How do you report conversations with Iraqis who agree to meet you in dark fish restaurants by the Tigris and who take that critical leap of faith as they sit with you drinking beer, munching on river trout, glancing warily at the door every time it opens. You can talk about it over pictures of people walking in the street, but in a country like Iraq, you never know whether some hapless soul who strolled into the shot is going to get arrested and accused of saying things he would hardly have permitted himself to dream. You can do it in a stand-up, but try watching a stand-up that lasts more than a minute.

"The Americans let us down," he said. "We saw them as our saviors, we counted on them for deliverance, and they betrayed us. Can you tell me why? Can you explain to me why they did that? The Kuwaitis suffered under Saddam for seven months. We've had him for twenty-three years. People pretend they are indifferent or stupid. They're just trying to survive. It's like Eastern Europe was, at least the richer countries. It's the covenant à la Czech. You get a tolerable life-style in exchange for silence. But the silence swells inside you like a balloon until it bursts. It burst those days in March, you know. There was a carnival atmosphere here for three, four days. Posters of Saddam were defaced. We talked about him. Can you imagine that? We actually talked about him on the street. We had to take the chance. It was now or never. Schwarzkopf was on his way. We believed that. We really believed it. Do you know, can you begin to know how he would have been received? Like a messiah, that's how."

"There would have been garlands and kisses," another man said the next night. "It would have been like Rome after the war. But the GIs wouldn't have needed nylons or chewing gum. You say life looks like it's returning to normal. Of course it is. What else could you expect? We're back where we were. We're going through the motions of living again. But we're not really alive. Our moment has passed. The window has been slammed shut. We're sitting at the same table, but we're not, not really. There's a screen between us. You had forty days and now you're out. We're still there."

I flew into New York on June tenth, just in time to run into the victory parade as I crossed town. I watched for a while and saw, clearer than ever, what the war had been about. It had been about winning, that's all. The military needed a clean victory to recover finally from the catastrophe of Vietnam. President Bush needed a victory for more parochial reasons. And the only thing that was worth going to war for, the overthrow of Saddam Hussein, remained unachieved, an ineradicable blot on George Bush, a rainstorm on the victory parades.

Scharansky had said that only in prison are moral choices possible; the free world is doomed to realpolitik. I didn't know if, with the approach of my birthday, I was turning moral after a half century of wisecracks, but I felt strange urgings in that direction. It just seemed to me that letting Saddam live to please the Saudis, to save the Turks from an independent Kurdistan, to save the world from another Shiite republic, might have had a certain logic to it. But morally it was little different than to have joined forces with Hitler in 1945 to face down the Soviets to the east. No, realpolitik is acceptable, inevitable perhaps, unless you're up against absolute evil. And that was the only possible definition of Saddam's regime as it had been of Nazi Germany half a century earlier. There was no rain on those parades.

THE END

❖

"No one who knew Bob Simon seemed surprised when he ventured into enemy territory. That was a very Simon thing to do. He was always seeking an edge to his work, pushing himself, moving the story along."

"What's that?" It was Françoise. She was in the kitchen.

"Shh, it's my obit. Let's see what they say about me now that I'm dead."

"Simon was among the best of war correspondents, up there with Murrow and Cronkite. He learned his trade in Vietnam. Ever since then, he longed to be where the action was. We sent him everywhere and for one reason. He was the best we had."

Rather was speaking slowly. He seemed a bit choked up.

"Didn't I tell you he'd do my eulogy? He did it for Collingwood, he's doing it for me."

"Bob was probably the most competitive correspondent working in this business, a longtime veteran of CBS News who covered stories for us all over the world, and covered them with a style all his own; the voice was unmistakably New York but the poetry shined through."

"See, I told you to work on your accent." That was Françoise.

"Shh. I'm listening."

"Simon loved opera and literature, loved putting words together, he spoke French fluently, he was a great tennis player."

"Did you hear that?" I shout to Françoise, hitting the pause button. "Did Bernstein write that? A great tennis player? He wrote that just because I can beat him. I've never met anyone who can't beat him. My uncle Irving can beat Bernstein and he's been dead for twenty years."

"Obits are supposed to say nice things."

"Obits are bullshit. This one is, anyway."

Don't try to figure out how you feel. Watch what you do. That's the only way I can understand anything anymore. I didn't jump up and down to go to Yugoslavia. So maybe there's hope. I am buying that big motorcycle. So maybe there isn't. I still prowl around the tennis court like an enraged bull, cursing and throwing my racket around. But that was only to be expected.

It is 1992 now and I still haven't seen Peter's fucking tree. In fact, I haven't seen Peter or Juan or Roberto since we said "see you soon" that night in London. As Ahmad might have said, "Would you believe?"

Writing a book was liberating in a way, the way Scharansky said it would be. I don't dream much about any of it anymore. But when I walk on the beach sometimes, I find myself in that room in the White Ship where they never took me; the courtroom where Ahmad signed his confession. The judge isn't Iraqi. He doesn't even have a mustache. I'm not sure who he is, in fact, but he does have white hair and he's wearing glasses. It might be Earl Warren.

We were just getting some shots, Your Honor, like I told you, some sheep bones and stuff. So what if I wanted to be the first guy in Kuwait? Is that a crime? Show me the statute. Look, I'm not denying that there is a pathology here, but I'll tell you what. You show me a happy human being with a healthy respect for authority and no illusions of invulnerability and I'll show you someone who has no business going into journalism. OK, he might make it in Washington, if he likes hanging out with those stiffs. But he'll never make it overseas. He just won't come up with the goods. And while we're at it, Your Honor, if you'll permit me a brief digression, if it weren't for crazies like us, if it weren't for bands of suicidal depressives roaming the desert and crossing borders, if that's how you choose to see us, who would tell you what's going on, Your Honor? That is, if you care. And you do care, don't you? You were watching television during the war, weren't you? Who would keep you posted? Those guys behind the podium? Forget it.

I understand, Your Honor, you've never been there and I'll never be able to explain it to you, but there is this thing about borders, about crossing over, about leaving the neat lines behind. When you've done it once, you'll do it again and again. Because there's nothing like it; not Verdi, not sex, not even ordinary danger. That's pretty powerful too. But a border adds another dimension, or, rather, it does away with dimensions. You're throwing yourself against the tender indifference of the world. You're poised, suspended. . . .

Look, I know I'm not doing very well, but I've been off a ski jump a few times and that's the sensation I'm trying so clumsily to convey: not the schuss down the chute, not the return to the hard-packed snow, but that instant of takeoff; that split second when you open your arms and soar into space, when your skis are pointing to the sky and you have ripped through the fabric of time. You don't know how or where you will land and, if you ski like I do, you have every reason to expect the worst. But it doesn't matter. Not for that infinitesimal instant. Because even if you break your bones, you will have experienced that one instant of immeasurable grace. You will have sailed with the birds.

But, when I leave the docket and stroll down the dark streets of Bourg-en-Bresse, past women rushing home, their shopping bags packed to the brim, what I mull over is not the drive to the border or the crossing over or the moment we were captured and why it happened and whether we could have avoided it. What I see is that man in the cell five weeks later, the night the White Ship got torpedoed from the sky. There he is, waiting for the last bomb to fall, the one he thinks has his name on it. But what's strange is that I don't see a gaunt middle-aged prisoner with a white beard and filthy pajamas. I see a little boy on his knees in that cell, a well-scrubbed little boy in his bathrobe, his hair neatly parted, saying his bedtime prayers. And sometimes I am so overwhelmed with affection for him that I want to hop on the next bus to

Baghdad, to find him, to see if he is still there, to take him in my arms, and tell him everything will be all right. I know he will be glad to see me.

That obituary for Simon showed clips of him in his various disguises: safari jackets, blazers, tuxedos, covering wars, uprisings, galas. It was well produced, well edited, and well written, even if it did go a bit overboard about the tennis thing. It was a first-rate television piece. Clearly, it deserved to make air.

AN EPILOGUE:
THE RESCUE

�֍✖

T_{HEY} were in a quandary at CBS. A four-man team had been missing for three days and they didn't know what to do. The team could have hooked up with an American unit near the border. The newsmen could have found a way to get into Kuwait. Blow the whistle and blow their cover. For now the most prudent course was to do nothing at all. Just wait.

Françoise Simon had been in New York since January thirteenth. Her diary entry for Monday, January twenty-first, reads, "Evening at Bob's Uncle Peter's. We play bridge and I win $5.95." That was the night her husband and three others were expected back at the CBS bureau in Dhahran.

Tuesday evening she went to the theater with her daughter, Tanya, to see Six Degrees of Separation. When she returned to her room at the Parker Meridien at 11:20 P.M., there was a voice message from CBS News vice president Joe Peyronnin. "Nothing urgent. Just wanted to chat." Françoise returned the call. Joe told her he was a little concerned but not worried. "You know Bob," he said. "They're probably off getting a great story." Françoise was not convinced. She knew from a message Bob had left on Tanya's machine that he had planned to be back in Dhahran on Monday. It didn't make sense for him to spend so many days without getting on the air.

At 5:40 in the morning, Thursday, January 24, Joe called again. "Their car has been found abandoned at the border," he said. Françoise was unable to reply. On the "CBS Evening News" that night, Dan Rather reported, "Questions were asked today about CBS News correspondent Bob Simon and his crew. They were last heard from Monday in northern Saudi Arabia, near the border with Kuwait. Today a Saudi patrol reported finding their vehicle and following the tracks of four men up to the Kuwaiti border. They said they did not see the crew."

Thursday night, CBS News vice president Don De-Cesare was dispatched to the Middle East. He had been there many times and knew the area well. He had, in fact, set up CBS News coverage of the Gulf crisis.

On Monday morning, January 28, the phone rang in the office of Sam Roberts, executive director of CBS's international broadcast services. It was Peyronnin. "Drop what you are doing and come to my office," he said. "We want you to run the search and make it a full-time job." Roberts was a logical choice. A former foreign editor and national editor, he had been with CBS News for twenty-nine years, knew every nook and cranny of the organization.

Over the next three days, dozens of letters were fired off under the signatures of Laurence Tisch, the CEO of CBS, and Eric Ober, president of CBS News, to heads of state, diplomats, Washington officials, the Pope, the PLO. Frank Stanton, the former president of CBS, used his contacts in the Red Cross to try to get to the Red Crescent, the Arab Red Cross. The State Department called in the Iraqi chargé. King Hussein sent a personal message to Saddam Hussein asking for information. A "Fellow Journalists Petition" was circulated in the United States, Europe, and the Middle East, collecting four thousand signatures. Ron Koven of the World Free Press Committee in Paris organized a letter-writing campaign. Robert MacNeil, co-anchor of "The MacNeil/Lehrer News-Hour," sent a letter to Saddam signed by forty of the biggest names in American journalism. The BBC began broadcasting news stories on the missing team on its Arabic Service. Henry Kissinger contacted National Security Adviser Brent Scowcroft. Bishop Tutu contacted Zambian president Kenneth Kaunda. Judge Abraham Sofaer was enlisted by CBS to go to Paris to see Iraq's ambassador to France. Jack Smith was sent to London to help Bluff's fiancée, Geraldine Sharpe-Newton, mount a campaign in Europe.

One of Roberts's first calls that Monday was to CBS News Moscow bureau chief Joe Ritchey, who approached Vitaly Ignatenko, the presidential spokesman, asked him to solicit Gorbachev's help. Joe was surprised by how quickly Ignatenko got back to him. The answer was positive. "Yes, we must do something," Gorbachev had told Ignatenko. "I want you to do it on my behalf."

Ignatenko then got everyone involved: the KGB, the Defense Ministry, Foreign Minister Bessmertnykh, special Mideastern envoy Yevgeny Primakov. By that evening the Soviet ambassador in Baghdad, Viktor Pasovoluk, had been briefed. During the next five weeks, Joe Ritchey had a new and pleasant experience. For the first time in his five years in Moscow, Ignatenko always took his calls.

Sam Roberts' phone was ringing off the hook. The pigeons were coming home to roost. From Tunis, the PLO said Iraq denied knowing anything about the four. From Paris, Pierre Salinger reported that the Iraqi ambassador said the journalists were not in Iraq. From Amman, King Hussein said Saddam had not answered his inquiries. From Algerian intelligence, there was a report, communicated by Alain Debos, that the Iraqis had launched a search for the newsmen and concluded that they were not in the country. From Baghdad, Ramsey Clark reported that Tariq Aziz, Iraq's Foreign Minister, claimed he'd never heard of them.

But there was other intelligence. In Riyadh, General Schwarzkopf told CBS people that Iraqi deserters had seen the four being driven to regimental headquarters near Kuwait. In London, British Intelligence told Jack Smith their own sources confirmed that the CBS team was in Iraqi hands. ABC's John Cooley called to say a good source claimed they were being held in a building in Kuwait City called "the Jewel of the Gulf."

On Friday, February 8, Roberts received a call from a man in Amman who would not reveal his name. He said the four had been sentenced to death in retaliation for all the Iraqis killed by Americans. He had heard it from his cousin in Baghdad. Roberts did not communicate that one to the families.

On Sunday, Don DeCesare, armed with photographs of the four, went from tent to tent in a Jordanian refugee camp near the Iraqi border. "It was a United Nations of the desperate out there," he told New York. "Arabs, Iranians, Filipinos, Vietnamese, Sudanese and more. No one had seen our guys."

Three blocks east of CBS News headquarters in New York, another operation was being manned around the clock in room 2601 of the Parker Meridien Hotel. Françoise Simon did not try to sleep. She ate only when someone remembered to bring her food. She subsisted on cigarettes and black coffee and telephone calls. She wrote in her diary, "What I discovered, not immediately, but by and by, was that not only did I talk to people, but people talked to me. It's amazing how you change from 'the wife of someone,' a pleasant enough person, perhaps, to somebody everyone wants a piece of. People do want to help. There's a lot of genuine concern. But they have their own agendas as well."

The turning point for Françoise came on Friday, February 8, when she was contacted by a man who had no personal agenda at all. Former Assistant Secretary of State Richard Holbrooke invited her to lunch at Lehman Brothers, where he is a managing director. "I can tell you're not doing enough," he said. "I don't see you on television. I don't hear you on the radio. I want this thing to be visible, because visibility will be their shield." He advised Françoise not to rely solely on CBS. "For them, it's a problem," he said. "For you, it's your husband. You have the moral authority. You must call everyone, and everyone will answer your call. No one will tell you you're rude or pushy. You have to push every button because, if he is freed, you will never know which one has done it, and if he isn't, you will always blame yourself for not having pushed them all."

Françoise felt she had been given the green light. That night she wrote a dozen letters to world leaders. She phoned Najeeb Halaby, the father of Queen Noor of Jordan, and got the fax number of the Royal Palace in Amman. She phoned Sam Roberts and told him she wanted to appear on "CBS This Morning" and CNN as soon as possible. It was arranged for Monday, February 11.

There were transatlantic phone calls every night. Françoise coordinated strategy with Geraldine Sharpe-Newton. It was difficult to mount a four-family campaign. Roberto and Juan were not married. Both sets of parents were divorced.

Wednesday, February 13, Geraldine went to the PLO headquarters in London with a letter addressed: "Yassir Arafat, Tunis." Afif Safieh, the PLO chief in London, faxed it immediately and said, "The act is done. We will know something soon and we will let you know."

On Friday, February 15, Françoise took the Metroliner to Washington to meet the French and Yemeni ambassadors. Charlie Wolfson, a close friend of the Simons' and a producer in the CBS Washington Bureau, was waiting at the end of the platform. Françoise panicked when she saw him. But Charlie was smiling. "There's good news," he said. "Arnett says they're alive."

"I can confirm that the four CBS News staffers are being held in Baghdad by the Iraqi government," Peter Arnett had broadcast on CNN. "According to my sources, which I consider to be reliable, they're being held in a building in the Karada district of the city on 52nd Street." (Later that day, Arnett told Roberts in a private phone call that the building is the headquarters of the Muhabarat, Saddam's secret police, and is referred to as "The White Ship.")

"Apparently there are three categories they can fall under. Innocents who can be released, prisoners of war, or spies. I am told that President Saddam Hussein will personally determine the outcome of the cases.

"My sources say that the health of all four is good. They're being fed three meals a day, the same food as their investigators."

Charlie was surprised that Françoise did not find this news as uplifting as he did. But she had already concluded that her husband was alive. If he had been killed, a body would have been found by now. And she was fixated on the word "spy." It was in that CBS car, heading toward the Embassy of Yemen in the Watergate Hotel, that Françoise sketched a scenario that was to stay with her for weeks: Roberto and Juan would be set free, Peter would be held as a POW, Bob would be hanged as a spy. That same night she wrote, "That's all I saw, Bazoft at the end of a rope."

The session with the ambassador made matters worse.

He asked many insinuating questions—where was Bob based, how many passports did he have—implying that he knew Bob was Jewish. And if he knew, everyone else must know, too. That afternoon Françoise decided that writing letters, talking to people, and appearing on television was not enough. She had to go to Baghdad.

Sunday night, when Françoise returned to her hotel room, there was a message on the answering machine, a deep, melodious voice: "Honey, I think of you all the time." It was Jesse Jackson.

That night, Tariq Aziz was arriving in Moscow on an Aeroflot jet from Iran. He was forced to travel overland from Baghdad to Teheran because the Allies would not guarantee him safe passage through the air.

Monday morning, February 18, Aziz and Iraqi deputy premier Sadoun Hammadi walked down a long, dimly lit corridor, past Lenin's apartment, to the office of Soviet president Mikhail Gorbachev. Bessmertnykh, Primakov, and Ignatenko were already there. It was Gorbachev who raised the issue of the missing journalists, expressing his personal concern. Primakov told Tariq Aziz, "Much of what you do will be forgiven. But no one will forget if some harm comes to these journalists."

Later, at a press briefing, Ignatenko said, "For the first time, we heard from Aziz that he is familiar with the issue, that he is knowledgeable."

Roberts wrote, "This was a chance for the Russians to gain some goodwill and retain a foothold for themselves in Iraq and in the Middle East. Our four men had become pawns in an international chess game."

Prospects seemed to be brightening for the four pawns. In London, Jack Smith lined up facilities and a team of specialists at the Humana Hospital Wellington. The team was headed by Bluff's personal physician, Dr. Stuart Sanders, and included a psychiatrist, Dr. Antony Fry, who told Smith, "The fact that they are journalists will help them in captivity, as they are keeping track of the story in their minds as something they will have to report.

On Tuesday, February 19, Don DeCesare and Larry Doyle drove to Baghdad from Amman. They arrived at the darkened Al-Rasheed Hotel at 9 P.M., in the middle of an air raid. A man sought them out in the corridor with a flashlight. Don thought he looked like Peter Sellers, but it was Naji al-Hadithi, the deputy information minister. "I don't know what you're doing here," he said. "You should leave. These men are not here. If you want to find them, ask the Saudis. We told your people that."

In the morning, accompanied by an Iraqi "minder," as he always would be when he left the hotel, Don went to the Soviet Embassy. Ambassador Viktor Pasovoluk was extremely friendly, told Don, "You can come by anytime and I will be communicating with you."

In Washington that afternoon, Pentagon spokesman Pete Williams got a phone call from Peyronnin. Williams assured Joe that the White Ship had not been bombed, which was true. It was not to happen for twenty-four hours.

In New York, switchboard operators at the Parker Meridien said that some days room 2601 got more phone calls than all the other rooms combined. They were fielded by Françoise's good friend Harriet Weiss, a public relations executive. Toby Bernstein, a ceramicist, also belonged to what had become a standing committee. So did Tanya, who dropped some of her classes at Columbia and spent most nights with her mother. The women were discovering that gallows humor is not experienced only by the intended victim. Family and friends feel it, too. They had begun judging the relative importance of Françoise's many new contacts by the quality of their carpets. So far Holbrooke was in the lead.

But there was another development which Françoise did not find amusing. Articles were appearing in the Palestinian and Jordanian press alleging that she, a French Catholic, was a Jew and an Israeli. This was potentially dangerous enough to' require rectification, Françoise thought. It was another reason to go to the area quickly; to stop off in Amman and talk to Bob's contacts there.

CBS was not enthusiastic about Françoise's trip. There was a distinct possibility Bob was dead, and the front office shuddered at the thought of Françoise discovering that in Baghdad. But she told Roberts she was determined. And if CBS didn't want to send someone with her, there were other possibilities. Jesse Jackson had told her, "If you want to go to Baghdad, count me in." Sarkis Soghanalian, an arms dealer under indictment in Miami for a customs violation, was making a similar offer. "60 Minutes" producer Lowell Bergman had put Françoise in touch with him because of his claim to have excellent contacts in Baghdad. If necessary Françoise was willing to go alone.

CBS decided to send London producer Doug Sefton

with her. It was a lucky break for more than one reason. When Roberts was briefing Sefton, Doug came up with a shrewd idea. Since the Russians want to help, and the Iraqis need the Russians, why not suggest that the four be turned over to the Soviet ambassador in Baghdad? Roberts wrote, "It was one of those ideas so brilliant and so simple, you say to yourself, why didn't I think of that?"

Roberts called Ritchey in Moscow, Ritchey called Ignatenko, who jumped on the idea, said he would recommend it to Gorbachev. He said a letter from Kissinger would help.

CBS president Howard Stringer contacted Dr. Kissinger, who is a member of the CBS board. Roberts drafted a letter to Gorbachev to be signed by Larry Tisch. It offered precise suggestions as to how the maneuver could be executed. Within hours Jay Kriegel, Tisch's closest adviser, was on the phone to Roberts. "Kissinger doesn't like your letter," he said. "He says it's too specific. You don't talk to a head of state that way."

"Give me a break," Roberts said. "I've never written to a head of state before. Change it however Kissinger says to change it." The revised letters went out that afternoon.

Saturday morning, February 23, Tariq Aziz, who was back in Moscow to accept a Soviet peace plan, told Gorbachev he knew nothing of reports that the journalists were being held by the Muhabarat. He denied knowing anything about their whereabouts. Gorbachev nailed him. "We know you know," he said.

Saturday afternoon, Françoise left the Parker Meridien for JFK to board British Airways flight 174 to London, in transit to Vienna and Amman. When she was checking in, Roberts paged her. There was news.

For weeks, Sam had been in touch with a group of Armenians in Fresno, California. They had relatives trapped in Baghdad and through an underground network were trying to extract them one at a time. They also had a lot of street gossip from Baghdad and on preset days and times called Roberts to fill him in.

Now they reported that all the Jews in Baghdad were being rounded up and killed indiscriminately. They had word that Bob's life was in danger because he was Jewish; that people were also out to get his family. Sam told Françoise all this. She said she was going ahead. Sam said he would put a bodyguard on her in Amman and one on Tanya in New York. Françoise agreed.

Early Sunday morning, Geraldine and Jack Smith drove out to London's Heathrow Airport to meet Françoise. They told her that while she had been in the air the war had begun on the ground. Geraldine told Françoise, "They will slip from the headlines now. Peter and Bob would be the first to understand that."

At the Vienna airport Sunday afternoon, Françoise went to the duty-free jewelry shop and bought a small gold cross on a thin gold chain. She would arrive in Amman a properly accredited Catholic. Françoise had never worn a cross in her life. Her mother would have gone into shock.

In New York, Tanya was given the choice of going to her classes at Columbia with a bodyguard or not going at all. "Are you kidding?" she told her mother. "Turn up with a bodyguard?" She changed her phone number and her lock and disappeared, went underground for a week, spending each night in the apartment of a different friend.

What neither Françoise nor Tanya knew was that the Armenian network had come up with another very hot story. Geraldine Sharpe-Newton didn't know it either, which was probably just as well.

On Sunday, February 24, Roberts got a call on his car phone from Fresno. The Armenians had freed one of their relatives in Baghdad. They had also liberated a westerner who fit Peter Bluff's description. He was near death; high fever, very weak, could barely talk. Roberts wrote, "I was stunned. Could one of our men be in the hands of friendly Iraqis? What would happen to the others? Would this man live? Is it really Bluff?"

Over the next few days Roberts got more information about this man, who was unconscious most of the time and delirious when awake. It began sounding more and more like Bluff.

In Baghdad, Soviet ambassador Pasovoluk was having communications problems. His only link to the outside world was one overloaded data line to Moscow. Three days after DeCesare's arrival, he still had not received specific instructions regarding the missing journalists. Don offered him the use of the CBS satellite phone on the terrace of the Al-Rasheed Hotel. The ambassador accepted. Don patched him through to the Foreign Ministry through the CBS switchboard in New York. It was a terrible connection. The ambassador was shouting in Russian. But he told Don, with considerable satisfaction, that the message was received. Then he asked if he could try to call his home in Moscow. He hadn't talked to his family since the beginning of the war. Don agreed. He got through to his mother, and was delighted.

The next day the ambassador's deputy, Alexander Guzmin, dropped by CBS to call his home across the Urals. He told Don: "The ambassador talked about your friends in an important place yesterday."

In Amman, Françoise was beginning her rounds. First stop: arms dealer Sarkis Soghanalian in his suite at the Marriott Hotel. Françoise thought she was walking into an Eric Ambler novel. Sarkis was fat, lurid, and charming; he could be played only by Sydney Greenstreet. A creature of the Levant, Sarkis spoke in cryptic metaphors. "We don't want to meet the gardener," he said. "We just want to eat the fruit." Sarkis told Françoise he would send a courier to Baghdad with a message about us, but she never heard from him again. The merchant couldn't deliver.

That afternoon Roberts got a call from John Lane, an old CBS hand, now an executive at CNN. Roberts knew there was something wrong from the tone of his voice. Lane put Steve Emerson, one of his reporters, on the phone. Emerson said he had received a reliable report that Bob Simon had just been executed. Roberts spoke to Emerson's source, a retired Marine colonel in Washington who, Sam said, was clearly in the intelligence business. The colonel's source in Iraq, someone he trusted, said Simon had been killed two hours earlier and that two others were hanged with him.

Roberts wrote, "The information sounded very true. I was crushed, decided not to tell anyone, certainly not the families. I was afraid that the Armenians had indeed rescued Bluff and that Simon and the others had been executed in retaliation."

But diplomacy continued along a separate track, forging through the fog of rumors which might have suggested that it was too late. In Moscow, Tuesday morning, February 26, Ignatenko addressed the issue in a briefing. In Washington, the State Department called in the Soviet chargé to request that the four be turned over to Soviet custody. In Baghdad, Soviet ambassador Pasovoluk told DeCesare, "I'm very optimistic this is going to be resolved within a day or two."

"Can you tell me more?" DeCesare asked.

"No," he replied. "I can't tell you how I know."

Don got word to New York. Roberts put a jet in Zurich on standby.

Wednesday afternoon, February 27, Françoise was picked up by an unmarked Mercedes and driven to a grand estate in downtown Amman. She was led down a long corridor and into a salon which seemed to have been lifted from the pages of Architectural Digest: very elegant, very California: light-cream-colored sofas and oriental rugs. No question about it; they were the best yet. After a few moments Queen Noor came into the room in a simple beige silk dress, perfectly offsetting her long blonde hair. Françoise was struck by her beauty, her porcelain complexion.

A Jordanian friend advised Françoise not even to at-

tempt a curtsy. The Queen will extend her hand, Françoise had been told, you will say "Your Majesty" once, and
she will say, Please don't call me "Your Majesty." It
happened just like that.

They were very close. Françoise was on a sofa; the
Queen pulled up a chair, sat next to her, and took charge
of the conversation, asking Françoise what she had done,
what she knew, and talking about what they had done and
were prepared to do. She was careful to put parameters
around that, but His Majesty, she said, was very concerned and had been extremely active.

The Queen wanted to talk about the Middle East. She
complained bitterly about how the Americans misunder-
stood Jordan; how in fact they understood so very little
about the whole region. She asked Françoise to describe
the mood in Israel. What do the Israelis want? Why is
Shamir so intransigent? Françoise explained how all her
Israeli friends want peace, how it does not require a giant
leap of the imagination to understand why Israelis are
worried about their security. Françoise had the impression
that the Queen didn't normally have this kind of exchange
with a stranger.

The Queen did not ask point-blank whether or not Bob
was Jewish, nor did she remark on Françoise's cross. But,
Françoise said later, "She sure saw it."

The meeting had gone on for two hours. It was getting
dark. Françoise didn't know how these things end, so she
looked at her watch. The Queen said, "Relax. These
interviews are over when I say they're over." It was said
with a certain irony, and to soften it, she added, "My

husband very much wants to meet you, so we have to wait
for him."

They were having tea when he came in. The King
collapsed in an armchair, his hand on his brow, and said,
"Oh, I don't know what he wants from us." The Queen
looked startled. He continued. "President Bush, President
Bush—what does he want from us?" Allied troops had
just paraded triumphantly through Kuwait City,
Baghdad had announced it would drop all claims to
Kuwait if the allies halted the offensive, and yet Schwarzkopf marched on.

The Queen said, "But, dear—we have Mrs. Simon
with us." He snapped out of it.

He told Françoise, "Let me be frank with you. We don't
have much contact with Saddam Hussein anymore. Tariq
Aziz is coming soon and we will give him messages, but
we don't know how far he can take them." The King
wished Françoise good luck, which at that moment she
felt she needed more than ever. What she had learned was
bad news: neither King Hussein nor Tariq Aziz had access
to the bunker. That entire thrust of the campaign had
gotten lost in the woods. Françoise would never forget her
day at court, but it hadn't taken her any closer to her
husband.

As she was being driven back to the Intercontinental,
Sam Roberts was getting a call from Fresno. The man the
Armenians had freed in Baghdad was not Peter Bluff.

The perverse roller coaster that had been rocketing
Françoise from hope to despair and back again for close to
six weeks now dropped her off Thursday afternoon at the

office of the Red Crescent. Dr. al-Hadid, their Amman representative, was far from encouraging. He had a convoy leaving for Baghdad Saturday morning, and he told Françoise it was imperative she compile letters and affidavits from Palestinians attesting to Bob's status as a journalist. He would hand them over to the Iraqi authorities. "We don't care what other people write," he said. "Forget about Dan Rather and Walter Cronkite. Your husband is in Arab hands and we need letters from Arabs because . . . he is Jewish, isn't he?" Françoise didn't answer. She had never been asked point-blank before, and she didn't know how to respond because she couldn't know what Bob was telling the Iraqis. But it was clear that he knew—which meant it was common knowledge.

She rushed back to the hotel and got a message through to Joram Rozov, Bob's good friend in Jerusalem. "Drive to our house," she said. "Look through Bob's desk. There are hundreds of notebooks. Find one marked 'Amman, December 1987.' That's when Bob was covering the Arab summit here. Get me all the names in that notebook."

Thursday evening, February 28, Françoise wrote in her diary, "It had not been articulated but I knew this was the final push. The war ended this morning, but the noose is tightening. If I can't come up with those affidavits, I will have failed to do my part. I will have lost him."

In Washington on Friday, March 1, President Bush announced that General Schwarzkopf would meet Iraqi commanders the following afternoon to discuss the return of the POWs. In Baghdad, Alexander Guzmin, the Soviet ambassador's deputy, dropped by the Al-Rasheed Hotel.

He took DeCesare out on the terrace and told him the ambassador had met with Saddam Hussein Thursday night. When Pasovoluk raised the question of the journalists, Saddam got very annoyed. "Why do you keep bothering me about these four men when there is a war going on and there are so many people under my control?"

Pasovoluk replied, "Because Gorbachev has a personal interest in these journalists and in journalists everywhere."

Alexander Guzmin told Don it was his impression Saddam had finally understood that the issue wasn't going to go away, that he might as well deal with it. He said Ambassador Pasovoluk believed the four would be released within twenty-four hours. Don was not authorized to phone New York without an Iraqi minder listening in. He decided this would be the wrong time to try.

It wasn't important. At 5 P.M. New York time, Friday, March 1, Eric Ober came into Sam Roberts' office. Ober had just gotten a call from Peter Jennings. A friend of Jennings', an Iraqi diplomat, had told him the men would be released very soon.

At 9 P.M., Joe Peyronnin was beeped at a dinner party. It was a message to call Secretary of State James Baker. Baker told Joe, "I just want to inform you we have been told your team will be set free in the next couple of hours."

At 9:30, Ober called Sam, said the Soviet ambassador in Washington had just phoned him with word that Moscow had been told a release was imminent. Roberts called the CBS traffic desk, told them to move the chartered jet from Zurich to Amman.

Roberts decided not to tell the families. He didn't want to raise false hopes and, "Frankly," he wrote, "we didn't know who might be alive and who might not be."

Forty-five minutes later Roberts received grisly confirmation that he had made the right call. Juan Caldera's brother-in-law phoned, said former Nicaraguan president Daniel Ortega had called Juan's mother to say that Juan was dead.

Françoise was feeling desperate when she went to bed in Amman Friday night. The Red Crescent convoy was leaving for Baghdad in the morning with no documents from her. Joram Rozov had spent Thursday combing through the messiest desk in the Middle East and had not come up trumps. No notebooks, no names. Nothing. For the first time Françoise did not know what she would do in the morning. She had no appointments, no plans, no ideas.

When DeCesare went to bed in Baghdad, he had a hard time falling asleep. He expected the Russians to knock on his door, to come and take him to the missing men. An air raid lasted until one in the morning. He listened to some hard rock on his CD player, finally dozed off, he figured at about three. When he was awakened by persistent knocking at the door, he was disoriented. He thought Iraqis had come to take him away. He struggled out of bed and opened the door. The four lost men were there.

The last entry in Sam Roberts' fifty-six-page-long log reads, "3/01/91 12:50 A.M. Foreign Editor Ortiz calls. All are safe with DeCesare in Baghdad."

It was 8 A.M. Saturday morning in Amman when

Roberts called Françoise. He told her the news and stayed on the phone a minute but didn't hear any words, just the sound of weeping. Then the line was cut. Fifteen minutes later Sefton was at the door, said they had to leave for the border right away. Françoise, knowing the departure was premature, said, "I'm not nearly ready yet. I am going to have breakfast and wash my hair." She was free.

Geraldine got the call at 6:05 A.M. London time. Roberts told her she couldn't tell anyone yet. So she stood in the middle of the room and said it to the light bulbs, the walls, the bed. "He's free. He's free," she told them. Then she said, "Thank you, God. Thank you. Thank you. Thank you."

Saturday night, on the plane to London, while Bob was sleeping in the aisle and Roberto was chatting up the doctor, while Juan was sprawled on the sofa and Peter was sipping champagne, Françoise wrote in her diary, "It ended with a phone call and a car, just as it had begun. A small and dirty car came through a cloud of dust and he walked out of it. I imagined this meeting for weeks. I built mountains around this moment, thinking: What will he look like? What will we say to each other? And then it went by in a flash, like smoke in the wind. Just as, in ten seconds, my life stopped when they told me a deserted car was found in the middle of the desert; six weeks later a car came from the desert and my life came back to me."

On July 12, Sam Roberts gave a talk to his synagogue in Rye, New York. This is what he said:

"When Bob Simon got off that charter plane at the old RAF field near London, Bob put his arm around me and said, 'Thanks. I know what you did.'

"'Forget it,' I replied. 'You would have done the same for me.'

"But the best of all—for me—is a postcard I have framed in my office. It's from Peter Bluff. There's a picture of the tulips in full bloom at the Botanical Gardens in Sheffield, near where he grew up in the north of England. A snapshot of pristine beauty filled with greens and reds and yellows. Exquisite flowers and trees and lawn. His message is an understatement of gratitude from a free man.

"It says simply:

"'Thank you for the Spring.'"